I0700788

Marked by Fate

The Marked Series, Book 1

Jayme Hunt

This book is a work of fiction. Names, characters, places, and incidents are the product of the author's imagination or are used fictitiously. None are intended as a faithful representation of any one country or culture at any point in history.

Copyright @ 2023 by Jayme Hunt

Cover art designed by Etheric Tales (etherictales.com)

Editorial services provided by Eden Northover (edennorthoverfictioneditor.uk)

The scanning, uploading, and distribution of this book without permission is a theft of the author's intellectual property. No part of this book may be reproduced without the permission of the author except in brief quotations or a review or a blog. Thank you for your support of the author's rights.

ISBNs: 979-8-9874208-0-5 (pbk), 979-8-9874208-5-0 (ebook)

Contents

To those who feel most alive
squinting at the pages of a book
at three in the morning
escaping into a world that becomes theirs
if only in those quiet moments

Chapter 1

Staring at the near-empty room in front of me, as the sun gleamed temptingly through the window, I realized one very important and soul-crushing fact: I wasn't getting a tan this summer.

I ran a hand through my hair in frustration. Summer vacation was supposed to involve a tan, trips to the beach, new hobbies, or even just catching up on TV shows or books that had been neglected throughout the school year. It was not meant to involve a life-altering move.

My eyes drifted over the cardboard boxes scattered about my room, identified by the half-hearted labels generalizing their contents. I stalked over to a box labeled Barn Clothes and ripped it open, throwing on a comfy pair of jeans and an orange tank top. Stopping for a moment, I assessed myself in the mirror. Dark crescents sat under my amber eyes, betraying fatigue, and my long, brunette hair was in desperate need of brushing. The paleness of my skin reflected the long freshman year of college I'd endured, spent mostly indoors knocking out the cursed general coursework.

Pursing my lips, I tore my eyes away from the mirror and made my way outside. The rest of my clothes would be staying put in their boxes for the foreseeable future. I had better things to attend to.

"Kate! There you are. I'm surprised it took you this long to go visit the pals," my mom commented as I breezed past her, stacking boxes in the kitchen. My heart lifted at her affectionate use of the term 'pals' for our two horses, Chester and Coyote. I flashed her a halfhearted grin as I tugged on my boots.

The summer sun tried its best to warm me, despite the chill that clung stubbornly to the crisp mountain air. I crossed my arms as I walked, refusing to cave and go back inside for a jacket. Two velvet noses spun toward me as I shrugged the barn door open, flaring with curiosity.

I clicked my tongue softly in greeting, and my heart swelled as a nicker of recognition rumbled through the space. I may have been away at school for the better part of five months, and while this may be a new place, Chester and Coyote would recognize me in any terrain. I located a half-open moving box full of grooming supplies and slid into Coyote's stall, combing his dark brown coat in circular motions as I mulled things over.

Though I was admittedly upset by our move, deep down, I understood. Ever since my father passed away, over ten years ago now, my mom fought tooth and nail to keep our ranch in California afloat. She didn't have the same knack with animals as my father — truthfully, no one did — but she was an incredibly hard worker and had established connections that carried us on.

Patiently, she'd waited — selling off bit by bit to keep us afloat, until she knew I was settled in at college to finally make the move. It was only my home for the holidays now, but it still pained me to see so much of our old life disappear. We now only had our two most beloved horses, our cattle dog Scout, and a little piece of land high in the mountains of Colorado.

The place was beautiful but isolated, and though my mother claimed excitedly that our new home had *character* because of its age, all I saw was something small and objectively decrepit. But I suppose beauty is in the eye of its beholder and all that jazz.

As I moved on to brush Chester, stress and resentment rushed out of me. There was something inherently peaceful about spending time with animals, especially horses. It was part of the reason I decided to study equine science at the university, the other part being how it made me feel more connected to my father.

He had been my idol — the one I followed without hesitation as I grew up, breathing in everything he said and did. I leaned into Chester and closed my eyes as tears pricked them, taking in the scents of hay, dirt, and sweet horse grain as I envisioned him.

My dad had uniquely deep amber eyes like mine and, despite his tall and strong stature, his movements were nothing but graceful when he moved and rode. He handled all the animals on our ranch, using a lifetime of knowledge to spot anything amiss, knowing exactly what was needed to nurse them back to health. He'd been there for every moment of my childhood — flying me like an airplane, gifting me ponies, and reading me books when I was little. As I grew older, he remained steadfast, cheering me on at every softball game and taking me to the movies, spoiling me with as much popcorn or candy as I'd wanted.

I felt the ache of loss but opted to press into it, burning the memories into my brain. Grieving my dad meant remembering him, and I wanted to remember every piece that I could, for as long as I could.

After I finished grooming the horses, my gaze caught on a horseshoe above the barn door as I closed it behind me. It certainly wasn't uncommon to see — it was a symbol of good luck, intended to ward off evil spirits — but, for some reason, I found my hand reaching up to touch it. The nails used seemed to be the originals, painstakingly preserved and straightened to secure it in place. My fingers traced the seven nails in their arched pattern, and I felt a chill rush through me, cold but somehow not uncomfortable. My eyes widened at the accompanying shiver.

A sound tore through the moment, and I ripped my gaze away to find Scout barking frantically at me, his ashy fur ruffled into points. Glancing back at the horseshoe to where my fingertips remained, I frowned as I found myself wanting to lean into it rather than move away. I hesitated, but brushed off the ridiculous feeling, lowering my hand instead to greet Scout, his hackles still raised. Scout had been my mother's solution to my father's passing — a puppy, surely meant to distract me from bringing up my father in the months that followed his death. Now I realized, he was likely a gift for her as much as he was for me.

"Hey, buddy. What's up?" I murmured, bending over and extending my hand to him. He quieted and gave me a pointed look but, after a reproachful sniff of my hand, his tail wagged in greeting. "That was a bit weird, wasn't it?"

He simply panted in response.

"Alright. Let's go see what we can scrounge up for dinner in this place. We need some fuel to make unpacking a little more enjoyable."

I straightened with a stretch as he sprinted toward the house in response to the word 'dinner'. I followed but halted by the door as the back of my neck prickled. I turned back toward the barn, in time to glimpse a flash of some large, dark figure dart behind it. I stiffened and waited several long heartbeats to see if I could catch any more movement, but the only sounds and stirrings came from the soft whooshing of the wind.

"Remind me again what happened to the family here before us?" I asked my mom through a muffled bite of pasta. It wasn't anything fancy, but the large pot was at the top of one of our kitchen moving boxes, and we'd been too hungry to rummage for anything else.

She finished her bite thoughtfully, and I took the opportunity to survey her. She had my dark brown hair, but lovely, simmering green eyes; she was slender, whereas I was muscled and, though I tended to be cold and distant, she lived for striking up conversations with both strangers and friends. Surely, she'd discussed the previous owner with our realtor.

"They all passed away. The man who lived here last held out until the last second but, eventually, he caved and had to visit the nearby hospital. I believe he died shortly after arriving there. The realtor heard he was a stubborn old man, Scottish blood: a firm believer that all he needed was some good mountain air to live a long healthy life." My mom paused. "I suppose he was right though. The man had been retired for over a decade before he passed."

"Did he not have any children that wanted this place?" I questioned, but my mom shook her head in response. "What about pets? Did he leave any animals here?"

"Not that I heard. He probably couldn't take care of them in his last few years," my mom replied, shooting me a curious look. "Why the twenty questions, Kate?"

I shrugged in response as the image of the mysterious creature burned behind my eyes. "Just thought I saw one earlier. I thought it might be a dog he left behind. But maybe it was a wolf."

"It's a possibility. That, or a coyote. But no, I don't think the previous owner left any pets around the area." My mom fixed me with her attempt at a 'stern-mom' expression, one she was too nice to ever deliver properly. "In that case, be sure to keep your head on a swivel when you take the pals out riding. I'm sure you'll be fine, but better safe than sorry."

Her voice wavered a bit as she lightly cautioned me, the tone and her words tugging at my heart. The silence that followed was weighted and as I spun pasta around my fork, I knew what we were both thinking.

She'd been the one to find my father, submerged in the creek running alongside our California property, after suffering a fall and head injury. Technically, they'd labeled his death a drowning due to the amount of water found in his lungs. I wasn't sure if it made it better or worse, considering he had always loved the water. She dealt with it by avoiding reminders of him — photos, songs, water, and lastly, the ranch.

Instead, I preferred pushing the boundaries to feel as close to him and his memory as I could. I hoarded every photo of him I could find, and every article of clothing I could slip from his closet before my mother sold most of it off in garage sales. I made a mental note to explore any nearby bodies of water, to see if I could feel his presence in the shimmering surface of a pond or hear his soft laughter in the rush of a creek.

But even if I resented the fact she pushed his memory away, I couldn't imagine my mother's pain after losing him. The older I got, the more I realized that while I had lost a father, she had lost a friend, a partner — a soulmate. I knew it haunted her daily, even over a decade later. I was certain it was a part of the reason why she threw herself into friendships so easily, filling the void my father had left. I knew, because it was the reason why I did the exact opposite. As I studied her anxious expression, I realized she wasn't just worried for my safety — she was nervous I was going to do the same to her; push her away for uprooting our home.

"Do you want to join me for a ride tomorrow?" I asked softly. She nodded across the table at me, a slow smile spreading across her face.

"Absolutely. Especially if it means we can put off unpacking and cleaning this kitchen for a few more hours."

I groaned in response to her teasing. "Who is this 'we' you speak of? I thought we had an 'I cook, you clean' system in place."

She chuckled and, dark mood lifted, we finished our meal in contented silence.

Chapter 2

Twice over the past few weeks, I swore I'd caught glimpses of a large, brown creature darting around our barn. Both times, it appeared in the early hours of the morning, as I was leaving for the new job I'd scored in town at the local coffee shop. I wasn't particularly happy to be up before the sun, but both of my run-ins with the creature woke me up more effectively than any cup of coffee could.

I'd done an egregious amount of research on local animal populations after first spotting the creature — even putting up with some very passionate lectures from a fellow barista, Lynn, who studied wildlife conservation — but I was no closer to discovering what it was. The local wildlife was bountiful, so it could have been any myriad of creatures — elk, bison, bears, foxes. The only animals I could exclude were smaller in size, as it was much too large to be any of those.

Perhaps it wasn't the smartest move, but I was determined to discover what was lurking around our barn. My curiosity compelled me to explore all the hiking paths around our home, and it was only an added bonus that it thrilled my mother. She happily mistook my intrigue as excitement over our move, whereas the truth was simply that I wanted answers.

I was like a dog with a bone – a very dark, mysterious bone that had me equal parts intrigued and worried. It could be a lost dog I needed to return to its owner or some starved, rabid animal; either way, I felt an obligation to protect our pets from this creature lurking around our house and barn.

I thought of that as I glanced down at Scout, ambling the path alongside my mother and me. He glanced up, his grayed face stretched in a doggish smile as he panted happily. I couldn't leave him at home while we hiked, not without sparking questions from my mom, but I kept his leash on as a precaution.

"I'm happy you picked a shorter hike today," my mother was saying. "I don't know how you keep doing these back-to-back daylong hikes. Even one of those would cripple me for a week!"

"To be fair," I returned with a smile, "I did half of those on horseback. The horses need exercise too, you know."

She rolled her eyes, murmuring some excuse in response to my light jab. She knew she needed to ride Coyote more often, but she'd been too excited about meeting the local townsfolk to direct much of her attention at home so far. Admittedly, I'd been more than happy to pick up the slack, returning home between shifts at the coffee shop. The company of my horses suited me much better than that of talkative Lynn.

While Lynn's knowledge on the local wildlife was sometimes interesting, it always disintegrated into topics involving trash TV, fashion, or recent arguments with her father. In her defense, I hadn't told her about mine, but it still stung. I'd give anything to have another argument with my dad, even over something silly like a curfew.

I brushed aside those negative thoughts and focused on the path instead, as the forest stretched into an expanse of lush green, flowered fields, beautifully juxtaposed against the gray, bare slab of mountain tops in the distance. My mom let out a happy sigh and bent over to pick one of several colorful flowers that bloomed along our path.

"Look," she exclaimed. She straightened and extended her palm to show me a tiny, scarlet-orange flower. "A fairy trumpet!"

I smiled and scanned the field, naming the other various flowers dotting the area – columbines, lupines, fireweed. I wasn't an avid floral collector like my mom, but I could appreciate their allure nonetheless. My thoughts were suddenly interrupted, however, by movement out of the corner of my eye. I tensed, moving slowly back to my mother's side.

"I won't take them home; they're poisonous to pets, but aren't they pretty? The trumpet flower symbolizes a fresh start, did you know that?" She carried on, her tone jovial, but halted as I grabbed her arm tightly.

"Mom," I murmured, tightening my hold on Scout's leash. She followed my gaze, and I heard the breath whoosh from her lips.

Across the field, a massive moose stood still, gaze locked on us. That fact alone would be both beautiful and unnerving, if it weren't for what stood at its side: a young calf, likely a month or two old. It didn't take being a local to know that a moose, especially a mother, was one of the most dangerous things you could encounter — the stories didn't do them justice. The mother was massive, easily a foot taller than our horses, and packed with thick muscle.

I felt a brush against my thigh as Scout took notice of the creatures. The blood drained from my face as I felt the rumble against my leg, and I knew what was coming before I even heard his deep growl. The moose's large ears swiveled, and she snorted in alarm, lowering her head.

Fuck.

"Scout," I muttered in desperation. *"No."*

"Kate...we need to back away...slowly." My mother's order came in a low tone, and I silently complied. As we backed up, the moose deliberately stepped in front of her calf before turning to face us once more. Its legs were long and spindly, but the power was all inside, evidenced only by the way her muscles rippled in her broad chest. Scout's growls intensified as it moved, inciting the moose further.

"Scout!" I hissed, the word a fatal mistake.

The moose lowered its head and, in one swift movement, charged. It took me a precious second to react, the speed of the large creature causing all thoughts to disappear from my brain. My mom tugged my arm, pulling me back to the tree line as we searched desperately for a large tree to either scale or hide behind. We could hear the moose clearing the field, approaching rapidly.

"Oh my god," my mom whispered anxiously as we pressed our backs against the largest tree we could find. I picked Scout up, pressing him tightly against my chest. My gut dropped as I mentally braced for the impact, and I wondered how much the creature weighed. Eight hundred, maybe a thousand pounds? Not to mention the addition of protective, animalistic rage.

Suddenly, Scout's growl erupted — only the sound was much deeper this time, more terrifying than before. I glanced down and saw he remained still and uneasy in my arms, no growl brewing between his teeth. Looking around in confusion, my eyes caught on a dark figure between two trees, further down the path. It didn't emerge fully into the clearing, but it was a large creature, round enough to be a bear.

You've got to be kidding me.

A dark brown muzzle appeared from the trees and into the light, revealing lips peeled back enough to expose large, dagger-like fangs. A vicious snarl rose over the sound of the approaching moose, causing a small squeal of terror to escape me.

"What? What? What do you see?" My mom asked, her voice breaking slightly with its shrill alarm. She whipped her head around and I watched in wild confusion as her eyes skirted several times over the figure, still mostly shadowed but clearly visible.

"You don't see that? Or hear it?" I asked, and pointed with a shaking finger, but she simply continued her panicked turning, confusion clouding her expression.

The approaching steps slowed with uncertainty, and then stopped entirely. My mother and I exchanged breathless looks as we waited. With the moose's charge halted, the snarling of the fanged creature stopped too, and I watched as the figure slipped back into the depths of the trees.

I released the breath I'd been holding as I heard the moose's movements shift back toward the field and noted my mother doing the same. We waited long after the sounds of its steps disappeared before moving, taking some much-needed time to recollect ourselves before shakily beginning our hike back down the pathway.

"I wonder if Scout somehow scared it off," my mom mused as we crossed back out of the tree line and into the yard of our home. I raised my brows, bewildered at her apparent disregard for the additional creature that appeared during the excitement earlier. Had she really not seen or heard it at all?

"It might have been the moose you saw near the house earlier," she considered, opening the door wide for me to go inside. I glanced back at the barn, thinking of the figure that had passed by a while back, comparing it to what we encountered today.

"Maybe," I hedged, but what I pictured in my mind was something entirely different, a creature that apparently only I had seen. One fearsome enough to put a charging moose at bay.

Chapter 3

I shook my head as I set up the wildlife camera, thinking — not for the first time — that the amount of time I invested in this was well and truly crazy. I had promised myself I'd be open to getting to know this new place, to build at least a few genuine connections with new people. Since the hiking mishap, I'd been out riding, sure, but otherwise, I had spent most of my time working or reading. Honestly, I wasn't too upset about it. Making friends was not my strong suit.

I just didn't seem to quite connect with the same hobbies, or with the same passion, like the rest of my classmates growing up. I floated in between social circles, always friendly but never forming anything lasting. My natural beauty helped: my curves, piercing eyes, and full lips attracted the attention of classmates as I grew older.

My curiosity over this new-found power was short-lived, however — I soon learned that any interest others took in me was merely skin deep. Anyone intrigued by my excitement over sports was interested, but only so that they could feed their ego by explaining them to me. The second they realized I not only participated in those sports, but could run faster, aim better, jump higher, and get more attention than them, they pulled away. I soon dropped any sports so that I could pretend to disappear. The only person who had ever cheered at those successes was my father.

Once college came around, it was even easier to fall into the shadows as an observer, rather than force friendships. At twenty, I wasn't yet old enough to go to the bars, and I felt no desire to make small talk with my classmates at house parties. I simply worked to keep my head down and receive good grades, if only to give my mother one less thing to worry about.

Gritting my teeth, I wondered what was worse – the hopeful look on my mother's face as I played up mere acquaintances as new best friends, just to calm her anxious mind, or the fact I couldn't care less that they were no more than lab partners.

I shoved those thoughts back as I fiddled with the camera, ensuring the power was on. If this creature was a coyote, I reasoned, I had enough experience with hunting to push away the guilt if I discovered it was posing a threat to the horses or Scout. Though we didn't see that much death on the ranch — mostly due to my father's expert handling of the animals — there was still a natural order to things, and I had long ago learned to compartmentalize.

I tapped the antenna and turned to my phone, checking the connection to the feed. Satisfied with the picture, I whistled to Scout and we both went inside. I grabbed some chips and flopped down on my bed, my eyes trained on the video feed.

As minute after minute passed, I found my attention waning, and decided to eventually prop my phone up with the live feed next to my laptop. To pass the time, I researched my fall semester courses. I was excited to finally take some classes outside of generals. Perhaps I'd even find a solo sport I could get involved with once more.

A bit of motion caught my attention, and my eyes whipped back to my phone. My whole body stilled, as if I could startle the creature outside from the safety of my bedroom. The sun was just beginning to set, casting a golden glow over the thick line of trees that surrounded the outskirts of our yard. From those trees, I watched as a large, russet-brown dog – scratch that, *wolf* – stepped calmly out of the tree line towards our barn.

It was massive, muscled like a grizzly bear rather than a wolf, and completely alone. The sun gleamed off its thick coat, nearly one solid color that looked like warm cinnamon. Its steps were slow and purposeful, head swaying from side to side. Then suddenly, it stopped and peered upward, almost as if it was assessing the horseshoe above our barn. After a moment, it emitted a low, mournful howl. The hair on my arms rose as I simply breathed two words.

"No way."

The wolf's head whipped around, fixing its eyes directly on the camera. My breath caught as I found myself staring into two very accusatory eyes: a piercing, unnatural azure blue. Even though it defied logic, with me sitting in the room looking at my phone screen, I felt as though I'd been caught, staring directly into this beautiful beast's soul. Time froze for one beat, and then two. Slowly, I exhaled and blinked for the first time since setting eyes on the wolf. The second I opened them again, he was gone.

"And you're sure, there's no such thing as brown wolves out here?" I asked the next day at work.

"Yes, Kate, I'm positive. Especially the way you described it. I've never heard of a thing like that." My coworker, Lynn, replied as she refilled the coffee sleeves, spilling several across the counter in the process. She groaned, and I flashed her a sympathetic grin. Her apron was already covered in syrup and wet coffee grounds, and we had only been open for an hour. "Are you sure it wasn't a stray dog or something?"

"Nope, it definitely wasn't," I replied. "But you're making me wish I'd spent the extra money for cloud storage to prove I'm not crazy."

She laughed, and I chuckled too, though my stomach churned as I remembered the eyes staring at me through the screen. I hadn't mentioned it to my mom, not wanting to worry her, but I had gone outside to check if there was any trace of the creature left in the area. I hadn't seen anything, but the eerie feeling still hadn't quite gone away. Part of me wondered if I'd really experienced any of it at all.

Gradually, our conversation shifted to more mundane topics, and I was able to bury myself in work. Tourists poured through, seeking caffeine to start or end their hikes, and I absorbed every route they discussed, making a mental bucket list of places to take the horses.

I was excited to learn there was a beautiful lake only a few miles outside of town, and I instantly placed it at the top of the list, planning to go on that ride after work. It was officially the longest day of the year today, and I could think of no better way to celebrate the official start of summer than with a nice dip.

As late afternoon rolled around and my shift came to a close, I poured a coffee for the road and tossed a goodbye to Lynn, hearing her yell "be safe!" as I darted out the door.

Once I arrived home, I threw a few snacks and a bottle of water into my saddle bag. Lynn's words rang in my ears, so I slid a hunting knife in the bag as well. I sent my mom a quick text to let her know where I'd be as I headed for the front door. Scout assessed my packing and decided he wanted to join, but the image of his last interaction with wild animals on a hike seared across my mind, and I tucked him back inside the house, apologizing as I heard his whines of complaint.

"Come on, Cheddy, ready for a ride?" I murmured as I slid into the barn, giving Chester a quick groom and saddling up. By my calculations, we had a solid six hours before sunset even began, so I enjoyed the trail up to the lake, letting Chester take his time picking the path and absorbing the sounds of nature. The birds chirped, the wind rustled, and slow footfalls came from Chester's hooves, lulling me into a full state of relaxation. I even gave begrudging kudos to my mom — nature *was* healing, and we were absolutely surrounded by it here.

However, as we approached the lake, I felt the hairs on the back of my neck slowly rise, as though I was being watched. I pulled Chester up and took a few beats to look around, but saw nothing. After a minute, I brushed it off. The tourists at the coffee shop had said the area was always busy.

When the lake came into view, though, I found it completely empty. There was nobody in sight fishing, kayaking, or camping at all, despite it being a relatively large lake. I knew it should have unnerved me, but the sight of such a large, shimmering body of water all to myself was insanely tempting. My eyes fixated on it as I urged Chester forward, allowing him to drink deeply from the clear glacial water.

He stepped into the water without hesitation and crashed his hooves down, sending large puddles up his stomach to cool off. He was clearly unfazed and I felt myself loosen at the sight, bringing back memories of similar outings with my father. When I was little, I had a pony that always tried to lie down in the water with me still on top. Instead of trying to bail before he laid down, I would cling on, splashing around with the pony. My father never chastised me in those moments; rather, he simply laughed at the sight and splashed more water on both of us, until all of us were soaked.

I grinned at the memory and turned Chester back to the shore to dismount, stooping to pull off my shoes and socks. Rolling up my jeans, I waded back into the water with Chester, wiggling my toes as cool water rushed over the tops of my feet.

I was debating dipping further in for a good float when all at once, the entire sky turned cloudy. I stiffened and tightened my hold on Chester's reins, looking up for further signs of a storm passing through.

Instead of rain, a layer of fog gradually rolled in, settling around us as if the lake was suddenly a hot spring in winter. I backed out of the lake nervously and crouched to put my shoes and socks back on.

I straightened, though, as I glimpsed a figure across the lake. After a jolt of surprise, I realized it wasn't human – it was a horse.

Chester realized it too, snorting while his ears swiveled in confusion. He let out a whinny to announce himself, and I strained my eyes to watch the strange horse's response. It made no sound, but seemed to pick its way across the lake towards us, body language alert and friendly. I didn't see an owner anywhere in sight.

As it got closer, I was completely awed by its beauty. It was a large dappled stallion, more white than gray, with a long, ashy mane and tail, and piercing black eyes. He appeared well taken care of, clearly not a wild horse or a runaway. He didn't have any tack on, though, so I wasn't sure what he was doing alone all the way out here. All worry about aggression washed away as he approached, and I found myself extending a hand in greeting.

"Hey, boy," I whispered, and his ears immediately pricked at my tone.

Chester clearly wanted to meet him as well as he strained against the reins, making whuffling noises in greeting. The stallion completely ignored him, eyes trained on me. He finally reached me and, as his dark, velvet muzzle reached the palm of my hand, a jolt of electricity rushed through me. If I didn't know any better, I could have sworn a golden — almost white — spark lit the space where our touches met, skittering out over my arm. Time seemed to stand still.

A strangled sound emanated from behind us, breaking the trance. I whirled to find a man in a cream tunic standing at the clearing of the lake, his eyes wide and mouth open. The stallion tossed his head and snorted, dancing a few steps away.

Automatically, I sidled to Chester's back, my hand reaching to the saddle bag to locate the hilt of the knife I'd packed. The man made no move, instead seeming to have difficulty grasping for words. We stood in a silent face-off and I simply glared, waiting for him to announce what he was doing here.

Eventually, he managed to choke out three words. "By the gods."

Chapter 4

"Who are you?" I demanded as I hid behind Chester, my hand fumbling for the hilt of my hunting knife. My heart thundered as I realized we were the only humans here at the lake.

The man was busy struggling to find words as my gaze scraped over him, assessing his strange outfit. He didn't seem much older than me, perhaps in his late twenties. His tunic was old-fashioned, but certainly not ragged. Maybe there was a Renaissance Faire passing through town? I'd heard Lynn talking about one down she wanted to go to, taking place near Denver later in the summer.

As my gaze shifted upward, I took in the scruff on his chin, somewhere between a beard and a five o'clock shadow, matching his shaggy auburn hair. His eyes were wide with shock, and I was taken aback by the deep, almost unnaturally blue nature of his stare. I blinked rapidly, trying to place what it reminded me of.

"Who are *you?*" He finally managed to get out, and my mouth turned into a defensive sneer as I noted my question remained unanswered.

"I'm the one minding my own business out here. You seem to be the one who followed a girl alone to the lake." I retorted brazenly. My brain scrambled to remember any tips I gleaned over the years while listening to true crime. I was good at being an asshole, but I couldn't remember if that was a good or a bad thing. I clutched the knife tighter just in case.

The man blinked, though his mouth twitched at the savage tone in my response, seemingly amused rather than hostile.

"Fair enough. My name is Kipp. Now, an answer for an answer – is this your horse?" He motioned to the stallion on my right, who I now noticed had made no move to leave this strange situation.

"No," I admitted. "He's not yours?"

I had the fleeting thought that perhaps the man had been chasing this horse, and embarrassment flushed my cheeks at my abrasive tone, if that were true. He certainly could be a jousting horse — a beautiful one at that — which made the Renaissance Faire idea much more plausible.

The man — Kipp — shook his head in response. "He certainly seems to have taken to you, though, if this is your first time seeing him," he pointed out cautiously, a curious gleam shimmering in his eyes, as if the statement held a thousand more questions. He spoke like he was much older and wiser than he looked, which couldn't have been a day over twenty-nine. I clenched my jaw, unnerved once more by the scrutiny.

"So, Kipp, you just decided to take a stroll through nature, alone, in a medieval costume?" I asked hesitantly.

"A – hmm? Oh," Kipp peered down, pursing his lips together. "You really must not know anything, then." He fixed his gaze on me incredulously.

A knee-jerk spiteful response bubbled up at his comment, and I glowered at him. The response died in my throat before I could voice it, however, lost while studying the azure blue color of his eyes. My gaze rose to his auburn brown hair, and a strange, aching familiarity struck me.

"Do — do I know you?" I choked out, and my stomach lurched as he nodded and smiled, his pointed canines gleaming white.

His canines.

"The wolf," I whispered under my breath, not daring to say something so ludicrous out loud. The man's smile widened as if he heard me, dipping his head as if to confirm my outlandish accusation. My heartbeat thudded wildly in my ears, and my weight shifted as I considered how quickly I could swing my boot back into Chester's saddle for a quick getaway.

"So, I suppose your new question is," he started, filling in the silence before I could fully leap onto Chester's back. "Not *who*, but *what* I am."

I lowered the foot I had started to lift toward my stirrup but remained silent, face taut. I was torn between the rational decision to leave, and the morbid curiosity that kept me rooted to the spot.

He paused, contemplating his next words. "It's much more complex than this, but for now, I believe this primitive explanation should suffice," he mused.

"I am a Faerie. And so, it seems, are you."

I laughed — maniacally. The absurdity of the comment landed, washing over me, and the only reaction I could possibly dredge up was to dissolve into stitches. I tried to stop, but ended up snorting, falling into another fit of laughter.

I just couldn't reconcile the warring in my head. What I'd heard logically had no stake in reality. Yet it was no less rational than my clear-as-day discovery of a shapeshifting wolf standing in front of me. I worked to push down the laughter still building in my throat, coughing.

Kipp cocked his head in what was an unmistakably lupine-like manner, blue eyes simply assessing me. He said nothing and stepped no further. I felt the heat spread up my neck and to my cheeks, growing defensive beneath his assessing gaze. I sucked in a steadying breath.

"What, you just expect me to believe I dropped into a children's book?" I snapped. "You're either the world's worst practical joker, or you have terrible social skills, because that's not how you drop a bomb on someone."

"Well, I'm no Pixie. I'm sure you'd find many more humorous creatures than me." Kipp deadpanned. All I could do was blink. "But fine. Let's see if I can do one better."

I stepped back in alarm, but before I could question his ominous words, the air around him rippled. It wavered like a mirage cast in the light between the sky and a hot pavement. I watched as every one of Kipp's limbs bent and shrank, the cinnamon color of his hair expanding to cover the entirety of his body as he dove to the ground. The whites of his eyes disappeared as his pupils shrunk, the piercing blue of his irises widening as his eyes became almond-shaped.

A strangled gasp escaped me as I stumbled back, the force of Kipp's heavy padded claws thudding loudly against the forest floor. The fog suddenly seemed heavier all around me as I found myself facing off with the same large, brown wolf I'd seen on my camera only a day prior.

He could have easily looked vicious in this massive form, but it was almost like he did his best to appear docile; his ears swiveled and his tail swished as he allowed me to absorb the scene in front of me. He waited several long moments for me to grasp what had materialized before me, and then shifted back. The air trembled once more as he leapt forward, my heart lurching in alarm before he transformed midair, adopting his human form once more. He took a few steps to right himself before coming to a stop and straightening on his, now, two feet.

Kipp lightly brushed off his tunic and pants, which were still somehow impeccably placed, before continuing. "I can assure you, this is no joke. For starters, the fact that you can even *see* me proves your Faerie blood. I had suspicions after you set up the camera."

My mind darted back to the memory of the wolf's eyes, staring directly into the camera. The breath whooshed out of me as though I'd been punched. "It *was* you! I knew you'd somehow heard me!" I exclaimed incredulously.

His mouth twitched, amused, and he nodded. "I have hearing far superior to yours in my wolf form."

"And...and it was you that helped fend off that charging moose," I murmured. His face went grim as he gave a serious nod, lips pursing at the memory.

I was still reeling, but my mind latched onto part of his previous comment.

"Wait." I shook my head. "You said that *I* have Faerie blood? Because I can see you?" My breaths were coming faster now, my chest rising and falling as the information I'd been presented with over the last few moments all clashed together.

"That doesn't make any sense. None of this does. I grew up *here,* with a very human life, with a very human family." My voice raised slightly, shaking, as if arguing would change the truth.

He simply shrugged in response. "There are many ways a person can become immersed in the Fae world. Perhaps you're a changeling; a Faerie child swapped for a human child at birth. Or even a faeling – half human, half Faerie."

He peered at me as if he could find the answer by simply mentioning the creatures, and my gut twisted uncomfortably at his casual use of those words to describe what he thought I was. It was inconceivable that everything I thought I knew about my family, my upbringing — my very *being* — could be entirely false. I crossed my arms as a shiver ran rampant through my body.

"Though," he mused further. "None of that explains *Liath Macha.*"

I was just about to ask what he meant when the gray stallion beside me tossed his head and let out a piercing whinny. He bobbed his head a few times, then trotted toward Kipp. I expected Kipp to simply stroke his thick neck, but was baffled when he dropped his head instead, almost bowing.

"May the strength of the wind and the light of the sun always surround you," he murmured nervously, in what sounded like a blessing.

I raised my eyebrows, readying my tongue for some snarky comment on the ridiculousness unfolding before me, when the stallion dipped its huge nose directly to Kipp's forehead, pressing the black velvet against it in a distinctly non-animal-like gesture.

Everything stilled for a moment, to the point where I realized I couldn't even hear the birds or bugs around the lake. It was as though the world had closed off to everything except the two of us and the horses. After several long seconds, the stallion backed away and pointedly returned to his place next to me. Kipp raised his head, eyes shimmering.

"Liath Macha is one of the most revered animals in our history," he finally spoke, answering the question that hung in the air after their unique exchange.

"It translates to 'gray of Macha'. His size and beauty are unparalleled. He was a gift from the goddess Macha to one of our greatest heroes, to be used as a chariot horse. He's also the best war horse from the past millennium."

His voice caught on the last sentence and, as he recovered, my mind spun at the casual use of the word 'millennium.' How old was this horse? Was it some sort of demigod? Furthermore, to know this story as if firsthand, though he *looked* young ... how old was Kipp?

"Fifty soldiers killed with his teeth," Kipp went on, his expression faraway as he recounted the story. "Thirty with his hooves. Some said Liath Macha died in the battle with his master, but others believed he went back to Gray Lake, where he first appeared. Either way, he hasn't been seen since."

Until now, I finished internally.

My skin prickled, mentally envisioning the puzzle pieces coming together as to why Kipp drew this conclusion around the revered war horse. I took in the empty lake, the fog surrounding us, and finally, the large, gray stallion, whose deep black eyes were assessing only me.

My gaze traveled to his muzzle and his large hooves, wondering if he truly harnessed the ability to kill multiple people in battle – let alone eighty. He was larger than most horses I'd seen, and certainly more muscular. But past that, I didn't see anything particularly mythical about him. My fingers twitched as I remembered the light that passed from his muzzle up my arm, and I reconsidered. Suddenly, another thought struck me.

"It makes sense for him to appear at a lake, and in front of a Faerie like yourself," I began haltingly. "But ... why me?"

Kipp fixed me with another one of his appraising looks, eyes flashing. "I can only see one reason. He's chosen you, specifically, because he knows that something is about to happen. What that is, I do not know. But I imagine it will be something monumental, and possibly devastating."

Chapter 5

Part of me wanted to leave Kipp in the dust and try to pretend this strange encounter never happened. Another part of me wanted to grab and grill him on this whole different life, separate from the one I knew — a life I was, allegedly, supposed to be a part of.

I opted for neither, instead facing away from him so he couldn't use that piercing gaze of his to analyze the warring emotions I was sure ran rampant across my face. I took my time to calm down, fiddling with Chester's tack and finally slinging my leg over the saddle, squirming to get comfortable.

As I gathered my reins in my hands and clicked for Chester to move forward, I heard Kipp blurt out behind me, "What are you doing?"

I tossed him a look before turning back to the trail in front of me, taking in his shock and confusion.

"You come here and tell me I'm at least part Faerie and that this war horse chose me for something," I responded, gritting my teeth. "Excuse me if I need a little while to digest this information. And in the meantime, I figured I'd take Lia-Liatch –" I fumbled over the word he'd used for 'gray' and cleared my throat.

"I figured I'd take Gray back to the barn with me to figure out exactly what purpose he has with me." I finished. The stallion's ears pricked as I focused my attention on him, and I swore he gave a whicker of approval at my less-than-clever nickname.

"You can't just take him back to your human barn!" Kipp exclaimed, scrambling after us. "He's meant for the Faerie realm. If anything, that's where we need to be headed now." I jolted in my saddle, grabbing the back of it and twisting around to face him.

"There's another *realm?*" I questioned, astonished. I was pretty sure my heart was close to collapsing from this overload of information, and if it hadn't been for the wolf exploding to life in front of me, I would have blamed this all on a strange dream. I slid a hand to my arm subconsciously, giving it a pinch, just in case.

"Of course! There's a reason why you don't just see hordes of Fae folk in your daily life," he replied matter-of-factly.

I faced forward once more, shaking my head. "Well, I've got a life here. I won't just drop everything on a whim in case I might be summoned to another realm. Especially a realm I just heard about from a stranger two seconds ago." I clucked my tongue to urge Chester forward, and Gray followed alongside us.

I heard a distressed snarl from behind me, and suddenly, Kipp was in front of Chester, teeth flashing. Chester shied, and I cursed as I grabbed for the saddle horn. "What the hell do you think you're doing?" I demanded, balking at his sudden change in temper.

"What I think," he hissed in a low tone, "is that I protected a family for centuries, only to have them die out a few months ago. And now, you come along. And though you apparently know nothing about the Fae folk, you can *see me,* making you one of us. Not only that, but your presence summons one of the greatest hero's steeds that has not been seen in nearly a millennium." He fixed me with a determined look, letting the words sink in.

My mouth opened and closed, but no words came out. A family he protected? A hero?

Kipp pressed on, ignoring me. "As for your role in this? I cannot say. But fate seems to be clear with mine. I have no more family to protect, and you have no idea of the world you're being thrust into. So, I will be your guide and your protector."

He stated it so simply that it left no room for discussion. For several long moments, we squared off, waiting for each other's next move – me, from my perch on Chester's back, and Kipp, from his wolfish stance on the ground. I realized that no matter what, from here on out, I had a big thorn in my side that I would be unable to shake. A thorn with cinnamon-colored hair and blue eyes.

"Fine, you big canine brute," I muttered. "What is it you want me to do?"

He noticeably perked up and stepped out of my way, peering up at me excitedly. "Well, first off, I should probably know your name."

"It's Katherine. My friends call me Kate."

"Well, Katherine — Kate. We're in luck. It's the summer solstice."

"What does that have to do with anything?"

"The Faerie realm. The portals for travel between our realms only open every so often, and the solstice is one of those times," he explained. "It's probably why Laith – erm, *Gray* – appeared to you today of all days."

"But it's just luck that I learned about the lake today. Sheer luck that I went today." I muttered, my head spinning. Kipp fixed me with a somber expression.

"There is no luck. Only fate. Fate decided to lead you here today." He stated seriously. "And it's fate for me to guide you through the portal today as well."

Realization dawned on me with those words.

"Today? We're leaving today? What about my mom? My job, my entire life here? How long would we be gone?" I sputtered with rising panic. A trip through the portal to a new realm didn't sound like a quick excursion to merely ask some questions. And yet, I realized, my hesitations were simply of a rational sort, trying to tie up loose ends. Some deeper, more intrinsic part of me was already blossoming with intrigue — and if I were being honest, my sudden curiosity frightened me more than anything else did.

Kipp shrugged, clearly unbothered by my barrage of frenzied questions. He turned away and began walking down the trail, tossing words over his shoulder.

"Impossible to say. However, we'll still make a trip back to the farm. I have some things to gather there, and we can ensure your absence makes sense for your family. You can ask your — presumably many — other questions as we go."

The tightness in my chest lessened slightly at his nonchalance, and I followed as we started back home. The first question that came to me was sparked by his comments. "How can this possibly be explained to my mom?" I questioned, exasperated.

Kipp didn't miss a beat, expecting the follow-up. "With magic, of course."

I rolled my eyes, muttering sarcastically, "Of course. *Magic.* How come I didn't think of that?"

Though his back was turned to me, I was pretty sure I heard him chuckle.

The ride back was filled with questions, just as Kipp expected, but he answered each with ease. Apparently, he was incredibly adept at enchanting items and could enchant a few objects of my mother's so that if she — or anyone else — questioned where I was, I would either be on a ride, at work, or back at school, depending on the circumstances. My mom always wore her wedding band, but Kipp would enchant a few other items, just in case.

I would call work and let them know my mom needed me at home for the foreseeable future. As for school – well, my heart jumped nervously at the idea of being gone so long. I just hoped I would be back in time for the fall semester. I had to be.

My immediate concerns covered, I redirected my curiosity back to Kipp. Though he wasn't exceptionally tall, he walked gracefully, keeping pace easily with the horses. His mass of shaggy hair curled around his ears, and it shifted between a rich dark brown and an almost reddish hue as the sun hit it between trees. I squinted, but couldn't tell if his ears had a curve to them like in the stories I'd heard. It didn't appear so.

Muscles rippled underneath his tunic as he moved. His arms, I realized, were incredibly toned. He wasn't stocky by any means, but his strength clearly surpassed your average athletic twentysomething – though I knew he only looked that age. I wondered briefly how old he truly was, but bit my lip. I wasn't sure I was mentally prepared to learn yet.

Kipp's skin was a deep tan, as though he spent most of his time outdoors and yet, as I scanned over his limbs, there was not a single sunspot on him. I glanced down at my arms, noticing a handful of freckles, and frowned.

"So, what makes a Faerie a Faerie? What specific ... qualities do you – do we – have?" I asked, stumbling over the term 'we'. He smiled at me gently, clearly noting the stumble.

"There's no singular definition. Faeries come from different races and different regions. As humans have different backgrounds and qualities, so do the Fae folk. I, for example, am an *Ùruisg*."

I snorted at the strange word, but received a sharp look from Kipp, which made me quickly straighten in the saddle, coughing to disguise the sound. "Okay, I'll bite. What's an ... Urisk?" I asked, using a simpler pronunciation of the word he'd said.

"Simply put, we are household protectors. The lore states we do chores around the house, but it's much more than that." He paused for a moment. "We find purpose in supporting the distressed and relieving the work that weary hands let fall. Whenever and however that assistance may be deemed necessary." My heart squeezed at his selfless tone as he recited the definition and I remembered his words from earlier.

"And you had a specific family you helped," I stated softly, prompting but not wanting to push the subject.

"I did." His reply came easily, but I couldn't help but notice the tension in his shoulders as he responded. "Most of us do. And if we're lucky, we follow their bloodline for the rest of our lives. But it doesn't always – work out."

I nodded. If anybody understood the intricacies of luck, family, and death, it was me. "I wish it had, for you." I responded sincerely.

His expression was one of surprise when he turned to me, before looking down for several moments.

"And you, then?" He ventured suddenly, changing the subject. "You never heard any family tales? Or suspected you were otherwise different from other humans?"

I shook my head in response. "I grew up in California. I had a normal childhood. A normal family that did normal things." I fiddled with my reins, stomach clenching. "I suppose I always preferred my family and animals to most other people, but that's not exactly an inhuman red flag."

"Not all people are worth your time and devotion," Kipp reasoned. I shifted in my saddle slightly at his response. Such a simple explanation for a lifetime of distress. "So, your mother and father are your only family?"

My heart squeezed, as it always did when the topic was broached. "My mother only. My father passed away when I was ten."

"I see," he replied, and I stole a curious look as he avoided any sort of apology. I wasn't offended, I found myself realizing – only surprised. It was refreshing, in a way, to simply have the moment remembering him, and not be pitied for it. Having to reply that it was 'okay' was exhausting, and somehow seemed to tarnish his memory, while my body screamed how *not okay* it really was. But the lie came out each time anyway, if only to placate the other person rather than myself.

"And how old are you now?" He asked, navigating to safer topics.

"Twenty. Almost twenty-one." I replied and heard the breath whistle in his teeth as he sucked in, surprised. "What?"

"You're just – so young." He wiped a hand across his face. "I mean, I understand how human lifespans work, better than most Fae. But you've hardly begun to experience anything."

"You only look maybe nine or ten years older than me," I began cautiously, wanting – but unsure I would fully grasp – the answer. His lip curled in amusement at that.

"After a certain age, Faerie aging slows. Roughly around twenty. I'm sure in a few years' time, you would have begun to realize the differences between you and the humans you surround yourself with."

"So, you're not immortal?" I asked, surprised.

He shook his head. "Not immortal, no. But we do have immensely longer lifespans. For example, I was born about three hundred years ago."

Chester's head tossed as my hand jerked from sheer surprise. Guiltily, I murmured to him and stroked his neck as my mind backtracked through old history lessons. Both World Wars, the Civil War, the Revolutionary War...

It was too much to get into, and I was sure it wouldn't be Kipp's first choice to discuss human history with me, especially given his sensitivity to discussions involving his old family. Opting to move on, I said, "So if you're an Urisk, what does that make...me?"

He studied me for a moment, blue eyes glimmering. "It's hard to say. Here in the human world, there's nothing really to put a shine on your defining characteristics. Magic is severely dampened here."

I deflated slightly, eager to know more about my heritage, which appeared to be straightforward until about an hour prior. "What are my – options?" I asked.

Kipp released a long breath, clearly underestimating the number of questions I would have during the ride home, yet continued good-naturedly.

"Many I'm sure you've heard of, though the human world often muddles the races. Nymphs, Leprechauns, Dwarves, Pixies, Selkies, Boggarts, Sirens..." He tapped off a finger for each as if reading off an invisible checklist. "The list goes on."

My head swirled. "What about elves? Or sprites?"

"All one and the same. Interchangeable words for Faeries. Magical creatures." He shrugged. "Call us what you will. We're a Folk with common denominators, but unique in many ways within. Magic that expresses itself in vastly different ways."

"And I'll have magic? When I get into the other realm?" I questioned wondrously.

Kipp hummed in affirmation. "A great deal of it, if I had to wager a guess."

Chapter 6

Three-hundred-year-old Urisks hoarded some weird items, I soon discovered. My brow lifted as I watched Kipp cram a seemingly bottomless bag with various things: cups, stones, and what looked like a bag of sand. However, both of my eyebrows raised as he cupped an old wooden toy that looked like a tipper truck. Kipp paused, then dropped it into the bag.

He caught my eye and cleared his throat. "Your turn."

I entered the house and headed straight to my bedroom. There I stood, assessing. Clothes were piled in their respective drawers, with trinkets spread across the top of the dresser. I had only finished unpacking a week earlier, and now, here I was, packing once more. My pulse quickened at the uncertainty that lay before me, but I shook it off and grabbed a backpack, stuffing shorts, shirts, and undergarments into it, refusing to allow myself too much time to think.

As I lifted the bag to my shoulder, my eyes snagged on a photo tucked into the corner of my mirror. The photo was of my parents and a much younger me during a trip to Badlands National Park.

Striped rocks colored the background, but my gaze focused solely on my parents, grinning from ear to ear. Both had a hand placed on my shoulder: a mark of protection. Love.

I snatched the photo on impulse and tucked it into the back of my jeans. I fixed my face into an expression of nonchalance as I exited the room, running into my mom lugging some grocery bags into the kitchen.

"Hey, mom," I greeted her as casually as I could. "How was your day?"

"Great!" She replied enthusiastically, setting the bags on the counter. She launched into a story about a new friend she'd made as she unpacked, accompanying the tale with comically exaggerated gestures as I smiled, using the opportunity to study her closely.

Smile lines etched her face, but even as she began to age, it adapted her beauty into something new, and just as stunning. Though her attractiveness and warm personality drew men to her like moths to a flame, she only ever had eyes for my father. Following his death, she allowed her personality to dim for several years, but even I noticed how she had blossomed since moving here, putting down roots and meeting new people.

A shadow materialized behind my mother as she spoke, and I realized with a start that Kipp was standing behind her. My eyes darted between him and my mother, breath held, waiting to see if my mother would notice his presence. What that would possibly mean for my heritage, if she had Faerie blood as well.

She simply carried on with her story without pause.

Kipp softly placed a finger on her ring as her hand lay resting on the kitchen table. His lips moved in a silent spell, and he retreated a moment later with a nod. It was done.

I flew forward to embrace my mom, who seemed startled but accepted it without question.

"What's this for?" She asked, laughing. I breathed in the comforting smell of her – freshly laundered clothes and pine.

"Nothing," I breathed in response. "I just – I'm glad to have you as my mom."

"And I'm lucky to have you, kiddo," she replied. I soaked in those words as her hand instinctively went to the back of my head, brushing my hair. My eyes pricked with tears and I pulled away, shrugging my backpack further on my shoulder.

"I'm going to take Scout for a quick walk," I said, proudly noting the steadiness of my voice. I didn't wait for her response as I walked out the door, whistling for Scout.

He came running instantly. I dropped on the front porch and scooped him up into my arms, taking deep breaths into his fur as I reminded myself it would be a couple of weeks at most. Just enough time to figure out my role in whatever this was. He was none the wiser and wiggled happily in the embrace, twisting around in an effort to kiss my face.

Kipp was inspecting the kitchen window as I straightened.

"It's taking effect," he murmured.

I peered into the window and saw her. She was in the middle of emptying the dishwasher, frozen with a plate poised in hand, a blank expression clouding her features. It passed after a moment, and she shook her head, continuing with the dishes. I swallowed back the rising guilt, reminding myself that it was only temporary — a safety precaution, ensuring she'd be none the wiser.

Kipp turned to me. "Time to go."

I told Scout to stay, then checked to ensure Gray was still hanging about. He was, looking out of place with his size and elegance in front of our small barn, where Chester and Coyote safely resided. His alert expression told me he was ready to continue our adventure and I turned as the realization sunk in. I had no idea where we were actually going.

As if reading my mind, Kipp started ahead and tossed back, "We need to find a ley line. That's where we'll pass through to the other realm."

"What's a ley line?" I asked, scrambling to follow. Gray trotted along behind me.

"Think of it like...your series of roads connecting on a map, but instead of transporting cars, they transport energy. Where lines converge, they carry enough energy to act as a conduit to our world on sacred days, when our worlds are pressed closer together."

"Ah," I replied, glancing down at the ground. I'd never picked up on any unique energies, but then again – I'd never been searching.

We picked our way through the forest, Kipp pausing every now and then as his body worked like some sort of ley line GPS. His satchel rustled every now and then as we scaled rocks and fallen trees, until finally I blurted, "Why were you packing old toys and sand?"

He glanced up, startled, and then gave a guilty sort of smile. "Urisks are natural hoarders," he admitted, "and my old family was incredibly superstitious." I thought of the old horseshoe on the barn, wondering if that may explain the pull of it.

"Most of what they collected was just junk, but every now and then, they came across a truly magical object. When Gerry passed," he continued, eyes shadowing, "I wanted to ensure those special items didn't end up in the wrong hands."

"So, the sand...?" I began carefully, not wanting to pry.

"Magical – it helps people sleep soundly." He slowed to analyze a spot in front of us.

"And the toy?"

He stopped. "Not magical. But still special." Before I could reply, he pointed to the ground. "We're here."

I looked down and saw – nothing. We were surrounded by rock and greenery, no trail in sight. And though I gave my body a quick scan, I noticed nothing different. Kipp noticed my frustrated expression and chuckled softly, reaching out his hand.

"Grab onto me – and Gray," he said. I slid my hand into his, realizing with a start how warm and large it was. I reached back for Gray, who came up beside me without hesitation.

As I touched his mane again, a slightly smaller spark than the first one danced across my palm again. I felt Kipp shudder next to me, emitting a low guttural noise from his throat. I glanced at him quizzically, and saw his jaw was tightly clenched.

Kipp didn't even look at me as he replied. "I felt your magic just now. It's – buried, certainly. But it's definitely there." He straightened. "This will probably feel strange for you, but just keep contact with me, and you won't get lost."

Wait – lost? Panic bubbled up in me, and I opened my mouth to protest, but before I could, my stomach squeezed as though I were hurtling down a rollercoaster — one that was abruptly spinning, twirling, and dropping, and then —

Then we were there.

I blinked once, slowly, and then several times in rapid succession as the saturated effect on the surrounding land around me remained. It was all I could do to breathe.

It was as if we were still in the Colorado mountain range, but somehow – not. The grass was greener, the sounds of animals in the surrounding trees were louder, and even the dirt seemed to have more color and contrast to it.

Warmth radiated off my face as I peered into the sky, where the sun was beginning its slow descent. The pinkish hues started where sky and earth met, blending in an exotic dance of pink, orange, and cobalt blue.

I glanced at Kipp, who was silently observing me as I took in the world, and I let out a soft gasp. His skin looked warmer, his eyes more piercing, but the greatest difference was a gentle – *energy* now emanating from him as I focused on his face. And that's when I felt it.

Humming was the best word to describe it. I felt a humming from the inside out, as if I had drunk more coffee than humanly possible, yet without the urge to twitch or fidget. I felt like I was burning with the heat pulsating through my veins, desperately aching for release. I lowered my gaze to my hands and rotated my palms where the energy buzzed.

"Oh," was all I could say.

"How does it feel?" Kipp asked softly, almost nervously. I hesitated before answering.

"Uncomfortable," I admitted. A nose pressed into my shoulder, and I glanced over to see Gray, looking even more impressive in stature than before as he nuzzled me.

I smiled and stroked my palm down his large face. Even the touch — from his coarse hair down to his soft, velvet muzzle — felt elevated. I shivered.

"If I didn't believe you before, I do now."

He smiled a little in response, but it didn't quite reach his eyes. "Now it's just a question of who we go to next." His lips pursed in contemplation. Then, he sighed. "I suppose the only logical answer is to go straight to the queen."

I felt my pulse quicken as his words registered. "There's a — a queen here? Why do I need to visit her?"

"You'll want to announce yourself. Someone in her court will have already received notice of your unregistered magical signature entering her lands."

Queens, and courts, and lands...it was all so much, and we had only *just* arrived. I bit my lip and pulled my light jacket in tighter around myself like a protective shield. I suddenly feared that this had been a huge mistake. My mouth opened as I considered making the request to return home.

"She will also likely set you up with a place to stay in the palace." Kipp added before I could voice my concerns. He ran a hand over his face, as if wondering whether to divulge his next thoughts and, despite the endless new information whirring about in my head, I latched onto that movement like a warning bell. My eyes narrowed as I realized there was more.

"Why would she do that?" I demanded, my hand dropping from Gray. Kipp cleared his throat and averted his eyes.

"Because now that you're here, I see what you are. You're one of the *Aes Sídhe* race. And so is she."

Everything went quiet for a moment as he allowed the weight of those words to sink in. But all I felt was confusion.

"Huh?" I responded weakly. Kipp's brows furrowed, as if I was a riddle he couldn't figure out.

"What is – an ay shee?" I fumbled over the term phonetically, and felt my cheeks burn at the intensity of his stare.

His eyebrows went from furrowed to straight up. "I keep forgetting that you probably haven't even heard Celtic stories; those words must be completely foreign to you."

He laughed and glanced at the sky, noting the setting sun as he looked around. His eyes locked on a large, flat rock, and he hopped onto it in a heartbeat – even more gracefully than before, I noted.

"Alright. Settle in," he said, smiling. "I suppose you should know a bit about your history before I throw you right into it."

Chapter 7

"All humans are direct descendants of Faeries," Kipp began. "We look similar in our most basic forms, and we have the same languages, thought processes, and emotions. In turn, Faeries are direct descendants of deities. There are many, many gods of varying power levels and magical qualities. That's why our races are so diverse with our numerous, albeit toned down, versions of magic."

I sat cross-legged in the grass, enraptured in his story. "So, there are multiple gods?" I asked.

Kipp nodded. "There were. From local gods to all-powerful deities. They're known in your world as well – mostly identified by the Celts, the Romans, and the Greeks. However, it's an older concept muddled together over time. But this was back when humankind was more connected to nature, their hearts more open to the idea of something greater than themselves."

I thought of what I'd learned briefly in history class about Greek and Roman gods, and my mind churned as names flitted through my brain. Apollo, Artemis Jupiter, Hades...it had been interesting, certainly, but nothing I'd ever taken seriously. I leaned in, propping my chin in my hands and my elbows on my knees in silent encouragement for him to continue.

"The Aes Sídhe are descended specifically from the goddess Danu — *Tuatha Dé Danann* is the name of the specific folk. They were a supernatural race of gods, so strong that some wonder if they were fallen angels.

"These gods ruled for five ages of the world before an army of humans conquered and settled the land. Some stories say the Tuatha Dé Danann fought and lost the battle for the human realm, but others say prophecy showed that the humans were meant to live and rule in their realm instead, so they willingly moved.

"Either way, the Tuatha Dé Danann built these kingdoms in this realm for the sixth age, and here all Fae folk dwell today. Parallels in some senses, but fully split from the human world."

My eyes were wide. "How do you know all of this?" I breathed. "About Gray? About my race's entire upbringing?"

"Everyone learns basic history about the Tuatha Dé Danann growing up here," he said, shrugging. "But I do descend from a line of *seanchaí*. We are born storytellers, taught to remember and pass down oral Faerie legends as part of our duty to our kind.

"And on that note," Kipp leaned so far forward that he almost fell off his perch. "I wouldn't mention who Gray is to those who do not know. I saw it in the way he chose you: the location, your connection with each other...only someone who knows the story like I do, and saw what I did, would understand. To those around here, he can pass as a normal — if large — stallion.

"The last time he was seen, it was during one of the darkest and bloodiest times of our history. People will fear his presence, and in turn, you. They could try to hold you hostage, interrogate you, or perhaps worse if they know the truth."

I swallowed thickly as Kipp continued.

"Knowledge is currency, and power is just as often manipulated here as it is earned. You're here to learn how to harness yours and discover if you've been called for something important. Please, don't share more information than necessary with someone who you don't trust." His eyes sharpened into their lupine slits until I nodded in understanding, glancing back at Gray, who munched happily at the emerald green grass. He seemed innocent, but the weight of his appearance was beginning to settle on me.

"So, you learn about the Aes Sídhe specifically because their kind created the Faerie realm?" I asked after several moments, returning to the original story.

"For that reason, and our rulers. They are all Aes Sídhe, and have been since the creation of our realm. Though now far removed from their original gods, they are still among the most cunning and powerful of the Fae."

If it were possible, my eyes widened further. I pressed my hands into fists, trying to feel the power that supposedly lay beneath my skin. "Are there a lot of ...of us?" I whispered. Kipp visibly winced and shook his head.

"Actually, no. There are not many of your kind left." His mouth opened as if to continue, but was cut off by a new, gravelly voice from behind him.

"And that's what makes this discovery *so* intriguing."

Kipp whirled, instantly placing himself between me and the voice. Gray tossed his head with a snort, ears swiveling, but didn't move.

I rose to my feet, uneasy at Kipp's reaction, and watched as a figure appeared from the forest.

A man, appearing to be the same age as Kipp, stepped smoothly out from the trees, and leaned against one to assess us. He moved with a cocky swagger and, as I followed his movements, I understood why.

His stance was somehow both lazy and lethal; it was as though he knew he would win if it came to hand-to-hand combat against us, but wanted to let that strength peek through just enough in warning. He was taller than both of us, trim but fit in a way that told me tight muscles rippled underneath his clothes.

He was dressed in a billowy white shirt that flowed in the slight breeze, tucked beneath a brown leather vest. The shirt was slightly open, exposing the slope of his muscular, tanned chest. My eyes traveled down to his legs, dressed in tanned leather pants that hugged his powerful thighs and dark combat boots. A blade was strapped to the side of his thigh, and my heartbeat quickened. He was not simply a stranger passing through the forest.

Finally, I let my eyes travel to his face, and felt my mouth go dry. His mouth was set in a firm line, his eyes a deep hazel, flashing more green than brown, as though he borrowed color straight from the lushness of the forest. They were slightly narrowed, as if constantly assessing the world around him and finding it lacking.

Even with traces of a dark beard shadowing his face, I could see the sharpness of his jawline beneath. His hair was dark brown, nearly black, cut short and brushed to one side – a statement that he didn't care all that much about his looks at all.

His entire appearance had me unsure if I wanted to bristle in the face of his cocky indifference, or work to crack through the defenses he clearly had up, to see if what was underneath was worth the battle. I took a final look at his expression and chose the former.

"Who are you," I said in a low voice: a demand, not a question. He straightened at my tone but didn't break his dark and unamused expression.

Instead of replying to me, his gaze slid to Kipp. "Little dog," he said, broad lips curving into a wicked smile. I took note of the slightly condescending tone, and my eyes narrowed. "How long has it been, fifty years?"

"Commander Reinold," Kipp responded flatly. "Not long enough." He didn't move from his position, shielding most of me from sight. Regardless, the commander tilted his head to get a better view of me, and I felt an angry heat flush through my body, settling low in my stomach as his pale hazel eyes met mine.

"What have you brought home, Callaghan? This is more interesting than your usual knickknacks," he purred, his voice a deep rumble. Kipp opened his mouth, but I answered for myself.

"My name is Katherine." I said, crossing my arms. "And I'm here to see the queen."

For the first time, the commander's firm expression broke as his eyebrows rose. He ran a knuckle down his cheek, brushing the side of his mouth, where his hand stopped as he surveyed me. I tried to keep my eyes off his full mouth, and instead meet his gaze with a furious one of my own. Finally, he grinned, the perfect row of white teeth unnerving against the darkness cast across the rest of his face.

"It's a lucky thing I found you, then. Your wish is my command." His eyes twinkled, and for the first time since his arrival, Kipp visibly relaxed.

"Blaise is commander-in-chief of the queen's army." Kipp explained softly. "I'm guessing he was sent as a response to your unidentified magical signature entering the land."

"You would be correct in that assumption. I'm here to take you both to the palace." Blaise responded, retrieving a pouch from his pocket. He eyed Gray, eyes again narrowing. I held my breath, waiting to see if he'd notice anything amiss. But all he said was, "Is the horse coming with us, then?"

"Yes," I responded quickly, leaving no room for discussion. "He's mine."

Blaise simply shrugged. "Alright, call him over. I'll need to use a big handful in that case."

I clucked for Gray, who trotted over, still eyeing Blaise with caution. "Big handful of what?" I inquired.

He pulled out a handful of sand in answer. It was an ashen, twilight blue color, but it shimmered as if flecks of silver lay within.

"Faerie dust," he replied. "We use it to travel quickly from place to place. And you three decided to enter quite far from the palace."

I blinked, a grin tugging at the corner of my lips. Before I could stop myself, I said sardonically, "So, you're like a real-life Tinker Bell, huh?"

Kipp tensed, and I wondered a moment too late if it was really the best idea to taunt this soldier looming in front of us. My breath caught as a long moment passed. Blaise's expression went blank, until a flicker of pure amusement broke across his face. He stalked toward the three of us, and it was all I could do not to shrink away as he leaned in close.

When he smiled this time, light green and brown orbs shone dangerously within his gaze.

"A good comparison, sunshine. Truly. But I am much more dangerous than Tinker Bell," he growled, and the sound reverberated through my whole body. Before I could respond, he tossed the sand over us. Clouds of blue and silver danced across my vision for a moment before the world swirled away.

Chapter 8

We landed in front of a colossal stable, made completely of stone. Vines wound tastefully around the open windows of each stall – easily forty stalls at least, though I couldn't even begin to count – and though they were plentiful, the vines never seemed out of control.

Luscious rose bushes adorned the grand wooden doors that stood at the entrance of the barn, an array of colors on display. I watched as beautiful horses were guided to the fields.

As I scanned the endless lush meadows beyond, I noticed a small young female approach us. She was olive-skinned, with raven-black hair, and though she wore a simple brown tunic, she had it belted with a beautiful ring of leaves. Flowers adorned her hair, remaining impeccably in place even as she bowed.

"Commander," she murmured respectfully, eyes averted.

"Wren," he acknowledged simply. "I'd like for you to find a space for this stallion."

She avoided his eyes and immediately found the stallion, mouth falling open in awe. I shot a panicked glance at Kipp who, returned my look with his lips pursed.

"Where –" she began, and I hurried to cut her off.

"He's mine," I said firmly, putting a hand on Gray's massive, muscled neck. "His name is Gray. If you have a pasture where he can be out, alone, I would greatly appreciate it while the commander takes my friend and me to meet with the queen."

She looked at me for the first time, and I watched her expression closely as she absorbed my words. Glancing between me and Gray, she bowed her head again.

"Certainly, ma'am," she replied, and as I watched, a flash of green lit her hands. When the glow faded, there was a halter in her grasp, crafted only of soft vine. I gasped softly, shooting Kipp a look of alarm, but it was Blaise who answered for me, his gravelly voice close enough that I felt his warm breath fan across my ear.

"Wren is a Dryad – a Faerie that possesses earth magic. She has been our stable manager for many decades. Gray –" I heard the amusement in his tone at the simple name, "– will be in the best hands."

I watched as she extended a hand to the stallion, palm flat. His nostrils flared as he inspected her, but he accepted her touch and lowered his head so she could slip the halter over his ears. After she knotted the halter, she tickled his muzzle and giggled as his lips whuffled over her hand in response.

I instantly relaxed at the sound, smiling as her eyes met mine once more, shimmering with silent communication. She knew the truth, but would keep the secret safe nonetheless.

As Gray's hoof steps faded, Blaise turned to me and scanned my entire body. I felt my face flush at his scrutinization, and wrapped my arms around my chest.

"You'll want to change out of those human clothes," he stated gruffly. "I will see to it that you've cleaned up to meet the queen." He spun on his heel before I could think of a snarky response, forcing Kipp and me to follow hurriedly.

If I thought the stables were massive, the palace was ... *ornate* beyond comparison. We walked alongside a large pond, carved into an otherwise perfectly groomed lawn. The water was an endless turquoise, rippling from the large, flower-shaped water fountain that fed into it from one end. Immaculate shrubs adorned the lawn.

The palace itself was a work of art, its stone matching the stables behind us, winding into a long rectangular pattern. Columns spiraled on the four corners of the structure, with pure white window sills standing out against the stonework.

A large archway invited us in, adorned by swirling pillars on either side. Blaise nodded at the two guards, who bowed their heads and moved aside without a word.

A large courtyard greeted us in the center, decorated with a massive, ancient maple tree and quaint stone bench sitting in the center. A bell tower loomed above the surrounding structures, and my eyes followed it upward as it stretched toward the sky. The sun had almost completely set, so only a soft orange glow illuminated the bell at the very peak.

"Corryn!" Blaise barked, making me jump. A pale, redheaded woman appeared, again donning a simple tunic and leather pants. She inclined her head in greeting, and I wondered curiously what kind of Faerie she was, and if I would ever be able to tell, the way Kipp and Blaise had instantly seen with me.

"Find these two a room, a bath, and some new clothes." Blaise turned his gaze to me. "I will summon you when the queen is ready to meet." He slipped away without another word.

As we turned to follow Corryn down a hallway, I muttered, "Well, he certainly isn't looking to win any popularity contests."

I saw Corryn visibly jolt ahead of us, and Kipp simply snorted in response. "A bit of advice, Kate," he murmured, low enough so only I could hear, "I would keep that witty tongue of yours in check with the queen."

I peered into the massive cauldron Corryn deemed a *bath* dubiously. The washroom was attached to my bedroom, and like all else, it was stunning. It was circular and recessed into the white stone wall, with privacy curtains draping from the two stone columns on either side. Steam rose from it temptingly, and a lemon-sage smell emanated from the tub. Still ...

"I'm more of a shower person," I hedged, glancing back at Corryn. She simply raised her eyebrows at me, puzzled.

"A shower? Like a – rain shower?" She asked. I decided it wasn't worth explaining, and dismissed her gently to undress, easing myself into the tub. A groan slipped past my lips as I was enveloped in the perfectly heated, softly scented abyss. Exhaustion hit when I realized how much had transpired in such a short amount of time.

The water tempted me to stay longer as I begrudgingly reemerged about twenty minutes later. Grabbing a towel, I eyed the clothes laid out before me. A simple maroon gown had been left on the bed, floor length and with long sleeves. I gritted my teeth as I held it up for inspection, my eyes wandering to my jeans and tank top, discarded in a pile on the floor.

Before I could make the decision, there was a soft knock at the door. I cursed and threw on the dress. Corryn stood there as the door opened, a tentative smile on her face. "May I help you with your hair?"

I nodded gratefully. I'd always had my mother to help with anything other than a ponytail, and it felt like a piece of home as Corryn combed and braided my hair. I shifted, feeling a pang of guilt as I thought of the blank look that had crossed her face before we left.

Almost the second she was done, another knock came at the door – this one louder and more insistent. I glanced in the mirror as Corryn opened the door, barely recognizing myself.

A cleared throat drew my attention to the door, and I saw Blaise standing there. His hair had been tamed into a more professional manner, though his expression was taut like usual. I scowled, instantly irritated by the sour look on his face.

"Are you ready to go?" He asked stiffly.

I nodded, and he turned in clear indication to follow. I rolled my eyes at his abrasiveness but trailed behind. We rounded corners and journeyed up endless sets of stairs, until I was well and truly lost.

We halted before a door garnished in gold and crystal, and it groaned as Blaise pushed it open. My mouth fell open as I took in the room.

The walls climbed high, a pale cream color with golden wainscoting which culminated at the top in elegant swirls of gold. It acted as a frame around the painted ceiling, decorated in clouds, set against a pale blue backdrop.

My eyes settled at the other end of the room, where an older woman sat on an equally stunning throne, imbued with crystals and imposing carvings. A large wolfhound lay next to her beside the throne, relaxed but alert.

The woman was older than the others I'd seen so far – perhaps in her late fifties – but still beautiful. Her hair was silver, though not from graying; rather, a shimmering, bluish hue, piled gracefully beneath a crystal tiara.

The gown she wore was relatively simple compared to the rest of the room: white, the corset embellished with gold and silver lace, with a soft tulle at the bottom. As we approached, I noticed her eyes were a pale blue, brimming with knowledge, wisdom, and — most of all — wariness. I shrunk back slightly at the sight.

"Your Majesty," Blaise started, giving a subtle bow. I found myself following suit with a stumbling curtsey. The queen gave a slight nod in return and rose.

"So, you're the one who set off alarms today in Muiranvia," she said smoothly, her voice holding an accent I couldn't quite place, as if etched from centuries of language reformations. *Muiranvia.* I hadn't even thought to ask the name of this new land — her land.

"And it would seem," she continued, cool gaze sweeping over me. "you are also one of the Aes Sídhe. How curious, to only be meeting you now."

"If it makes you feel any better," I replied, "that delightful little nugget of information is brand-new to me, too." I heard Blaise choke. *Shit.* I thought, recalling Kipp's words, and bit my lip. Maybe I shouldn't be so informal. "Your Majesty," I added belatedly, and winced. The addition made it sound even worse.

The queen simply smiled in response, moving back to her position on the throne. The wolfhound raised its pewter, wire-haired head for a long moment, then plopped its head down onto its paws once more. "It appears you've had quite the trialing day. If you do not mind sharing your story before you rest, I would love to hear it."

And so, I did — for the most part. I had prepped earlier in the bathtub, the words tumbling out now as I retold a slightly fabricated version of events. The story I crafted included everything needed for the explanation, without a single lie – discovering Kipp in his wolf form, his revelation that I could indeed see him – while carefully excluding Gray's mysterious appearance from the tale.

"We came in hopes that I could learn more about this side of me. My magic. Perhaps learn more about the mystery of my...heritage." I admitted. This last admission was a new one, and a true one as well.

The queen was silent for a long moment. Her hound yawned by her feet. Finally, she rose once more. "We are agreed, then, that there are many questions about you that need answering."

I nodded emphatically.

"You will train her in all physical matters," she addressed Blaise directly, "starting tomorrow morning."

"Excuse me," I blurted, and bit the inside of my cheek at my brazenness. The queen simply turned and faced me, a singular brow lifted. I took the motion as an invitation and asked, "Why would I need physical training?"

"My dear, did they not tell you?" She chuckled softly, though it was a sad sort of laugh. I dared a glance over at Blaise, whose hardened face betrayed no emotion.

"Our kind grows rarer every day. We are the most powerful of the Fae — able to wield all magical elements — and yet, we are the most fleeting. It seems that more of our kind disappear every year. For this reason, I should like you and every one of our kind protected, capable of defending ourselves by any means necessary."

"Protected from what?" I inquired, but the queen waved the question away.

"It's simply a precaution," she answered, her tone reserved. My cheeks blazed with a mixture of rage and panic. Was this why Kipp had hesitated earlier, when I asked him if there were a lot of us? What wasn't I being told?

The queen continued, oblivious. "I will ask around this week and assign you a mentor to learn how to summon your magic." She turned in a clear sign of dismissal, but paused suddenly. A curious glint sparkled in her pale blue eyes. "I do not believe I ever caught your name, child."

"Katherine." The answer didn't come from me, and I glanced over at Blaise, startled that he even recalled my name. His response was stony as ever, dangerous in its tone — but somehow seductive in a way that beckoned me to accept its call.

I blinked, willing it away. "Katherine Doyle." I specified. "Er, Your Majesty."

The queen glanced between Blaise and me for a moment. "It is good to meet you, Katherine. I hope you find comfort and answers here."

"Thank you," I breathed, and in a graceful flow of tulle, the queen disappeared, the guards and hound close on her heels. I pressed my hands against my dress, both to straighten it as I turned and to brush away the cold sweat accumulating in my palms.

"We should get you something to eat before bedtime," Blaise's voice murmured behind me, roughly. "You, and especially your little *dog,* must be starving by now."

I whirled to him, eyes flashing. "Do *not* refer to Kipp as a little dog." I snapped. "I can hear the condescension dripping from your voice. I don't care if you're a commander; the next time you disrespect him, I will smack you so hard your head will spin."

His eyes narrowed, but he remained silent as he turned and led me back to my room, where he ordered Corryn to bring dinner for Kipp and me. I seethed in equal silence. Where did he get off at treating people so poorly?

As I settled back into the room, Blaise made to leave, but caught my eye before the door closed. His eyes shifted from their normal glower into an almost mischievous smolder, and his lips curled into a half-smirk, quirked at one side.

"Should you ever smack me, Katherine, I can't promise I won't enjoy it," he drawled, and closed the door before I could respond, leaving me open-mouthed and staring. *Capricious prick.*

Several minutes later, Kipp knocked, uncannily timing his arrival with the food. But before he could dive in, I slammed the door and whirled on him. He caught my expression, azure eyes wide with alarm.

"Kipp, I need you to be honest with me," I began, voice deathly serious. He settled obediently onto a chair next to the table in my room, while I took the seat opposite and leaned in close. "Am I in danger here?"

To my dismay, he didn't look at all alarmed by the question — in fact, his answer was quick. "As long as you keep a low profile, no. The only Aes Sídhe that are truly in danger are those with royal blood. High power, high status." His voice was low and steady, a fact that only angered me further.

"*Truly* in danger?" I hissed, the rage singing through my veins, hot and uncomfortable. "What did you get me into here, Kipp?"

"Look, I didn't know you were one of the Aes Sídhe when I brought you here. And honestly, they're just rumors. Most agree your race is dying out naturally. The royal families like to keep their bloodlines pure, after all." Kipp backpedaled.

"Rumors of what?" I pressed, clutching my hands into fists, now pricked with cold sweat.

"There are rumors that someone is out there — out to get the royal families by picking them off over time. That's why the queen is so overly cautious about her bloodline. Any Aes Sídhe under her roof, really."

"Well, royal or not, that's some shit I don't want to be a part of, Kipp. Take me back!" I demanded, standing up and sending the chair thudding to the ground behind me.

"I'm so sorry, Kate. I can't do that," Kipp breathed, and I whirled on him. He flinched at the lethal look in my eyes, raising both hands.

"Look, I would if I could, I swear. I don't want to put you in harm's way, either. But...the solstice has passed now." He glanced at the window in my room, and my gaze followed, taking in the pitch black of the night. His voice was soft as he added, "There's no way back until fall."

I sank slowly back into the chair, a helpless feeling blossoming in the pit of my stomach.

"Look, like I said, it's only rumors about the royal families," Kipp continued in an attempt to reassure me. "And they're just that — *rumors.* It's nothing to worry about. Either way, I'll find a way to stay at the palace and protect you. And so will all the guards here."

When I didn't respond, Kipp sighed and lifted the silver lid on the food that had been brought for us. The incredible smells emanating from the trays urged me to lift my head and survey the food. My stomach grumbled at the sight as I realized how long it had been since I had last eaten.

Perfectly seasoned meats and cheeses, fresh fruits, bread, and bright salad greens lay before us. Saliva pooled in my mouth as I rushed to pile slices of ham, lettuce, and cheese onto a thick piece of bread, sighing at the rush of flavor. Everything was heightened here: just as the colors adorning each blade of grass and each ray of light were brighter here, even the food was packed with more flavor, bursting on my tongue.

"Other than giving you what I think was a *completely* unnecessary scare, what else happened with the queen?" Kipp asked eventually, his question followed by a strange sound. My eyes rose in time to see him tearing into a turkey leg, groaning happily. I snorted, realizing Blaise was possibly right about Kipp and his animalistic hunger. I relented and relayed the visit to him.

After hearing my story, Kipp gave me an impressed look. "For such a young person, you sure do have some wits about you. The queen's hound? It can smell a lie as easily as we can smell this food before us."

My eyes widened in surprise as I wondered what would have happened had I been caught hiding the truth. I decided not to dwell on it; instead, I'd just have to learn to be very careful with my word choices.

"So. Are you going to tell me why you and the commander are at each other's throats?" I asked, popping a strawberry in my mouth. Kipp stood and stretched, contemplating.

"Let's just say it involved a lady at a bar, many years ago. She decided to go home with me, the *little dog*, instead of the second-in-command — at least, he was back then. I believe his ego was rather hurt."

I scoffed. "Men. Seems you're the same in every realm."

Instead of being offended, Kipp flashed me a toothy grin. "Look. I'll stick around so long as you're here, and the second we're able, I'll take you back. I made a promise, and I'll stick to it." He said the words seriously, and I gave him a grateful smile. "I have friends here to catch up with. I can introduce you to them tomorrow, after your training."

"About that. If there's really no threat to me, do I need to do physical training on top of understanding my magic?" I asked, trying to erase the whine from my voice.

"It certainly won't hurt for you to learn how to defend yourself in every way possible. As much as I hate the commander, Blaise is the best person to teach you." Kipp reasoned. "I'll keep an eye on your training, though, to ensure your sharp tongue doesn't get you in trouble."

I laughed, and we said our goodnights. I was grateful to slip into a pair of my own pajamas, and my heart tinged as I wondered how my mother was doing. Even as I snuggled into the vast, soft blankets of this new bed, tummy full and laughter still in my head, I couldn't avoid the apprehension that grew as I recounted the day's events. I had left everything I knew and loved at home, and whatever danger lurked here, I wasn't entirely convinced it would leave me alone.

Chapter 9

If I thought any of the training sessions I had on my high school sports teams were hard, those rapidly became a distant memory with Blaise's training.

We began with basic fighting stances and, after merely a few punches, Blaise decided to focus on muscle building before any hand-to-hand combat. Interval after interval we went with full body workouts. My arms, shoulders, core, legs, and even my ass hurt as I staggered out of the palace with Kipp, who howled with laughter.

"I don't see you hitting the gym," I hissed as we followed the river that wound around the palace and led to the nearby town, Sairas. Muiranvia was the name of one of many lands in the Faerie realm, Kipp had informed me, and Sairas was its capital city.

I was almost too sore to note how cute the town was – almost. Birds sang as we navigated the narrow cobblestone streets that wound along the river, and the beautiful half-timbered houses boasted sloping roofs and balconies of cascading, colorful flowers.

Kipp simply barked another laugh and dipped into an alleyway. He knocked on a door to his right. Moments later, a slender, beautiful man opened the door – somewhere similar to Kipp's age, I suspected, but where Kipp looked more weathered and road-weary, this man radiated health and energy. His ebony-colored hair was wavy, shaved into a pattern on one side as his locks tumbled elegantly down the other.

His dark, almond-shaped eyes scanned Kipp carefully for a second, and then me. I noticed small, colorful gems placed artistically around his eyes, brightening his features, and I offered a hesitant smile.

He broke into a dazzling grin in return. There was a whoosh of colorful, billowy fabric as he embraced Kipp, the pair whooping together. I found myself grinning at the contagious joy radiating off the two of them, then yelped in surprise as I was pulled into a colorful embrace as well.

"I'm Castille," he said before I could recover. "And I am already *dying* to know how it is you dragged this mutt to my doorstep." Unlike the condescending tone used by Blaise, the warmth and affection in his jest was evident. Kipp returned the teasing with an affectionate smile of his own.

"Kate." I returned easily, my hesitant smile widening. "And it's a long story."

"So, we hope you can free your day up for us, Cas." Kipp ventured. Castille laughed, clapping his hands together.

"Twenty years since your last visit, and you think I'll drop everything for you?" He exclaimed. I held my breath. "You'd be completely right. Get your ass in here. Come on, come on."

I took in the cheerful living room as he ushered us in, the walls painted a warm maroon that accentuated the white cedar flooring. The furniture was cozy but antique, with flashy plaid pillows adorning each surface. I noted a framed photo of him and a familiar younger Faerie.

"Are you with Wren?" I blurted, surprised. Maybe I'd judged him improperly, maybe it was just different in the Faerie world –

"Oh, gods, no!" Castille roared with laughter. "For one thing, she's my half-sister. For another, she lacks the proper *equipment* for my standards."

Kipp snickered from behind, sniffing at a bottle of liquor before crinkling his nose and moving to test another. Glasses and bottles of various shapes and sizes were within easy reach, filled with either herbs or liquids. Castille clearly took his entertaining seriously.

"Your half-sister?" I spoke. "I met her last night. She's incredible. I watched her make a vine halter out of thin air!"

"You think that's incredible?" Kipp cut in, pouring glasses of what looked like whiskey. "You should see what Cas can do. He's a healer."

As if to prove Kipp's point, Castille waggled his painted fingers, and an orange-yellow glow danced across his palm, not dissimilar to the sunset we witnessed last night. He traced his hand across my shoulder, and I groaned as some of the soreness lightened.

"I can't eliminate the soreness entirely." Castille said as he continued down my arm, "Your muscles need to break down to rebuild stronger than before. But I can remove some of the swelling and usher along any regeneration that's already started."

I smiled in thanks, and Kipp handed me a glass as Castille worked his way over each limb. I eyed the glass suspiciously. "You know I'm not twenty-one yet, right? Is this – legal?"

I heard a low whistle and glanced down at Castille, who was shaking his head. "You are a *young* one, then." He tutted in dismay.

"And thought she was fully human, until about a day ago." Kipp supplied, collapsing casually on a couch at the other end of the room.

"You're fine, by the way," he directed at me. "Our rules and regulations are much fewer than in the human realm. You're going to be cussing up a storm the further you get into training. The least we can do to help is supply a little relief and joy in between."

My eyebrows lifted in surprise, but I raised my glass in silent cheers, and gulped down the brown liquid. It burned the back of my throat and I bit back a cough as tears pricked my eyes. It didn't go without notice, though, and I heard soft chuckles from both Faeries as I made another feeble attempt to feign indifference as I took another sip.

I watched with dismay as Castille's hands traveled over my body, his healing power taking away most of the freckles that adorned my arms and healing the damage inflicted by the sun. No wonder everyone I'd encountered so far had near-flawless skin.

"So, human-born, young, and a full Aes Sídhe." Castille straightened and grabbed a glass of whiskey. He swirled it and sipped, surveying me. My cheeks burned at the inspection. "And a lot of power in there." He plopped down on the couch, pointing for me to find a seat. "Have you felt it yet?"

I found a recliner across the room, feeling like I was in an interrogation chair as soon as I sat down. I remembered the hum in my veins from the day prior and twirled my hand subconsciously as though I could call it back to me. "Maybe a bit, when we first arrived."

"I saw it." Kipp said suddenly. I shot him a look, but he held my gaze, directing his next line at Castille. "It was almost pure white."

Castille hummed with interest. "Maybe air?"

Kipp shrugged in response.

"Excuse me," I cut in, irritation and helplessness flaring inside me. "Can someone please explain my potential magic *to* me, instead of *over* me?"

Castille laughed and threw me an appreciative look, as if he saw my sass and welcomed it with open arms. He crossed his legs, leaning back into his chair as he ticked the side of his whiskey glass.

"My apologies, Katie-cat," he said, designating the nickname warmly. "All Aes Sídhe have two things that set them apart from other Fae: unparalleled strength and magic. You'll find that you have more speed, stamina, and strength than most others. So much so that you could kick my sorry ass to the human realm and back, if I piss you off enough. Which I'm sure I will, eventually." He added with a grin, and I couldn't help but laugh.

"You also have nearly unlimited magical reserves. Other types of Fae have either one magical element, or need to tap into enchantments, spells, or magical items to feed their power. You can learn to master several – air, fire, water, earth – all the elemental magic. Every one of your kind has one signature magical element far more powerful than the other three, depending on your deity bloodlines."

I sank back into the recliner, feeling deflated. "But I have no idea what my bloodlines are," I muttered, looking down at my hands. I'd never known such a helpless feeling, like I'd been thrown into the ocean without knowing how to swim.

"The queen's mentor will help guide you. I'm sure whatever magic is strongest in you will give clues as to your heritage." Kipp said gently.

I glanced up from my hands and looked between the two of them. Gratefulness blossomed in my chest at their helpful and empathetic expressions: my two flotation devices, I decided, as I navigated these uncertain waters.

"So, if your power is healing," I said, nodding at Castille, "What is yours, Kipp?"

He answered with his wolfy grin.

"You've already seen it. Shapeshifting," he replied. "It's not elemental, but all Urisks are shapeshifters – normally into animals that can blend well onto a farm or near humanity." I nodded, understanding, and then shot Castille an inquisitive look.

Castille chuckled, pushing off the couch.

"Try not to be too blown away," he said mischievously, and suddenly, I was blinded by a shimmer of that sunset glow. I lifted my arm to my eyes, and when I lowered it, my jaw dropped.

Castille still stood there, but a set of wings gleamed behind him. Hues of his characteristic reds, yellows, and oranges all danced and merged in the multicolored sunset that adorned his back.

It reminded me of a dragonfly, with an intimidating main set of wings rising high over his shoulders, and a smaller set folded beneath.

The membrane — thin, but evidently strong — was fully iridescent, showing off the shades of his different colors with each movement. An intricate system of veins weaved throughout, a testament to their strength, despite their delicacy.

"Well, don't keep a Fae waiting," Castille purred. "What do you think?"

"You're beautiful," I breathed, and he clapped gleefully in response. "What – what are you?"

"He's a Pixie." Kipp answered for him. He appeared bored, as if he'd seen this countless times. "It looks cool and all, but it also gives him quite a bit of his pain-in-the-ass nature."

I remembered Kipp's mention of Pixies the other day by the lake. He'd referenced their playful attitude, and I couldn't help the smile that tugged at my lips as I surveyed Castille now, exhibiting that to the fullest.

"Don't lie. You know you love this ass." Castille replied as he shook the body part in question at him, darting out of the way as Kipp launched a pillow at him.

"I'll leave that to your rather dubious conquests. I know there are plenty." Kipp laughed good-naturedly, and Castille simply shrugged.

"I like to make a point to know the town gossip as much as possible. Who's to say I'm not supposed to have a little fun while I'm at it?"

My grin grew as I watched the pair interact, though a part of me ached for that friendship — a friendship I'd never had. But maybe now, I could. An odd friendship, perhaps, but one that sounded more inviting than the friendships I grew up with.

Fuzziness consumed my head as we all chatted, drank, and snacked. I began to realize Cas truly was the eyes and ears of the town as he caught Kipp up on all the goings-on since he'd last visited, asking us both tactful questions as well. We both noticed as Kipp skipped brusquely over the passing of Gerry, the older gentleman who lived in the home before my mother and I moved in. Instead, we moved on to lighter topics.

Despite the yearning I still felt for home, I found myself enjoying the way Cas and Kipp embraced me as part of their group without question. Cas's laughter was infectious and warm, as he joked with me in the same way as Kipp — without reserve, without judgment.

Dinnertime rolled around, and Wren appeared. We exchanged shy smiles across the table as the two men bickered. I fielded questions from Cas about the latest pop culture references, with Kipp throwing in the occasional dispute.

"I've heard the latest music, and let me tell you, it has all gone steadily downhill since the 90's." Kipp asserted.

"Well, I wouldn't know. I used to be able to pilfer cassette tapes or CD's when I visited the human realm. But now everything is on a 'streaming service,'" Cas complained, raising his fingers in air quotes.

"And excuse me for not taking music advice from someone who has had centuries to learn manners, yet still eats like a feral beast," he added pointedly. Kipp, who had indeed been busy shoveling food into his mouth, paused, a string bean hanging from the side of his mouth. We all burst out laughing.

"Life's too short to worry about how I eat my food. Even as a quasi-immortal." Kipp said unapologetically, and continued digging in.

Wren rolled her eyes and laughed. "He's just as bad as my father."

"At least your father can turn on the manners when he chooses. I'm not sure that button exists on Kippers here." Cas replied, flicking a piece of food at Kipp, who jokingly snarled in response.

"So, you two have different fathers?" I asked, remembering Cas's use of the term 'half-sister'. Wren nodded.

"We have the same mother, but different fathers. That's also why I'm a Dryad and Cas is a Pixie. Different genetics," she explained. I looked between them for a moment, noting how Cas's face was dimpled and round — almost cherubic — whereas Wren's was more elegant and angular. Despite their physical differences, the familial affection they shared for each other was obvious.

"Though since our mother is a Pixie, she could have been one too. Such a missed opportunity." Cas sighed dramatically, pretending to be wounded as Wren softly punched his arm.

"My father passed away when I was young. Same as yours." Cas added softly, eyes meeting mine. "My mother remarried about seventy years later to Wren's father."

I broke his gaze and looked at my half-eaten plate, appetite suddenly lost. The familiar feeling rushed back – as if gravity ceased to exist. It had taken losing my father to realize he was a large part of what kept me grounded in my childhood.

"Does it get any better?" I asked in a hushed tone. "Any – easier to forget and let go?"

Cas considered it deeply for a moment. "Letting go doesn't mean forgetting. It means recognizing your past in a way that empowers you to recover and redirect your power." He shifted his hand, palm facing upwards as his healing power danced across his flesh.

"My father was one of the strongest healers this city knew. I know the best way to honor his memory is to continue that legacy and leave the world a better place than I found it. I can't presume to know your father's wishes, Katie-cat, but I imagine he would want you, at the very least, to find your place and be happy."

I smiled, glancing down at my plate again to blink away the tears blurring my vision. A small piece of me hoped this journey was exactly what my father would have wished for me, and the people he would want to see me surrounded by.

"Vinyl records." I said suddenly, looking up. Everyone gave me a quizzical look.

"They're making a comeback." I explained. "If you want to hear the newest music, I bet you can find it on vinyl records."

Cas beamed, slapping his palm on the table in excitement. "Well, it seems like you and I will have an errand to run together the next time you head back to the human realm!"

I smiled, and the conversation settled back into easy topics for the remainder of dinner. By the time Kipp and I returned to the palace that night, both my heart and my belly were surprisingly full.

Chapter 10

"Fuck," I hissed, stumbling back and clutching my hand. Blaise quirked an eyebrow, but made no move to check if it was okay.

"You curse a lot for a lady," he said instead. I flexed my fingers and glared at him.

"I'm no *lady*," I corrected. "And I have just as much right to use cuss words as anyone else. Especially when someone pisses me off." I shot him a pointed look, which he chose to ignore.

Birds tittered in the trees nearby, though the sound barely registered as I focused on catching my breath. We were in the garden just outside the palace, training on the large clearing filled with tightly packed gravel. It was used regularly as a training ground but, at least for this morning, it seemed we were the only ones planning to use it. Bright green boxwood shrubs rose like thick walls around us. I was grateful for the privacy — or at least, the illusion of privacy — as we trained, especially since I was proving to be piss-poor at it.

"You keep cupping your thumb into your fist. All that will accomplish is injuring your thumb, possibly breaking it. Pull it out and tuck it between your first and second knuckle." Blaise explained, demonstrating. When I followed suit, he barked at me to resume my fighting stance.

I spread my feet shoulder-width apart, bending slightly at the knees. I pulled my left foot – my dominant foot – back, right foot pushed forward. Bouncing on my feet, I raised my hands once more, tucking my elbows in close to my ribs and lowering my chin.

Blaise nodded in what I'd already come to learn as his version of approval over my correct stance, raising his hands in silent encouragement to continue. A thought occurred to me, and I blurted, "Why don't you have a shield or anything?"

"Because you're not strong enough to do any damage," he replied simply, that half-cocked smirk twitching the corner of his mouth again. My left fist connected with his palm angrily, followed quickly by a right hook, which he intercepted with ease. His grin widened, showing dimples I hadn't yet seen.

"I'm an Aes Sídhe," I huffed in frustration, launching another one-two punch. "I thought I was supposed to be just as strong as you."

"Wrong on two points." Blaise straightened, and I paused. "First, hard work beats lazy talent, *always*. There are Fae out there that work hard enough to beat plenty of Aes Sídhe — especially one as untrained as you."

My cheeks blazed, though I wasn't sure which comment irked me the most — lazy or untrained. Perhaps what bothered me was the kernel of truth in both.

"Second," he continued. "I am not an Aes Sídhe. I am a *Daoine Sídhe*." He enunciated the word deliberately, drawing out the *'deen-ya shee'*, as if understanding it would be my first time hearing it.

"Similar – very similar – to your race. Essentially only a step removed," he explained. "The key difference is that we descend from the war gods and hold no magic. However, we make up for it with more speed and strength than your kind. And then we hone it to the hilt. Most of my forces are Daoine Sídhe."

Interesting. A race basically designed by nature to be warriors. I dragged my eyes over Blaise once more. He really was pure muscle, from the broad shoulders to the sharp cheekbones and, though he kept his posture relaxed, his expression was permanently tensed, as though waiting for some unknown danger to jump out at any moment.

He wore a similar outfit to the day we first met —leather pants and a plain cloth shirt — but had discarded the knife usually strapped to his leg. I was certain it was for my own safety as I fumbled through our lessons.

"So that's why the queen has to find someone else to mentor me in magic," I realized aloud. Blaise nodded, raising his hands once more as he motioned for me to continue.

"Hopefully, she can find someone you won't curse endlessly at," he muttered. I stumbled over my next punch and stared at him. His eyes crinkled as he smirked. The hazel color of his gaze glimmered more gold than green today.

"So, it makes jokes now?" I taunted. "I could use more of those to get through this torture."

"Tough. You've reached your limit," he grunted, but not without affection. "Now, get in position. Uppercut time. Remember the power is in the rotation of your hips: down, and drive up – Do you remember the weak points from yesterday's lesson?"

I groaned, spouting off answers as we continued the lesson. Over an hour later, as I walked back to the palace, my muscles trembled in places I hadn't known existed.

Instead of heading straight for a bath, I detoured to the barn to check on Gray. Wren said yesterday that he had settled in fine enough, but I wanted to see for myself. I scanned the land while hobbling to his pasture. The sun bathed the emerald grass for what seemed like miles, and I wondered how much land counted as the palace pastures. I watched the grass sway lightly in the wind and wondered if I'd be able to explore it on horseback. I loosed a piercing whistle.

My eyes were drawn back to Gray as his head shot up at my whistle, long, wavy mane tossing high in the air as his nostrils flared. He identified me and let the world know with a whinny that brought a grin to my face. He trotted across the pasture, his movements graceful, like he floated on the air.

"Hey, boy," I murmured when he reached me, giving the space between his eyes a good scratch. "You doing okay?"

He bobbed his nose against my shirt in response, shoving me a step backwards with his strength. "You might not want to do that," I warned with a laugh. "I *reek.*"

"Do you want a carrot for him?" A voice said behind me, and I turned to see Wren approach. She retrieved a handful of carrots from a leather pouch hanging at her side. Smiling gratefully, I took a few and moved over in open invitation for her to join me.

Gray's ears pricked, and he gleefully munched the carrots I offered him. Cautiously, Wren opened her palm to give him a few too, which he grabbed without hesitation. She giggled as he took a final bite, whuffling at her dark, braided hair with curiosity.

"He's really taken a liking to you," I observed, smiling gently. I hadn't forgotten her look of recognition the other day and decided to use this moment to open the door for that conversation. She looked at me and saw it too.

"How is it possible?" She breathed.

"I honestly don't know," I admitted, toying with Gray's forelock. "He just – *appeared* to me at a lake in the human realm. Kipp is the one who explained who he is and what he's done. Your guess is as good as mine as to why me, and why now."

Wren leaned over the paddock fence, lips pursed as she considered my words. "Whatever the reason, I don't think it's good," she ventured, then shot me a guilty look. "Not that it's bad that you're here. I mean, Liath Macha – sorry, Gray – belonged to a hero before. But your appearance also tells me that...something bad is coming."

Though her words were grave and her face grew dark, it wasn't something I hadn't already considered. Kipp had warned me Gray's recognition would cause this reaction. She tapped the fence post nervously for a few moments before continuing.

"In his last battle, it was said that he wouldn't let the charioteer strap him in to go to battle. He only let Cú Chulainn himself do it."

"Cú Chulainn?" I echoed.

"The hero he belonged to. Cú Chulainn died in that battle after Gray here fought so bravely to defend him. It is said Gray led them to his body after the battle, so that they could give him a proper burial and avenge him."

Gray snorted and tossed his head, as if in understanding of our conversation. A shiver ran through me, and I peered into his dark eyes, trying to envision the carnage he'd seen, and the terror of being in the middle of battle. The way he'd known what would happen and tried to warn his master.

"I'm so sorry that happened, boy," I murmured. "That's so tragic. How – how do you know all of this?"

"I've been at this stable for a long time. It's just a pastime of mine to study up on horses – both those that reside here and famous ones from long ago."

"Got it," I replied. We sat in silence for a moment. Gray grew bored of us and shifted to graze nearby.

After a while, I turned to Wren. "Look, about him – you and Kipp are the only ones that know –"

"Say less," she interrupted with a small wave. "I'm good at being discreet. I wouldn't want to put a target on either of your backs."

"Thanks," I answered gratefully. "So, uh, bad things to come. Do you have any idea what? Or how to ... prepare?" I hated the weak lilt in my voice.

Wren shrugged. "Honestly? I couldn't tell you. There are always small things here and there – no place is perfect – but I haven't heard of anything particularly dark brewing. Your work to tap into your power can't hurt, especially if you're at the center of this. In the meantime, I'll see what I can find out in the community."

Her mouth twitched into a small grin. "Or better yet, I can just bug Cas. He's certain to know these things before the rest of us."

I laughed, relieved to have a next step, no matter how small. Acting on impulse, I reached over to give Wren a brief side hug. "Thank you," I said earnestly. She looked surprised, but nodded.

"My pleasure. But one more thing first."

"What's that?"

Her nose wrinkled. "Go take a bath."

I laughed and pushed away from the fence, glancing a final time at Gray and waving goodbye to Wren.

My bright attitude faded, however, as I sat in the tub later, contemplating Wren's words, and when I slept that night, it was fitful. My dreams were cloaked with images of wars I'd never been in, and blood I'd never seen spilled across the battlefield plagued my psyche.

Chapter 11

Loud banging jerked me from my distressed sleep and I rolled over, moaning. The banging didn't relent as I contemplated throwing my pillow at the door, before remembering where I was.

"Alright, alright already!" I yelled, dragging myself from bed and yanking open the door.

Blaise stood on the other side of the door with a scorching expression, his hand still raised to unleash another furious knock. He froze, catching my eye.

"You'd better be waking me to tell me that Faerie realm coffee has the power to keep me from killing you right now." I seethed through gritted teeth, combing a hand through my wild bed hair.

Blaise didn't answer, his eyes skimming over my body instead, that scathing gaze turning a different kind of heated. I suddenly became very conscious of the fact that I was in a pair of pajamas I'd packed from home: silken blue night shorts, paired with a matching strappy tank top, both of which revealed quite a bit more than should probably be seen outside of bed. Especially considering the conservative way I'd seen Faeries dressed around the palace and Sairas.

I crossed my arms, willing my body to tone down the way it responded to Blaise's stare. He cleared his throat and peered down the hallway instead, leaning against the doorframe. A muscle in his jaw twitched.

"You're late for training," he said flatly. "Get dressed. We're doing cardio today." With that, he pushed off the doorframe and stalked off.

My jaw dropped and I slammed the door, hoping he heard it as I stomped to the bathroom to brush my teeth and hair. I cooled off as I gradually woke up, but even on a good day, I wasn't a morning person. A quick change into some leggings and tank top from home, and I was out the door to meet him. He didn't acknowledge me as I approached.

"So, no coffee then?" I asked to lighten the mood, but also with a little hope for a caffeine burst. His answer was a sidelong glance.

"Rough night?"

"You could say that," I replied warily.

He sensed my tone and diverted the topic. "I've found a good running route for us to take. We'll run it every third day, starting slow, then gradually increase the distance and mix in some sprints."

As it turned out, Blaise's version of *starting slow* was incredibly difficult. We took a path that weaved along the river and up and down rolling green hills, but as the distance dragged on and the pace remained just a touch above uncomfortable, I lost focus on the beauty of our surroundings and concentrated only on keeping my breathing.

By the time we arrived back at the palace, I was ready to collapse. I forced myself to keep walking to keep my legs from stiffening, and the gulping of my breaths was the only thing keeping me from dry heaving.

Blaise smirked down at me, as if he knew I would be cursing him out if I only had the extra breath for it. Suddenly, his eyes flickered from my glare to something behind me, and he bowed.

"Your Majesty," he murmured. I did my best to straighten and turned around, beholding the queen who stood behind us. I mimicked Blaise, wincing slightly.

Two soldiers flanked either side of her, standing a respectful few feet back, and her wolfhound sat loyally by her heels. A beautiful young woman stood beside her, with cunning brown eyes and dirty blonde hair that tumbled down her shoulders.

"Katherine," the queen started, "This is Darrya. She will be mentoring you in all things magic from here on out."

She turned to Darrya. "Please report back with your progress weekly."

Darrya bowed her head dutifully, and the queen made to leave, the rest of her entourage following in suit "Feel free to get acquainted."

With that, she floated gracefully away, like a leaf on a gentle breeze. Darrya, Blaise, and I were left standing awkwardly in the courtyard. Blaise nodded in acknowledgment at Darrya, who returned a wry smile. He brushed past me on his way out of the palace with a brusque, "Don't forget to stretch."

As soon as he left, I turned to size up Darrya, but was met with a crushing embrace.

"Gods, is it good to have a new face here!" She exclaimed, her expression now completely warm. "I swear I've been staring at the same old dusty faces for the past century."

She let go, holding me at arm's length to briefly examine me. I held back a flinch as her hands brushed over the fabric of my workout clothes, unfamiliar with such a close, friendly touch, especially from a near-stranger.

"Where did you get this training outfit? Ugh, whenever you head back to the human realm, I definitely need to hitch a ride. I know it might cause some stir around here, but we're due for a little pot-stirring every now and again," she gushed. All I could do was blink in response.

She smiled guiltily as she noticed. "Sorry, I'm just so used to being forced around all the royal Stuffs. When I heard someone young and new needed a magical catch-up, I jumped at the opportunity to peel that aristocratic, pain-in-the-ass mask off for a while."

Looking at this unabashedly energetic, happy Faerie before me, I relaxed slightly. I wasn't normally the exuberant type. I usually shied away from people like her in the human realm, but something about Darrya's openness rubbed off on me. She reminded me of Castille – both unashamedly willing to offer warm friendship without a lick of judgment. I offered a smile in return.

"So, you're a pot-stirrer? I didn't know the queen would allow those in the court." I said with a smirk, hoping my sharp tongue wouldn't change her tune. Darrya simply laughed in joyful approval, motioning for me to follow.

"If I ever stir the pot, I make sure nobody knows it's me," she replied mischievously, her brown eyes flashing.

Yep, I like her.

"You, on the other hand, stirred the pot good and hard, purely with your presence. It's impressive, truly."

I knew she meant it in jest, but my stomach flipped regardless, remembering my dream from last night. I followed her as we moved into the kitchen. She piled a plate full of eggs and ham, pushing it into my arms and snagging a croissant for herself on the way back out.

We ended up back in the courtyard. She leaned against the large maple tree and motioned for me to sit on the nearby bench. "Eat," she ordered. "You'll need protein to keep up with the physical training."

I obliged, feeling my self-consciousness fade in the face of hunger as she studied me. I wasn't sure if it was my heart still pounding as I recovered from my run, but I could have sworn I felt a light energy tap against me.

"You know," Darrya began, tilting her head. "Most times I can tell what signature magic a Fae possesses just from the energy they give off. It's like feeling for someone's magic, but squinting to see it with more detail. But you? You possess a great amount of magic. Possibly more than my cousin, who harnesses the most I know. More than me, certainly."

My eyes widened and I gulped down my bite of food, suddenly losing my appetite. I pushed the plate aside. "Can you tell what my signature magic is?" I breathed.

Darrya paused a beat, then shook her head. "Maybe it's because you haven't tested your magic yet, but no. Have you ever felt it?"

"Just once. When we first arrived. It was like a...a *hum*. Like something in my body urging for a release." I explained. Darrya nodded excitedly, pushing off the tree.

"Do you think you could will that feeling back into your body?" She asked encouragingly. I frowned in concentration as I dug deep inside myself. Watching my palms, I hoped to see some flicker of the white glow which had danced across them nights before.

The glow that danced around Gray.

A symbol of something foreboding to come. I had triggered it, somehow, bringing something terrible into the lives of these wonderful Fae folk.

My mind darted back to the battle I'd seen in my dreams the night before; the blood and the screams...

"You need to clear your head."

I glanced up at Darrya standing above me, her long blonde hair a waterfall that framed her concerned face. She turned to sit next to me, nudging me lightly in the ribs.

"Magic comes from the soul and, oftentimes, the thoughts in our head can be all-consuming. Everyone must empty their thoughts, even a little bit, to fully gain their souls." She took a deep breath, and I watched as a blueish-white hue grew in her palms.

Suddenly, a gust of wind danced around us. It gathered fallen leaves from around the tree, pulling them into a small tornado which rose higher and higher. Then suddenly, it disappeared, and the leaves fell softly to our feet once more.

I met Darrya's gaze, openmouthed. She beamed at me, hair tousled by her own magic, as leaves settled on her head like nature's own crown. Leaning back, she closed her eyes.

"It's a good thing to visit the human realm," she began, stretching. "I make a point to, whenever I can. Humans have empathy, comradery, complex emotions, and mortality that adds passion and purpose to every day.

"We Fae, on the other hand, have strength, speed, stamina, near eternal lifespans, and these magical bits and pieces. We...*feel* everything more and, for that reason, I'm grateful that we don't deal with the same types of struggles I've witnessed in the human world. But over time, it also means we tend to think and feel in black and white. We hold eternal grudges and lack the same type of purpose as humankind."

She rolled her head to face me. "You grew up in the human realm, and yet, you are fully Fae. As I see it, you can either let whatever heightened emotions you're feeling now consume you...or you can turn it into your own personal weapon. Someone who has passion, purpose, empathy. And the sheer strength to wield it."

I digested her words and rubbed the back of my arm. Until now, I had considered my human upbringing as a crutch: lacking physical strength and feeling ridiculous for my lack of knowledge in the Faerie realm.

Was it possible that barging into this realm, into all their lives, was actually a good thing? Did my humanity give me something I could wield positively?

I sighed and closed my eyes, pushing the snippets of the dream away. Instead, I focused on Darrya's words about humankind. Empathy. Comradery. Passion. Purpose. As it calmed my mind, I emptied those too, focusing instead on reaching into my body – exploring the depths of my *soul* – searching for the energy I'd once felt humming inside.

The moment I touched it, I felt the world shift.

Chapter 12

The first magic that came to me was earth.

I felt the trembling beneath my feet, though it was less like an earthquake and moreso a murmur within the ground as it told me a story — a story that extended between every root, every blade of grass, every pebble, and every tree in our proximity.

"Everything – *everything* – is connected," I gasped in realization. Darrya simply smiled.

"It's the power of the gods. They created everything with their respective magic – earth, fire, water, air. You're not only feeling the connection between nature, you're also feeling the connection to the gods themselves."

I scanned the foliage around us, looking more alive than ever as that intrinsic part of me awakened, as though from a long-dormant stupor. Power surged through me like an electrical current living in my very veins, and another thought occurred.

"So, you know what bloodline you're connected to? Is air your signature magic?"

Darrya nodded, a small gust breezing by once more. "My dominant bloodline stems from the goddess Cailleach. She ruled the winds and winters." She smiled mischievously. "Not a bad heritage, given the fact that most have powers that stem from male gods. Mine is one of the original feminists."

I laughed, then focused on summoning a flower from the earth. The energy welling in me wavered, and I bit my lip, pushing back in defiance as a small, single pink rose blossomed in front of us. Despite smiling softly at the triumph, I sagged back against the bench.

Darrya patted my knee. "Magic wielding is like any other muscle. You'll need to practice. Repeatedly. I'll come to find you first thing tomorrow, after your training with Blaise."

She bent over to pluck the rose and handed it to me. "Don't forget to look back at where you started when you get frustrated at where you're going."

I looked down at the rose in amazement, twirling it in my fingers. I had *created* this, with a power I hadn't known existed just a few days prior. By the time I glanced up, Darrya was gone.

A full week had passed, packed with demanding training that honed my physical and magical abilities. I had brushes with water and air magic, much to Darrya's glee. When I'd asked how far her air magic extended, she had shot up into the air, golden hair merging with the sky as though another sun had risen. Jealousy coursed through me as

I wished desperately to have such a handle on my magic. I wondered if someday, I would be able to fly as well.

My progress felt agonizingly slow, especially as I worked voraciously to hone the different elements. However, I followed Darrya's advice religiously and looked at my single rose every night before bed. I reminded myself of my achievements so far: willing a wave in the river, growing a sapling tree, and beginning a small air current to carry the leaves. I was making progress.

I met with Cas, Wren, and Kipp almost nightly. While Cas fluttered around, healing what he could of my continuously sore body, Wren delighted in showing me her earth magic and worked with me where she could. She also promised to introduce me to a friend of hers, an Asrai — a water Faerie — in case I needed more help with other elements.

After discussing with Kipp and Wren, we all decided to let Cas in on the full story of Gray's appearance to me. He'd taken it in stride, simply telling me that I had to remember him when I became a legend. After a moment to think, he added that he had not heard of any potential unrest or anything out of the ordinary – though he would dig around.

I leaned over the fence, watching Gray roll happily in the pasture as I willed patches of grass to grow another inch or two for him to munch on.

Wren appeared behind me. "Have you ever thought about riding him?" She asked.

I shook my head, but eyed Gray curiously. With his size and history – a deity in his own right – he surely possessed supernatural speed and strength. My pulse quickened at the thought of galloping down a trail on his back, hair whipping behind me as his hooves thundered against the ground.

"Want to give it a try?" She asked, reading my mind.

My small smile was the only encouragement needed as she disappeared into the barn. I whistled like I had a few days before, my heart lifting as Gray shook the grass from his back and trotted enthusiastically to me.

Wren slung the saddle pad, saddle, and bridle across the fence, but as she moved to create another halter, I stopped her.

"Let me try," I said, and focused my energy on the power needed to produce a vine, which I slowly let take the shape needed. My hand trembled, and it took a lot longer than it had taken Wren but, eventually, I held a halter formed entirely of vines.

Wren let out a low whistle. "You may be frustrated with your progress," she said earnestly, "But it took me the better part of two months to learn that one." Pride swelled in me at her words, and I tied the new halter around Gray and led him out of the paddock. Exhaustion tugged at me, but it was overpowered by my satisfaction, knowing how far I'd come in my training.

I ran my hand haltingly over his back, as much to check for any sores as to test if he was comfortable with this. His ears remained relaxed as I tacked him up, and I gave Wren a look of surprise. She shrugged in response.

Taking a deep breath, I placed one foot in the stirrup. A pause – no reaction. I hopped and swung my leg over him, now fully astride, and though his ears swiveled, he made no move. I swallowed and surveyed the ground below us, realizing he was indeed much taller than any of the horses at my family ranch.

"Well, that went better than expected," Wren admitted. I exhaled and nodded in agreement, looking down at her now much smaller figure on the ground.

I cracked a grin and squeezed gently, guiding Gray into a walk, which he did obligingly. We walked a few circles around Wren before I urged him into a trot. She watched us, grinning, before ushering us off to go find a trail along the river for him to let off a little speed.

I was more than happy to let loose, too. I was completely right about Gray's strength, and found comfort in his power as I felt it buzz like magic between the two of us. It radiated out from him, and I felt it in the ground, the air, and the water rushing alongside us as we traveled down the river. Wherever I brushed his bare skin with my hands or legs, the electric buzz heightened.

On impulse, I pulled up at a boulder, slick with emerald moss and tiny, red-capped mushrooms. I slid off and proceeded to remove Gray's saddle and saddle pad. The ground surrounding the large rock was dotted with small, colorful wildflowers. I searched until I found a stray log to drape the tack over, finding the sight of the flowers too beautiful to trample on, especially now that I was more in tune with my earth magic.

Carefully, I climbed onto Gray's now bare back and leaned over his neck. I felt just as secure without the tack; if anything, I felt more in tune with him than before.

"You're like a damn couch, you know that?" I said playfully into his ears, which swiveled to pick up the sound. "I doubt you were ever meant to be ridden with a saddle." He tossed his head in response.

I took him through the paces until we cantered alongside the river, and I was laughing with sheer glee. He responded without hesitation to my every movement, seeming to guess what I would ask of him next the second the thought formed in my head. My heart thrummed in tune with his hoofsteps, the rush of the river echoing the joy in my head.

Finally, I dropped the reins and flung my arms wide, embracing every piece of bliss the moment had to offer. Closing my eyes, I tilted my head back and grinned wildly, letting the rock of the canter move us forward as one.

Until we weren't anymore.

Suddenly I was flying high, higher than I was supposed to. My eyes flashed open and I saw that Gray had leapt over a fallen tree trunk, yet I was too late to lean forward with the jump. Instead, I made the last-minute decision to tuck and roll off his side – right into the river.

It took all of a split second for me to realize the water was ice cold. It gushed faster and deeper than it appeared from above. I clambered for the surface, but my fingers struggled to find purchase on anything solid. Rocks slipped through my fingers and panic grew — too much panic to focus on any magic that could help. My limbs, sore from the day's training and now from riding, complained. My lungs began to burn.

Finally, my panicked kicking found rock, and I was consumed by a searing pain as the speed of the river, combined with my kick, slammed my knee back into its socket. I gasped out the last of my breath, but luckily, the force of my kick had sent me spiraling to the surface, where I gulped precious mouthfuls of air. Gray paced along the side of the river, his ears pinned back.

I sent my arms out, desperate to grab a passing branch. Instead, they found something warm and solid and before I could think, I was being dragged to the other side of the riverbank. I gasped, soaking wet, as I sprawled across the ground with my aching leg outstretched.

"Are you alright?" A concerned male voice loomed from above, and I looked up to see wide, pale blue eyes staring back at me. A mop of light blonde hair tumbled around his face, which he pushed back in clear distress as he scanned my drenched, shivering frame. He looked younger than most of the other Fae I'd met, maybe in his early twenties – which, I supposed, still meant he could be over a hundred years old.

"Are you hurt?" He asked again, but before I could respond, a loud thud interrupted me. We both jerked our heads to see Gray, who had jumped the river, rushing towards me. His head was low, almost predatory, as he eyed up the Faerie standing over me. He arched his neck, and the gesture made his massive stature seem even larger.

"Holy shit!" The Faerie exclaimed, stumbling away as Gray came to nuzzle my shoulder. He instantly relaxed as I stroked him. "What kind of horse can make that jump?"

"This one," I said with affection. I snagged Gray's mane and pulled myself up somewhat unsteadily. The fair-haired man took another step toward me, as if to ensure I wouldn't fall, but I waved him away. He stood back, but his look of concern didn't fade.

"Thank you," I said earnestly. "There's no telling what would've happened if you hadn't been here."

He shrugged and gave me a small smile. "Just doing my small part. Though your acrobatics were something to be admired. You really boosted our fallen angel reputation with that one."

My face reddened at the realization that he'd seen my fall. He tilted his head, inspecting me with raised brows. "You're new."

"Yeah, uh…it's kind of a long story. I'm Katherine." I supplied, testing my weight on my bum knee. I bit my lip as pain shot through my leg again.

"Finlay," he responded, glancing down at my leg. He pulled a gold-encrusted flask from his pocket. He wore the most relaxed outfit I'd ever seen on a Faerie, I realized: loose dark leather pants and a billowy short-sleeved white tunic. He extended the flask to me and nodded to my injury. "Here. This might help."

Warily, I took it from him. Despite the casual attire Finlay wore, the flask was a rich thing of beauty. It was plated entirely in antique gold, with a Celtic symbol I didn't recognize embellished on the front. I unscrewed it and took a sniff. It smelled like whiskey, with hints of vanilla cutting through the strong charred odor of alcohol.

As I took a cautious swig, he withdrew a hand-rolled cigarette and lit it. I choked, though I wasn't sure if it was from the whiskey or the sight of him lighting up.

"I didn't realize you had cigarettes in the Faerie realm," I said, surprised.

He grinned, tendrils of smoke leaving his mouth on either side. "If it's a good enough vice, it's made its way from the human realm over here. Smoking, drinking..." His eyes twinkled, and he offered me the cigarette. "Though sex started with the gods first."

I shook my head, both at his offer and his words.

"So you're not just new to Sairas, then," he continued. "You're new to the Faerie world. You must be the one my cousin has been training."

"You're Darrya's cousin?" I blurted, and he nodded. I eyed him up again, trying to piece together the exquisite royalty Darrya exuded with this brash, unkempt cousin that stood toking up in front of me. He studied me as well, and I felt a slight tingling sensation at the scrutiny. Briefly, I recalled Darrya's mention of her cousin being the most powerful Aes Sídhe she knew.

"Hmmm. She was right. You do have some insane power in there, little fallen angel," he said, his voice silken as he flicked the ashes off his cigarette.

"*Katherine.*" I corrected, my lip curling at the nickname that mocked my fall. I shifted my leg, wincing again. "And how does everyone just see this?"

"Drink," he demanded, noting my wince. I obliged. "You just have to look in the right way. Call your power up, and reach it out like you would to get in touch with the natural elements around you. Extend it toward the other person."

He paused, taking another inhale. As I summoned my magic, he exhaled a puff and grinned. "Wrap it around me. I'll send mine out too, so you'll get the full extent of my power. Just as a comparison point."

I tucked the flask in the back of my pants and shook out my hands, trying to focus. Hesitantly, I reached out, embodying that now-familiar hum as my magic extended towards him.

The whispers of power along the edge of his skin were apparent the second my magic collided with his. I couldn't quite determine his level of power, having nothing for comparison, but I could tell his magic was warm — almost burning and chaotic — unlike any I had mastered so far...

"Fire," I realized out loud. Of course – I hadn't noticed a lighter in his hand as he'd lit his smokes. Finlay's eyes widened in impressed surprise, but he nodded.

"Very good. That's my signature magical element, thanks to the god, Belenos. The *'Bright One',* and all that."

I was barely listening as I continued exploring, poking around the edges of his magic, until mine fully encompassed him. That was when he let me in.

The torrent of energy that flowed into me melted my core, like an electrical current zapping at my very insides in the most delicious way. Our powers intertwined, dancing, becoming one with each other in a manner that offered me all the warmth of Finlay's power, but with the electric hum of my own as well. Every nerve ending tingled as I yearned to get closer to him and his power.

It was only when a soft moan slipped past my lips that the alarm at my body's response snapped me back to reality. Without even realizing it, I tugged my own magic back up close, confining it once more within myself.

"What the hell was that?" I snapped at Finlay, who simply blinked. "Well?"

He cleared his throat.

"That, little fallen angel, was what we Fae folk call power-sharing. Quite the experience, isn't it?" He purred tauntingly, as if he knew how it had set all my nerves on edge, and how part of me wished to do it again.

"It's *Katherine*. And do you just make a game out of violating others like that?" I snarled. He shrugged, but I could tell the comment struck home as his eyes widened briefly with remorse. He took an extra long drag before responding.

"I figured you could use your magic for a little fun to break up the monotony of your normal lessons. That's all." His expression suddenly turned mischievous, and I finally saw the resemblance to Darrya. "Come find me if you ever want to try again," he added cockily.

Ignoring both him and the shriek in my knee, I turned away. Grabbing two large chunks of Gray's mane, I used it as leverage to gain a running start and swung onto his bare back.

Given his height and my injury, it took some scrambling to fully sit astride him, but I lifted my chin to dispel any indignity as I glowered down at Finlay.

"Not likely," I replied, and with that, I guided Gray back toward town. I only glanced back once, startled to see Finlay still watching.

He saluted me as he caught my eye. In return, I raised my middle finger with my own personal salute.

Chapter 13

"You flipped him off?" Wren said, aghast, while Cas howled with laughter in the background and Kipp paced angrily by the door. Cas had immediately healed me when I'd appeared injured on his doorstep, while Wren had disappeared to return Gray to the stable. As soon as she returned, I relayed the whole story.

"I'd bet no one has ever done that to him before," Wren continued, wringing her hands nervously. "He is the queen's great-grandson, after all."

My eyes widened. "Well, I didn't know *that*. All I know is he was a royal pain in my ass." I felt an immediate flicker of shame at my tone. Wren was so sweet; sometimes I felt like I was corrupting her, even though she was decades older, despite looking my age. I tried to remind myself that her brother had the same devilish tendencies I did, especially as I watched his attempts to control his laughter now.

"I can't believe he tricked you into power-sharing with him," Kipp seethed, a low growl forming in his chest. "I should have been there to protect you. From the river, from him." His pacing increased.

"Kipp, calm down," Cas warned. Kipp simply snarled at him and stalked out the door. A moment later, a russet-colored shape darted off down the street. I pressed my lips together in a thin line, wondering if my actions were to blame for this strange outburst. It left me slightly distressed, but moreso, confused. Cas met my eyes, and as if reading the question there, released a weary sigh.

"It's not you, it's him. He'll be back. He just needs to work off some steam."

"What is...what is power-sharing supposed to feel like?" I asked hesitantly. Cas gave a small smile and came to sit down on the sofa beside me.

"It's typically something done between Fae that really trust each other. It can increase both of your powers temporarily. Since magic comes from the soul, it's like two souls meeting together in a long, comforting embrace. Since you can't hide your soul, it's like holding up a mirror to each other – you'll feel whatever you feel for the other person. Friends, enemies, lovers. It bares all."

I felt my cheeks redden as I remembered the delicious rush I felt at our souls meeting in their magical dance. My toes curled slightly.

Cas watched me carefully, then let out an amused laugh. "By the gods," he said. "Your cute little souls basically got it on!"

I heard Wren's strangled noise of surprise from across the room, and I ran a hand over my face in embarrassment. Cas shushed her with a snicker and offered me his hand.

"Here, let me show you a different example." His eyes glowed slightly as his magic extended to mine. I felt the hum as it approached and, as it touched the edge of my own, I realized I could tell from looking – truly *looking* – at his power, what and how much he held.

I was surprised by how much dimmer it was than Finlay's, a testament to how much power our race really did hold. Despite that, a peaceful joy radiated from his magic, a feeling that whispered of its healing qualities. I could feel it surrounding me, almost like it was tapping on the door of my magical source. I let him in.

As soon as I did, however, I felt his power disappear and Cas hissed, shaking his head.

"Sorry," he said, shifting in his seat. "I've just – I've just never power-shared with an Aes Sídhe. And certainly not one as powerful as you. It startled me." He chuckled and shook his limbs out. "Let's go again."

This time, when I let him in, it felt exactly how he'd explained. A calming, soothing embrace. I could feel our powers intertwine, less like a dance and more like a nuzzling sensation. I grinned, and he returned it, opening his free palm to show me his healing power. What was normally a low glow now made me squint, the power clearly surpassing his normal abilities.

"That was awesome!" I exclaimed giddily as Cas rescinded his magic. He simply winked.

"Well, Katie-cat, it helps that we're both awesome."

The door slammed as Kipp stalked in, back in his Faerie form, but covered in dust and sweat. He glanced at me, as if assuring himself I was still whole, and then stormed off to the bathroom. We all remained silent as we heard the start of running water, and the patter of footsteps as he paced between the guest room and the bathroom.

I caught a glimpse of his chest as he whisked his shirt off, and my mouth dropped open as I took in the marks there.

Several long scars ran down the right side of his ribcage, as if something had attempted to cleave him in two. Rage bubbled up in me on his behalf, and as he disappeared into the bathroom, I turned to Cas and whispered angrily, "What happened to him?"

Cas eyed the door where Kipp had disappeared, and then me. "Here, let me walk you back to the palace." He motioned with his head for us to move, and as we walked, he cleared his throat and began haltingly.

"The family that lived where you and your mother are now," he began, "had been Kipp's family the entire time he lived in the human realm. He followed them when they left Scotland, watching several generations grow old. But this last one..."

He rubbed the back of his neck, pausing. I glanced at his face. The skin around his eyes bunched, and his face was taut. I grabbed his hand out of impulse and, when he faced me, I gave him a small smile. He released a slow breath and continued.

"When he came back to visit about fifty years ago, he was a wreck. He'd been in a fight with a mountain lion, and he had been unable to portal his way back for my healing magic. He had to heal the normal, human way. He barely made it."

My hands curled into fists as I thought about the long gouges I'd seen across his ribcage. Cas continued.

"But much worse than that were the psychological scars. He'd been out there protecting Gerry's young son. But even in his wolf form, he didn't make it in time."

My throat constricted as I remembered what Kipp had packed from our home. Odds and ends, I'd thought – but also a small, wooden child's toy.

"He – he has to know – it wasn't his fault," I choked out. Cas's smile was sad this time.

"You know that, and I know that. But he doesn't see it that way. He sees it as not only his job, but his purpose in life, which he failed. And when he failed, he lost the lineage of the entire family he'd been sworn to protect."

I wrung Cas's hand in mine. "No wonder he's so torn up about me getting injured," I speculated out loud, and Cas nodded in agreement.

"We're his family now."

"A slightly fucked-up family, but one that can work to protect *each other*," I added emphatically, and I felt Cas's hand shake in my grasp as he laughed deeply.

"With your power, Katie-cat, I wouldn't doubt that most people will need protection from you." He gave my fingers one last squeeze as we reached the palace and said good night.

My sleep that night was fitful once more, with dreams of a rushing river and a golden-haired Fae with mischievous pale eyes. But those dreams were broken up by images of Kipp in wolf form, slashed and bleeding as yowls of a mountain lion tore through the distance. I felt the hum of my magic as I reached for it, desperate to protect Kipp. And to protect the little boy he, too, had sworn to protect.

Chapter 14

"Today, we introduce weapons." Blaise said, turning to grasp his discarded scabbard. I pulled my hair away from my shoulders, grimacing as it stuck to the sweat built up there.

In the week following my tumble off Gray, I'd thrown everything I had into my training. While the physical aspect had always come easier for me than others in the human realm, I was still pleasantly surprised to feel the movements that had been difficult or even nearly impossible in the first few days become much easier. My punches were hitting harder, my runs were longer, and my movements were more rapid.

I'd even managed to force Blaise into putting his fighting leathers on, to avoid bruising. I rode a high that day, proud of myself, but my progress stagnated at first as I attempted to avoid how attractive it made him look. Despite his perpetually stern expression, the rich brown leather strapped deliciously against his figure, making him look every bit the regal warrior he was.

I caught sight of Kipp, sunbathing in his wolf form. He looked relaxed, but I knew his constant shadowing of me this week was a form of therapy for him. I'd rolled my eyes the first day he said he would accompany me to and from the palace, though I said nothing, my heart jerking at the memory of what Cas had told me.

Blaise tightened the belt that held his scabbard and followed my gaze. "You can tell your little dog that you don't need babysitting when you're with me," he grumbled, as much in Kipp's direction as in mine.

It was Kipp who let his lip curl and ears flatten, those piercing blue eyes fixed on Blaise. But it was me who snarled. There was a resounding whack, and Blaise stumbled back a few steps, grabbing his jaw.

I gritted my teeth and clutched my fist. It twinged from the hit, but I'd taken his lessons to heart – my thumb perfectly placed, striking with my first two knuckles.

Blaise stared, bright hazel eyes wide with dismay. It took every fiber of my being not to flinch or take it back and say it was a mistake. My mother had raised me to be a proper lady; to hide in the shadows with a polite smile, to not raise conflict, and apologize for every inconvenience I might cause. All my life, I'd followed along for her peace of mind. But she had no idea I was here, and I was determined to embody my truest image in this new world — an image without even the faintest glimpse of a *proper lady*.

"I told you what I would do if you disrespected my friend again," I ground out, lifting my chin in a dare to rebuke it.

To my surprise, Blaise grinned — a wide, full grin, with his white teeth gleaming. I stood there in shock as he turned to Kipp, inclining his head slightly.

"My apologies, Callaghan. It won't happen again."

Kipp simply rose and spun a half circle before laying the other way, flapping his tail on the ground a few times in irritation.

"That was quite the punch. I have to say, I'm impressed." Blaise spoke directly to me, rubbing his jaw. "Alright. Come. It's time to pick your weapon." As we walked, he continued talking.

"In any case, you will learn how to fight with a standard sword and shield first. But Darrya will teach you how to wield an air shield so you can be protected and learn to use other weapons." Blaise explained, stopping. All I could do was nod and stare at the massive armory we now stood in.

It was underground, in a foreboding stone room that held endless wooden racks of weaponry: swords, shields, spears, bows, and countless other items I had no name for. Blaise paced around, lifting and weighing swords as he went, glancing at me every now and then to size me up.

"It's a good thing you're left-handed," he mused. "It's an unpopular opinion, but to me, it throws fighters off. They aren't used to fighting someone from the opposite side. It gives you the upper hand."

I stopped at a row of daggers and other short, curved knives. "Are these throwing knives?" I asked curiously. Blaise came up next to me, inspecting.

"These? No. These are your best friends when hand-to-hand combat begins to fail." He skimmed his hands over them, selecting one and handing it to me. "Easy to hide in your clothing. And use when necessary."

"It doesn't seem like it would do much," I replied dubiously and, before I knew it, I'd been spun around and tugged against Blaise's chest. Before I could ask what the hell he was doing, I felt the cold chill of a blade against my neck; it was light as a feather, but still present. My heart raced.

"Oh, it does. Because, sunshine," Blaise's breath was hot against the back of my neck, a stark contrast to the cold blade against the front. "anything can be a weapon. Even a small weapon can do damage. Especially one an enemy does not expect."

He lowered the blade, but neither of us moved. I felt keenly every point where our bodies touched, where his hand – strong but not painful – gripped my waist. Another shaky breath feathered against the nape of my neck, and I tilted my head back slightly. I felt him shift, leaning forward –

His hand met mine, and in it, he placed the dagger. He curled my fingers around it, and I felt how warm and calloused they were.

"Keep it," he said, his voice husky. "You never know when you might need it." With that, he pushed away, leaving me reeling.

"I'm sure Darrya will be looking for you soon," he continued, moving through the rows of weapons in clear dismissal. "I'll have a sword picked out for you for our next lesson."

I waited a heartbeat to see if he'd say anything else, and when he didn't, I huffed and slid away, rolling my eyes. I willed the confusing swirl of emotions out of my mind and body as I hunted for Darrya.

Once I found her, I relayed Blaise's request, and we began our work on an air shield. Her example was absolutely impenetrable. I threw sticks, punches, and – after some hesitation – large stones, only for them to bounce off an invisible force shield cast before her. She laughed with glee, explaining how it can be used like the shields carried by soldiers: wrapping your entire body, or extending to protect those around you.

I attempted to emulate hers until I was trembling, even sweatier than I was that morning, but it fell apart time and time again. I couldn't tell if it was because I wasn't yet capable, or if it was because my mindset wasn't on par with what it usually was.

By the time I stalked back to town for the evening, Kipp padding silently along beside me, I was thoroughly irritated and in dire need of the company of my friends.

"Wow, what a face. What's got you moping in here like a eunuch in a whorehouse?" Cas inquired breezily, pouring me a drink and topping off his own. I heard a bark of laughter from Kipp as he transformed behind me.

"I have been wondering that myself, considering she clocked Blaise a good one today," he said with a chuckle. Cas and Wren both wore the same shocked expression, looking more like siblings than ever before.

"Well, he had plenty of warning," I grumbled, shrugging. Kipp's shoulders shuddered as he held back a laugh.

"And then he gave me this," I added, twirling the dagger in my fingers. The memory of how it came to be mine still left me confused, but I reminded myself of why I'd hit him in the moments prior. He was nothing more than an arrogant musclehead, even if I felt slight goosebumps remembering the closeness of his lips to my neck.

"The commander-in-chief gives gifts now, huh? I'm not surprised it would be in the form of a weapon." Kipp said, taking it gently and inspecting it. He hummed in approval, and I shot him a look of surprise.

"What?" He shrugged. "Who knows when you'll need to stab someone. Maybe him."

I rolled my eyes and shoved him. Cas approached with a slight stumble, clearly having had a few drinks before we arrived. "I doubt he'd give her a real weapon if they haven't even been training with them. I bet it's not even sharpened."

"Cas, maybe don't – " Wren began as he snagged the dagger from Kipp's hands and ran his finger down it. "Oh gods, of course he did," she sighed.

"Yep. Okay. It's actually very sharp." Cas said as blood pooled across his finger. He made a fist and, in an instant, the wound was healed.

"You're lucky you're the one in the family with healing powers, considering how often you're injured as a result of your own stupidity." Wren scoffed, giving him an affectionate glare.

I laughed and settled in for the night, already feeling lighter. A shining piece of hope glimmered in my soul that this would always be the case.

Chapter 15

The next few weeks passed by fairly uneventfully. I trained, finding sword practice to be the most difficult part thus far. Despite Blaise finding one of the lightest and shortest swords available in the armory, it was deceptively heavy and left me feeling uncoordinated.

Neither Blaise nor I spoke of the moment in the armory; rather, he had a habit of disappearing right after our sessions for the remainder of the day. I noted it with a mixture of disappointment and relief.

Luckily, my magic practice had been improving greatly. I was now successfully building air shields, though they were nowhere near the strength of Darrya's. Soon, she reasoned, we could practice extending them to other people.

I had also been making leaps with my earth magic, now able to build and dismantle full bridges for Gray and I to pass across as we explored on our rides. Though, I hadn't made much progress with my water magic, and I hadn't been able to touch fire magic at all. I tried to ignore those particular facts and instead focus on my other triumphs. But it still irked me most days.

Darrya had a hunch that, since my earth magic seemed to be my strongest so far – already surpassing her own – perhaps my bloodline stemmed from the earth god Cernunnos. There were people coming in for the large festival this upcoming weekend that shared the same heritage, so she promised to ask some questions.

Lughnasadh – a harvest festival I had never heard of – was allegedly one of the four key festivals dominating the Faerie realm. It was used to pay reverence to one of the highest gods, Lugh. There would be large gatherings of Fae folk from surrounding areas, setting up tents for trade, contests, feasting, drinking, music...I was intrigued by the elation visibly spilling from my friends this week.

I couldn't help but feel some frustration, however, as I stalked toward the training ring for my morning session with Blaise. A rustle nearby alerted me to Kipp's presence as he shifted back into his Fae form.

"What's got you down in the mouth today?" He asked, appearing beside me as I walked toward the courtyard. I shrugged, and he didn't push the subject, allowing us to walk a few paces in silence.

"I just – it's just that I've been here *weeks.*" I finally admitted. "I'm excited to learn these new things, and to take Gray out, and to be with you, Cas, and Wren, even Darrya. But I don't see the point yet. I just figured whatever I was meant to do here would happen sooner."

The exasperation in my voice surprised even me. I hadn't realized how much it had been weighing on me until the words came out. Kipp placed a comforting hand on my shoulder in clear encouragement to continue.

"I'm supposed to start college again in two weeks. What am I supposed to do?" It was a plea, one I knew Kipp couldn't have the answer to, but I posed the question nonetheless. Emotion shimmered in his eyes as he considered my words.

"I'm honestly not sure. I expected more answers by now, too. Perhaps it is a blessing, though, as you've had some time to adjust to what it means to be Fae. But you do have a family and a life in the human realm. I understand that. Better than most here." He wrung his hands together and flashed me a sympathetic smile.

"It's a holy festival, marking the beginning of fall. That means the portal is open. How about you and I make a trip back to see your mother tomorrow? Perhaps things will become clearer then."

My heart lifted and I eagerly nodded at the offer. "Thank you."

He nodded and, in the moment it took to glance at Blaise doing warm-ups in the training ring and back to Kipp, he was already shifted back into wolf form, trotting to his usual spot of surveillance.

I settled in the movements that had become so familiar to me: the balance, the breathing, the striking and parrying. It was effortless for Blaise, who likely left to do his actual training after mine, but I took pride in the fact he no longer looked bored as he took on my blows.

As our training drew to a close, slow clapping sounded from the edge of the arena. Kipp leapt to his paws as Blaise and I both whirled around. I watched as Finlay appeared from behind a wall of green shrubbery, a cigarette dangling loosely from his mouth. A few courtiers hovered behind him, donning various colors of ruffled dresses. Gaudy jewelry flashed against the summer sun as they fanned themselves, clearly overheating but refusing to abandon their chances with royalty in the garden.

I quirked a brow at the tittering group hovering awkwardly behind him, then refocused on Finlay as he approached. He wore tight black pants and leather boots, but the only indication of his royal status was a long, thin cloth shirt, hanging loosely on his chest and embroidered in gold. He stopped in front of me with a lazy smile.

Kipp had shifted back into his Fae form, bowing respectfully from his position at the side of the arena. My entire body stood at attention as Blaise moved to stand behind me, a hair's breadth from our skin touching. He didn't bow, so I opted not to either, but I shivered as a bead of sweat dripped down my spine.

Finlay's pale blue eyes flicked to Kipp, acknowledging his bow, and I couldn't help but note the glassiness of his pupils. He cocked his head curiously, analyzing Kipp for a long moment.

"Have we met before?" He purred in question. "You look familiar...did we share a Selkie during the last solstice?"

"I'm flattered, your Highness, though I believe I would remember that, if it were the case." Kipp responded, a flush tinging his cheeks. Finlay hummed curiously but decided to drop it, turning his attention back to me.

"That was impressive," he commented. "It's been a while since I've trained. Perhaps I should take it back up. See what it's like to get my blood pumping again."

"Are you spying on me or something?" I asked, annoyance flitting through my veins. "Was the power-sharing not enough for you?" Blaise stiffened almost imperceptibly behind me.

"I apologized for that." Finlay said, his indifferent demeanor faltering for a moment. He took a long inhale, and continued on the exhale as smoke billowed around him, "I came for my flask."

I blinked. "Your flask?"

"You never gave it back after that day by the river. I've had others to make do, but that one is special to me. I'd like to have it for this weekend's festivities." His smirk returned, accompanied by a wink.

"I'll have Corryn deliver it to – well, wherever you're staying." I said flatly, and he inclined his head in mocking thanks. I could have left it at that, but the arrogant gesture had me unable to avoid a little mouthing off.

"I thought, being the queen's great-grandson, you might be busy with other things for Lughnasadh that don't involve being wasted. Like worshipping the gods, or whatever." I bit off.

I saw surprise flick across his pale blue eyes at the realization that I knew his relation to the queen. But there was no hurt at the condescending tone I used; rather, he simply schooled his expression back into that crooked, lazy grin of his.

"I prefer to do my worshipping in the bedroom," he drawled, his piercing expression burning into mine. My core turned slightly molten at the unbidden thought.

"What is it you hope to do? Wet her sheets with your sweaty despair?" The sharpness of Blaise's tone made me flinch. I glanced back at him, stretched tall and foreboding, a sneer on his face.

Finlay eyed Blaise for a moment, then simply shrugged. I released a breath. I supposed that only someone of Blaise's rank could make a comment like that and get away with it, knowing Finlay's status.

"I'll be waiting for Corryn," he said, turning and striding away. A billow of smoke trailed behind him, and my nose crinkled.

"I didn't realize you and he were acquainted," Blaise murmured from behind me.

"I didn't realize my social life was any of your concern," I quipped back without turning, and motioned for Kipp to join me as I stalked out of the arena. Admittedly, I was proud of the fact that I didn't look back once as I made my way to my room.

After handing the flask off to Corryn — whose expression was painted with several unasked questions — we made our way to the courtyard.

"What are you kids doing here?" A bemused voice sounded behind me. I turned to find Darrya, arms crossed, eyebrows raised.

"Training?" The word came out as a question, and Darrya grinned.

"Oh girl, no. It's a *holiday*. No training, just fun!" She stated with a laugh. I exchanged a surprised look with Kipp, who simply shrugged and smiled.

"She's not wrong," he hedged, and turned to her. "What are your plans for the rest of the evening, then, Darrya? Participating in any of the contests?"

"Gods, no," she responded emphatically, and I watched as the joy on her face was suddenly clouded with shadows. It was brief, concealed by an amused mask shortly after, but it was there. "I'll probably be spending it making small talk, building connections with other royal families. Trying to escape where possible."

Again, Kipp and I exchanged a look, one where I saw the same decision in his that was reflected in my own. I turned to Darrya and extended my hand.

"Come join us in town," I said with a smile. "You may still have to engage in small talk later, but the real party starts now."

Her brown eyes widened. "Are you sure?"

"Absolutely," I responded. "We'll have a great time. Though I make no promises about the behavior of the rest of them." I added with a warning glance at Kipp. His eyes simply danced mischievously, and I ruffled his hair affectionately in response.

Darrya was positively beaming. "Let me change and I'll meet you out front!" She turned, and I could've sworn she used a touch of her air magic to propel her strides, underscoring her excitement as she hurried into the palace.

As she went to change, I dipped out to check on Gray quickly before the festival. He seemed as happy as ever, almost as if the extra commotion suited him. Wren joined me in giving him a quick carrot and scratch, and then followed me back to the front of the palace, talking excitedly about tonight's events.

"You know that this festival is to honor Lugh, right? He's said to be the father of Cú Chulainn," she said, skipping alongside me. "I don't see how that gives you any answers, but it's just an interesting fact."

"I'm not sure either," I mused, studying her happy gait. "You certainly seem excited for tonight."

"I am! Dancing is my favorite, and the music at this festival is beyond comparison."

I grinned at her exuberance, and was about to ask what kind of music would be playing when the ground fell out from beneath us.

What the –" I coughed and brushed dirt off me, while Wren groaned and rolled over. Panic coursed through me as I picked at the dirt walls surrounding us. The soil was soft and damp, as though it had been carved rather recently and, as I peered up at the sky, I realized we had fallen into a massive hole. "Where did this come from?"

Wren grimaced, brushing herself off as well. "I think I know," she said with a sigh, and stood up, yelling with a tone I'd never heard from her before. "Maizie! Mereiah!"

After a moment, two identical faces peered over the edge of the hole. They were the first Fae children I'd seen here, probably around nine or ten. Their youthful faces were riddled with guilt. Wren put her hands on her hips. "You fix this, *right* now!"

A touch of fear flickered across their faces, and they disappeared again. After a moment, the earth began to tremble and we were rising back to the surface. Once the ground settled, I saw the two girls, wide-eyed and raven-haired, biting their lips as they glanced between Wren and the ground.

"You two! You could have seriously injured us. I thought you were over these types of pranks," she chastised, and they ducked their heads, muttering apologies while kicking their feet in the dirt.

"Now, get out of here before I think about telling your mother what you did." Wren pointed toward town, and they gasped, scrambling over each other as they ran. I covered my face to hide a grin.

"What the heck was that?" I asked.

Wren exhaled loudly. "Those were my nieces. They're in town for the festival, and they're always good for some trouble. They're Dryads, like me."

I surveyed the land behind us, which showed no lingering trace of a secret pit. "They're half my age, but probably just as powerful." I grumbled good-naturedly.

"Well, for starters, they grew up here. Everyone here learns how to master their powers as they progress through school. They're also twins," she added. "So, power-sharing between the two of them is as natural as breathing. Twice the power."

I considered this as we walked back to the front of the palace, wondering for a moment what it would have been like to grow up and attend school here. Would I have found a way to belong, in all the ways I hadn't in the human realm? What would I be capable of with my magic?

"That was the first time I've ever seen you get feisty, Wren," I teased as we approached Kipp and Darrya, who were patiently waiting. She blushed, muttering something about her family being annoying, but I continued. "No, seriously, that was hot! You should yell more often!" I laughed and darted away before she could smack my arm.

The other two gave us a quizzical look as they took in the mud smattering our clothes.

"We fell victim to two ten-year-olds and their pranks," I explained. "So, let's get going, because now I *really* need a drink."

"Do my eyes deceive me?" Cas droned from the kitchen, where he was making a special drink concoction with endless items I had no names for. "Or did I just witness the queen's gorgeous envoy pass through these doors?"

The beautiful blonde Fae in question breezed through the entryway in her typical devil-may-care manner, touching Wren's arm in a familiar greeting and passing into the kitchen to give Cas a warm embrace.

"It's nice to meet you, Castille. I've heard a lot about you from Kate." Over her shoulder, Cas glanced at me with a look of alarm.

"All good things," I laughed. "But don't let her fool you. I think she's a bigger, badder wolf on the inside than Kipp."

Darrya simply tutted and pulled away from Cas, waving a hand in my direction. "I prefer the term sheep in wolf's clothing."

Sheep or wolf, Darrya looked stunning. She had changed into a navy-blue asymmetrical dress, with a high, lacey neckline. Her hair was pulled back into a high bun and that, combined with her dress, spoke of class yet looked incredibly sexy on her.

"I didn't realize you were the queen's envoy," Kipp remarked curiously.

To be honest, I hadn't known that, either, but I could see the wheels in his mind turning. As the envoy, she would likely have access to any information about a potential war, or any unrest in the

Fae realm. Still, I met his gaze and narrowed my eyes, shaking my head. *Not tonight.* He ducked his head in understanding.

"Most days, yes. But tonight, I hope to just be a normal Fae, having some fun. Possibly with some gorgeous slice of Fae rolling in my sheets by the end of the night." Darrya said slyly. Wren's eyes widened, having never seen this side of her at the palace, and Kipp guffawed in approval.

"Ooooh," Cas crooned, licking some salt off his fingers and pointing at Darrya. "I like her style. I think I'll be looking for a bit of the same myself tonight."

"Speaking of," Darrya said, rummaging through the bag she'd brought. She pulled out a soft pink piece of fabric, patterned with a rose-gold lace overlay. "I figured, since I only ever see you in training clothes, you probably didn't have anything fancy for tonight."

She held it up to me, and I took it gingerly in my fingers. The fabric was soft and shimmered with the gilded lace that adorned it. "Darrya," I breathed in awe. "This is..."

"Well?" She urged. "Try it on!"

I obliged, not surprised in the least to find that it fit perfectly. It hugged my waist, now taut with muscle from all the training, and billowed out at the curve of my hips. It was still respectful, with short sleeves ruffling over my shoulders, but a slit in the skirt and the V that accentuated my chest were a pleasant surprise.

I entered back into the living room and was greeted with whistles and calls to spin. I did, smiling. When I stopped, I realized everyone else had changed as well. Wren wore a flowy emerald green dress that boasted a gold-beaded halter top; she also wore her hair in a bun, with tendrils of ebony locks framing her face.

I surveyed Kipp, who had pulled on knee-high black leather boots over loose white pants and wore a belted charcoal gray tunic. He'd even slicked back his normally messy, cinnamon-colored hair, though I still glimpsed a shadow of a beard.

He glanced at me curiously as I inspected him with a smirk. "What?"

"I'm just thinking about how different the style is here. It's such a strange mixture of old and new," I said, knowing he would understand after spending decades in the human world.

"Hey, you can't knock it until you've tried it. I happen to find these clothes much more comfortable than the nonsense you wear in the human world. Like jeans?" He groaned. "I don't know how you did it."

I snorted and turned my gaze to Castille. "At least he has the right idea."

Cas grinned, giving a comical bow in response. The pants he wore were tight black leather, a stark contrast to his long, puffy shirt, colored crimson and silver. It must have been specially made, because his wings were on full display. He wore orange and red jewels along his hairline where the shaved portion met his luscious waves, tumbling down the right side of his face.

Wren came to my side to fuss over my hair, and while I argued with her to keep it simple, Darrya brought me one of Cas's drinks. I sipped slowly, savoring the flavors that danced on my tongue. By the time I finished one, I was already lightheaded.

"Shit, Castille, these are strong." Darrya said, as if reading my mind.

"So, you don't want another one?" He teased, holding a freshly poured glass in front of her face, then whipping it away.

"I didn't say that," she responded, grabbing it in one quick motion and darting away. He laughed and went to pour more.

I stood up, feeling the braid Wren put in my hair and smiling at her appreciatively. I grabbed the glass Cas shoved my way.

"Drink up," he said, dancing away. "We have a festival to attend!"

Chapter 16

We traveled through the various booths, snickering and stumbling more than normal thanks to Cas's drinks, and I was awed by what I saw.

Wren pointed out all types of Fae folk as we walked, explaining in hushed tones. I was stunned by the unique elegance of each, noting some Pixies with their wings splayed, boasting a rainbow of colors. My heart warmed watching groups of Faeries greet each other with enthusiastic embraces, and children weaving in and out of booths, laughing. It felt like...home.

While the rest of the group sampled some cheeses, my eyes caught on the booth next door, and I found myself drawn in. The booth owner, who I identified from Wren's brief explanations as a Deva – a fire Faerie – explained her craft, but my ears didn't register the words.

Instead, I traced the intricate braiding of her torc necklaces and bracelets. They were beautifully unique, elegance crafted into such strong metal. I brushed my thumb over one bracelet in particular, both ends rounded with garnet-colored stones in the center, layered with white.

"Sardonyx," a silken voice whispered in my ear. I jumped, turning to see Finlay standing behind me. We both took a beat to absorb what the other was wearing.

Finlay wore the same type of outfit as Kipp, with the knee-high boots and billowing white pants, but his deep purple tunic was belted with a delicate chain of gold, further accentuating the gold of his hair. I noticed that he'd slicked it back, as if to calm the volume, but it had already started to fall back in front of his eyes.

"Come again?" I asked distractedly, blinking. His eyes, which had landed on my chest, rose to meet mine. I felt my face flush slightly at the obvious location of his scrutiny.

"Sardonyx," he repeated. I could smell the scent of vanilla and cigarettes on his breath. "The stone. It represents strength and protection. It also happens to be the birthstone for the month of August. Perfect for Lughnasadh."

"My birthstone," I murmured absentmindedly, tracing the bracelet. I'd never bothered to learn my birthstone.

"When is your birthday?" Finlay asked, raising his brows.

"In a week," I replied, eyeing him warily. He simply nodded and motioned toward the bracelet.

"You should get it," he said, and pulled out the flask I'd had Corryn deliver to him earlier in the day. He took a long swig and winked at me. "Thank you for returning this, by the way."

I rolled my eyes in response. "What do you have in there tonight?"

"Apple juice," he deadpanned without missing a beat. I couldn't help but throw him a small smirk, which he returned warmly.

"There you are! Oh, hey cuz." Darrya approached, draping her arm over my shoulders and sizing up Finlay. "Are you giving my girl any trouble?"

"Wouldn't dream of it," he replied smoothly.

"Good. Because I would love for you to help us with our training sometime. Kate here has yet to master the element of fire." Darrya continued. My cheeks flushed with embarrassment at her comment.

Finlay turned his assessing gaze back on me with a brief once-over. I expected to see disappointment in his expression, but instead, it was rife with amusement.

"That surprises me, given how much fire this little fallen angel here seems to have in her personality," he responded, eyes dancing. My own narrowed at his retort, the flush in my cheeks reddening further with the addition of irritation.

"*Katherine.*" I corrected, as Darrya laughed.

"So, you do know Kate, then," she said gleefully as the others came to join us.

"Come on, it's time for the dancing!" Wren said at an excitement level that was rare for her. She pulled at Darrya and me, and Darrya yelled a goodbye to her cousin as we were dragged away. I caught his eye as he gave a playful salute with his flask.

I heard the music before I saw the dancing; it was beautiful music that I felt thrumming in my veins. It reminded me of the way loud electric or disco music could beat straight into your soul, and yet, it was entirely different. The natural tunes rose and fell and, as I watched the Faeries dance, my whole body relaxed.

Everyone twirled and chanted shamelessly to the beat, different types of movement that bore no judgment, only joy. The bonfires that were lit in a large circle around the field swayed too, as if in time with the dancing of the Faeries.

I found myself grinning at the sight, sipping on a glass of wine that had mysteriously appeared the moment I was running low. I glanced at both Darrya and Castille with a grin. I'd told Kipp I was concerned about the dangerous friendship we'd put together between those two, and he'd chuckled in full agreement.

"Well, what are we waiting for?" Wren said, and dove merrily into the fray. Cas followed closely behind, but before Darrya could follow, she found herself drawn into a conversation with what looked like a member of a royal family. I tossed her a sympathetic look and stood with Kipp a while longer, sipping wine until my mind was hazy.

A beautiful Asrai approached Kipp, and I slyly excused myself to let them chat, flashing Kipp a wink as I left. He rolled his eyes, but I noticed he didn't argue.

I joined the dancing Faeries — awkwardly at first — but as the music made its way to my soul and the effects of the wine set in, my inhibitions lifted. I found myself spinning and flowing, crossing paths with Faeries I didn't know and the flashing faces of my friends as they twirled by.

At one point, I paused long enough to catch sight of a group of warriors, standing on the hill overlooking the dancing. They all wore the rich chestnut fighting leathers, golden designs embroidered on the shoulders; surely a means to impress those traveling to Sairas with the power of the queen's army, I thought.

One soldier stood out among the rest. The belt that sheathed his sword was embellished with a large buckle that looked like some sort of Celtic symbol — the same symbol on Finlay's flask, I realized. It was the only sign on his clothing that marked how he stood above the rest rank-wise, but the way he stood was sign enough: tall and stalwart, an unmoving force against any storm. His hair was perfectly coiffed and the unruly stubble normally gracing his jaw was shaved neatly.

Blaise's somber gaze seared straight into me. I ignored the pleasant feeling that grew in the pit of my stomach at having his attention. I continued dancing, watching as his eyes raked over my body. And once they reached my eyes once more, I threw him my middle finger and turned, disappearing into the crowd of gyrating figures.

Even if his body was chiseled by the gods themselves, he wasn't allowed to make me feel the things I'd felt, only to spurn me as he had in the armory.

My dancing became almost furious as I worked to sweat out my emotions. As the night darkened, with the only traces of light coming from the embers of the bonfires and the moon, I locked eyes on another Faerie in the masses. He fit every mark of tall, dark, and handsome, but his eyes were the most intriguing. They almost seemed to shift between blue, green, and gold, flashing treacherously.

I approached, breathing heavily. The male grinned, his perfect teeth a startling white. "You were dancing your little heart out on the field there," he noted, his voice somehow both raspy and silken.

I nodded, unable to speak. He motioned with his head for me to join as he turned to saunter down the hill. "Would you like to take a walk to cool off?"

I nodded once more, eyes wide. "Who are you?" I breathed as we strode away from the festivities.

"Me? My name is Flint," he purred. I rubbed my arm, a small part of me yearning to sidle closer at the sound of his voice.

"What kind of Faerie are you?" I asked.

"Same as you, but slightly different," he replied. I blinked in confusion, but before I could respond, he continued.

"My power isn't in the elements. It's in less tangible things."

I studied him curiously as we walked, noticing the sharp line of his jaw. He met my gaze with a knowing look of his own.

"I can read your thoughts. Understand your innermost wants. Your deepest desires," he crooned. "And I've been watching your desires be unmet all night."

He stopped, and I noticed we were on the other side of the hill, away from the now-dwindling dancing and music. A sweet mist began to spread across the field as I realized how *right* Flint was. I had been dancing to avoid the feelings inside me that were begging for release. Ones that had no real outlet. Until now.

"I can feel how you wanted more than just his eyes on your body. On your mouth," he murmured, voice ravenous. My lips parted as I stared at his, full and inviting. The mist around us became intoxicating.

"You were desperate for some release. I can give that to you. Do you want me to give that to you?" His eyes locked onto mine and I leaned forward, nodding and closing my eyes. He smiled a slow, sultry smile, and leaned in to meet me.

But my lips met nothing. Instead, I heard a gurgling sound, and when I opened my eyes, I saw Flint's surprised face as an inky substance dripped from his mouth. It took a split-second for me to realize it must be blood. I shrieked, stumbling backward.

The Faerie fell forward, and behind him stood Blaise, stone-faced, wiping the black blood off a short blade.

"What the hell?" I yelled, staring down at the body that now lay between us. The mist, which had hung heavily, began to clear, and I saw a dark pool of blood spilling from Flint's throat.

"That's a strange way to say thank you." Blaise ground out, shooting me a stern look.

"Thank you? Thank you for killing this *one* person who was interested in me? Are you insane?" I demanded. Blaise's jaw twitched, his expression unreadable.

"This was your suitor, hmm?" He rolled Flint's body onto its side, and I stared down at – something unrecognizable. The mist had fully cleared now, showing what lay beneath us. His face was no longer that of a handsome, dark stranger. It was grotesquely warped, pale, and sullen. My mouth opened and closed, but no words came out.

"This is a *Gean-Cánach*. The 'Love Talker', if you will. A type of dark Faerie." Blaise stepped over the now-bony structure that used to resemble Flint and stalked back up the hill. I scrambled after him.

"Dark Faerie? That doesn't make any sense. He looked – normal – and he had a normal name, and – " I stopped, embarrassed to admit that was all I had known about the Faerie I'd been ready to mack on a few minutes ago. The shock of witnessing a murder – was it a murder? – was sobering, and I wasn't entirely sure what I had been thinking in the first place.

We crested the hill back into the main dance area. Blaise stopped to give instructions to one of his fellow warriors to 'dispose of the body below,' and my stomach churned.

"Katie-cat! There you are!"

I wheeled at Cas's voice and saw him approach with Kipp. Their hands brushed against one another as they walked, and I observed a slight hesitation as they both moved to create distance. I cocked my head, trying to catch their expressions, but neither gave anything away.

"Are you good?" We all asked in unison, and laughed.

"If you don't mind, I'll be escorting Katherine back to the palace tonight." Blaise said, suddenly beside me. His tone was polite but left little room for discussion.

Kipp stiffened as his lip curled slightly, but I gently touched his arm. "I'll be fine," I reassured him, nodding towards the Asrai hovering in the distance, eyes glued on Kipp. "You go enjoy your night."

"And you enjoy *yours,*" Cas cut in mischievously, giving Blaise a deliberate once-over. Blaise cleared his throat and glanced away.

I shook my head softly. Cas lifted his hands up apologetically, but winked as he turned.

Blaise and I walked for a while in silence, but finally I ventured, "He said he could hear my wants and desires. Does that...does that type of magic really exist?"

"It's a dark type of magic. It shouldn't exist this close to the borders of town," he responded tightly. "My army works to keep it secure. I can only assume the festival made the creature forget the risks at the expense of so much potential prey."

I heard the disappointment and anger in his voice, that he and his army had failed to keep the borders secure. Silence consumed us once more, until we finally reached the entrance of the palace. Blaise nodded to the guards on duty, and as we approached the hallway where we would split ways, I turned to him.

"Wh – what would it have done to me?" I asked in a hushed tone.

Blaise took a moment, inspecting the ceiling before letting out a long breath.

"All it needed to do was kiss you. One kiss. It would have stolen a piece of your magic, then disappeared. You would have pined for it and nothing else, losing your will to eat, sleep, to do anything. Eventually, it would have caused you to die simply from desire."

I shuddered, and Blaise glanced at me.

"I wouldn't have let that happen, you know," he said in a low voice. "Its true face glimmered for a moment as it beckoned you, so I followed close behind. When I saw its words were enchanting you, I had to take action."

I can feel how you wanted more than just his eyes on your body. On your mouth.

My face burned as I realized Blaise had likely overheard the creature voicing my desires out loud. "Why didn't you step in sooner?"

Blaise shifted on his feet. "I assumed you would not fall captive to its charms. Are you not marked?"

"Excuse me? Marked?"

"The Shield Knot. It's a mark that wards off evil spirits from using dark magic to coerce you. It's also claimed to aid soldiers on the battlefield. My entire army has it. And so should you, clearly."

When my puzzled expression didn't lift, Blaise cleared his throat and began undoing his leathers. My pulse quickened when the vest slid apart, leaving the top of his white tunic flowing. He pulled the tunic down to the left, exposing his bare chest, his muscles arching with the movement.

My lips parted as I took in the exposed skin. A large circle wove in and out of itself to create four solid corners within the symbol, giving the impression of no beginning and no end.

I broke my stare to eye him dubiously. "That tattoo can ward off evil spirits?"

"When it's paired with a protection spell during creation? Yes," Blaise said, and when still I raised an eyebrow at him, he grabbed my hand. Before I knew it, he was pressing my palm flat against his mark. "Can you feel it?" he murmured.

It took a moment, but then I felt it – a similar feeling to Cas's energy when I'd tapped that wall, but more defensive. It exuded protective energy.

"I do," I whispered, surprised. Blaise didn't move, and I felt the normal energy past his mark – the heat of his naked flesh against my palm, the steady pounding of his heartbeat. My own pulse ramped from quickened to full-on skittering.

I gathered as much courage as I could, swallowing, then asked softly, "How much of my conversation with the Love Talker did you hear?"

Breathless, I kept my eyes averted as I waited for his answer. The seconds ticked by, agonizingly slow, and I was about to ask if he'd heard me when he replied, his voice raw.

"Enough to hope it was talking about me."

My eyes shot up to meet his, my heart leaping to my throat. His face was stony, expression guarded. His hand traveled up to meet mine, still on his chest. He took my wrist lightly, not quite moving it away, but shifting it a hair's breadth off his mark.

"Was it?" He asked hoarsely. I couldn't speak, but met his hazel eyes, now smoldering, and nodded.

In the next second, my back was pressed against the stone wall as Blaise's lips crushed against mine. They were full and soft but demanding as they claimed me. His one hand gripped my wrist, now pressing it above my head, while his other traveled down my waist. A desperate noise escaped me as his lips left my mouth and traveled to my neck, eliciting a groan from him.

"You look absolutely devastating tonight, Katherine," he growled.

I tugged my arm, begging to touch him with both hands, and he dropped my wrist, allowing my fingertips to explore that delicious piece of exposed skin, skimming over the glorious plains of his chest.

I closed my eyes, tilting my head to offer him more space while he trailed his kisses down my throat. I gasped as his teeth grazed the nape of my neck before his lips came crashing back onto mine, swallowing the sound and sinking his tongue into my mouth to caress my own.

Heat spread like the spill of a waterfall, rushing down my body and pooling in my belly. My hands traveled from his chest up to his face, my fingertips grazing over his faint stubble, tracing the sharp curve of his jaw. I sucked lightly on his bottom lip, and that was all it took for him to press me harder into the wall.

Grabbing my leg, he lifted it up to trail his rough hand up the soft fabric of my dress. His other hand clutched a fistful of my hair, lifting my chin in a demand for more from our kiss. I drank him in, tasting the spicy, oaky flavor of the alcohol he'd been drinking, mingling with the earthy scent of his leather.

Blaise pulled back, his jaw twitching and his pupils dilated as he restrained himself from venturing into more dangerous territory. Our heavy breaths mingled and echoed along the corridor.

Before either of us could make a move, the loud bang of a door somewhere in the palace made us jolt. We glanced down the hallway, then back at each other.

I swallowed. "We should – we should probably–"

Blaise nodded in understanding, lowering his arms. I felt their absence keenly.

"Goodnight, Katherine," he murmured softly, and after holding my gaze for a moment, he backed away, slipping into the darkness.

I found my way slowly to my room, my head reeling as I replayed the moments in the hallway. The door closed behind me, and I stood for a moment, allowing my heartbeat to slow. Eyes closed, I trailed my fingers over my mouth and neck, thinking of all of the places he had touched me.

Enough to hope it was talking about me.

I drew myself a cold bath in a pitiful attempt to relax from the night's events, and by the time I threw myself on the bed, I was so exhausted I almost missed it. There on my pillow lay a little black box, with a small, folded letter on top.

I rose to my elbows, grabbing the letter and eyeing it curiously. Inside was a simple sentence: *Happy early birthday.*

Confused, I reached for the box and opened it. A metal cuff bracelet, intricately braided, was placed inside. The ends, with their beautiful circular design, held two small orbs that boasted layers of red and white. Sardonyx.

Chapter 17

"Oomph!" I groaned as we landed back in the human realm. Kipp's landing was comically graceful compared to mine, and he chortled as I regained my footing and stuck my tongue out at him.

More jarring than the somersaults in my stomach from the crossing was the stunning emptiness I now felt in my body. I searched in me for that hum of my magic, but it was barely reachable, as if it were lulled into a deep slumber. I tried not to panic as the energy that had become such an integral part of me over the past month dissipated to near-nothingness.

"Yep. It's not pleasant." Kipp said, studying me. "Our magic is rendered nearly useless in the human world. We still have enough scraps of it to create stories about us, though. Mostly light practical jokes from temporary visitors, but some have stayed and used it for good. Think of those with an unbelievable green thumb, or nearly superhuman speed, or the countless stories of people being brought back from the brink of death in a miraculous way. Things that force people to contemplate whether life is unpredictable, or if magic really is at play."

Half of me wanted to ask about the presence of dark Faeries here, the shadow to the light he had mentioned, but that would only open the door to discussing what had transpired last night. I didn't want him to worry that he'd left me unattended. Instead, as we approached the barn, I asked, "Will she be able to see us?"

He shook his head in response. "No. I've cast an enchantment over us to keep us hidden from non-Fae folk. The one that didn't work on you." He tossed me a wry grin, and I responded by ruffling his unruly hair, the friendly gesture now so familiar to me.

We approached the house, and I took in the clearing, noting the dullness of the colors surrounding the area and the stale feeling that hung in the air. Despite the two decades I'd spent growing up here, I now knew what a world with magic was like. Returning to a world devoid of it was beyond strange.

I heard my mother's laughter before I saw her, the sound bright and cheery like the chime of bells. My heart twisted as I peered into the window. She sat at the dining room table and tossed her dark hair back as she laughed again, her smile stunning as she ran her hands over a deck of cards splayed out before her. A strange woman walked to her side of the table, topping off the drink in my mother's hand, while using her free hand to gesture emphatically as she told a story — one that clearly had my mother in stitches.

"Your mother is beautiful," Kipp murmured beside me. I nodded, my throat constricting.

"Especially when she laughs." I whispered, wringing my right wrist, where I now wore the cuff bracelet.

And there it was. She was happy. Finally finding friends, stepping into this new home and new life with none of the scars and dark memories of my father that our old home had — potentially even happier without me, another reminder of my father's passing.

Kipp stood silently at my side, letting me simply observe my mother for several long minutes. I allowed the emotions to whirl endlessly, contemplating what my life had been before, compared to now. I concluded that, against all odds, my mother and I both had more now than we had previously. We were both happier, fulfilled in a way we couldn't be when tied to each other. Even if a part of me broke at that realization.

I lowered my head and sighed. "I need to make a call." Kipp looked at me, those azure blue eyes wide and questioning. "I need to withdraw from the university."

He offered me a sympathetic smile and gave me space while I made the call. When it was done, he held out his hand, knowing I was ready to leave without having to ask. I took it gratefully, and we walked back to the ley lines.

"No matter what," he ventured after a beat. "You have a family with us. You know that, right?"

I nodded, giving his hand a squeeze. "Yeah, I know."

But when we got home, I decided to spend the rest of the evening in my room at the palace instead of joining him in Sairas. I turned restlessly in bed, trying to distinguish between my family in the human world and here, mulling over the finality of the choices I'd made.

I barely slept that night, and by the time I rose for training the next morning, I was well and truly flustered. My emotions, likely heightened now that I was back in the Faerie realm, toiled between guilt, anger, and sadness. As I saw Blaise, a warm rush of desire joined the mix, simply adding to the confusion.

My eyes pinned on his full lips, which flickered into a brief smile as he saw me, though our exchange of greetings was almost shy.

"So, should we warm up?" He asked, raising his hands. I bounced on my feet, feeling my limbs wake up, and began boxing lightly into his fists. I caught his eyes as I struck, his thoughts about the other night mirrored in them.

The night of Lughnasadh was the start down a dangerous road where feelings could get involved. Feelings that had already solidified my decision to be here, away from my own mother — who seemed happier without me, anyways.

Before I knew it, I was slamming my fists into the palms of Blaise's hands, possibly harder than I ever had, even with the training shield in place. I froze, panting, as tears brimming my eyes. Blaise didn't move a muscle, clearly willing to let me pummel his hands into a pulp if need be. His expression was indecipherable.

Gritting my teeth, I turned away, ashamed of the outburst of emotion. My fists curled and uncurled as I tilted my head back, as though I could will the tears to return to my eyes instead of spilling out the edges.

"I'm sorry if I overstepped the other day," Blaise murmured softly in my ear.

"What?" I blinked in confusion, causing a tear to fall from one eye. I brushed it away in irritation.

"If I overstepped my bounds, I apologize. I know what the Urisk means to you." Blaise cleared his throat. "And if what I did impacted your relationship, I am sorry for that."

"What are you talking about?" I whirled to face him. He held his arms behind his back, face pained. "Are you – are you talking about Kipp?"

He nodded, averting his eyes. I glanced over at Kipp in his wolf form, who had rolled over and was laying on his side, observing our interaction with amusement shining in his lupine eyes.

A short chuckle escaped me, and Blaise looked up in surprise. "Kipp and I are just friends. Nothing more. I consider him family, but more of the older brother sort."

His eyes darted to Kipp as if to confirm, and Kipp gave a pointed yawn. Then, Blaise turned his gaze to me, brows knitted in confusion.

"Look, I'm just not – not in a very good headspace today." I admitted, rubbing the back of my neck. "I had a rough day yesterday, and I didn't sleep well."

Blaise's pained look lifted somewhat, but he still studied me intently. "Would you like to take the day off?" He asked with surprising gentleness.

I shook my head vehemently.

"I think I need this." I asserted, and his mouth twitched in appreciation. He turned to pick up my sword, handing it to me and lifting one of his own.

"Good. Because you've survived all of your worst days so far. Today will be no different." With that, he swung his blade in a fluid, circular motion and landed in a fighter's stance. "Let's see what you've got."

I grinned in response and dove into training. The motions provided a sweet respite from my thoughts, and by the time I stumbled into the courtyard for my magical lessons, my mood had lifted considerably.

I slowed as I inhaled a familiar skunky scent — a reminder of my first year in college. My eyes widened as they landed on Darrya, rolling her eyes at Finlay, who leaned against the tree in the courtyard, a hand-rolled joint dangling lazily out of his mouth.

Darrya caught my eye, waving at me eagerly, and Finlay turned his head. His normal, slightly careless appearance had turned to fully unkempt, with his flowing locks lending a just-rolled-out-of-bed look. His oversized tunic, half-laced at the front, was completely undone, and my eyes traveled to the place where the V stopped, surprised at the amount of muscle that peeked out from underneath the fabric.

"Hello, little angel," he crooned, eyes crinkling as he gave me a lopsided smile. I decided to ignore his insistent use of the nickname, and instead eyed the joint as he took another drag.

"Seems like a new bad habit," I commented. He simply shrugged, exhaling. A trail of smoke climbed to the skies.

"I have several bad habits, as you know. Take your pick." He dropped the joint to the ground and twisted his foot on top of it, motioning to my arm. "Glad to see you got your birthday present."

"Birthday present? Kate, is it your birthday?" Darrya glanced between us, her expression going from excited to horrified as she feared the idea of missing it.

"It's in a few days," I muttered, shooting Finlay the best death glare I could muster. He merely winked in response. *Jerk.* Now I would never hear the end of it, and he knew it.

"Isn't it your twenty-first birthday? Kate, you'll be old enough to drink! Well, *officially* — in your human realm, anyways." Darrya gushed. Finlay raised an eyebrow at me.

"Twenty-one, is it?" He questioned. "You'll be an adult. Just let me know if you're ever in the mood to do any ... *adult* things."

"Ah, yes. I'll give you a holler if I ever need a new addition to my sewing circle." I quipped. Finlay's bright eyes widened and his lips parted in surprise before broadening into an impressed grin.

Darrya snickered, then cleared her throat. "All right, you two," she began. "I brought Finlay here in hopes he could show you a bit about fire magic. Since it's his dominant element, he should be able to explain it better than me."

I pursed my lips. "Funny. I knew that, but I really would have expected earth. What with the *grass* and all."

Finlay tossed that lilting smile my way and produced a delicate orb of fire on his fingertips, letting it dance across each finger before using it to light a normal cigarette.

"Fire is the most different from the other elements," he started. "It bears pieces of the others – especially air, since it needs oxygen to be fed – but has a completely different feel. Whereas the others feel bidden, inhibited, natural – fire is more chaotic."

He flicked his fingers, causing the fire to light across all of his fingers and grow, stretching several feet into the air. Even as it ascended, it never left its thin torrent, about the width of his hand.

"It doesn't want to be controlled, which makes the internal tug of war that much harder. You need to let go — enough to will it into existence, but never loosening the leash enough for it to flow unconstrained."

I watched as he let a small crack in the funnel appear, from which the tongues of fire lashed out. A wave of heat enveloped me, but as fast as I could blink, he had reeled it back in. I glanced at his face curiously, only to find his expression relaxed. Perhaps he was just never sober, so this was a natural state for him, wielding his fire powers half-cocked.

The fire disappeared, and he motioned to me. "Come on, let's have at it."

I concentrated, willing the now-familiar surge of magic to well inside of me, pushing it towards fire. But instead of feeling the connections I had with earth, air, and water, I met a brick wall. I bit the inside of my lip.

Darrya sighed softly, and Finlay flicked his cigarette to the ground. He stomped on it, then moved toward me. I tensed, and he tsked.

"You'll never be able to summon fire all tense like that," he admonished me, taking the back of my hand in his. I told myself not to pull back, instead leaving it in his unsurprisingly warm palm.

"Here. Take a moment to locate any heat inside you. Whatever heat it is – the warmth of friendship, the heat of anger, or the burn of desire."

His breath brushed past my ear as he spoke, and I smelled the ashy scent of his last cigarette, mixed with a faint note of that vanilla whiskey. I hated that I now associated that scent with him, almost like a devilish perfume. Some animalistic part deep in my body longed to taste it.

Nope. Cut that out.

"Take that heat. Close your eyes. Breathe. Let go." I did as he asked, closing my eyes and allowing the rush of heat, flowing unbidden. "Now imagine it lighting a spark with the outside world."

My feelings zeroed in on the contact between our hands. I felt the heat localize there, burning its way to my palm. There was a low murmur of encouragement in my ear and suddenly, I felt a spark ignite. I was quickly left with emptiness as his hand darted away from mine with a hiss. I whipped my eyes open, looking between Finlay and Darrya. The former gave me a guilty look.

"My apologies. It was there – the heat, the spark. It was just incredibly strong." He shook out his hand a few times. "You may need to try it without physical contact until you learn how to guide it into not causing harm."

My cheeks reddened, but I obliged. I was able to produce the same small spark a few more times before we called it quits, with Finlay sliding off to do gods knew what – likely more drinking – while Darrya and I moved on to the other elements for the remainder of the session. I made sizable progress with water, which softened the disappointing blow of my fire work.

When we were done, I invited her back into town for the evening. I felt a twinge of guilt as we walked into Sairas, knowing I had ulterior motives with the invite, but I pushed them down, remembering how she and Cas got along like kindred souls. I wasn't just shaking her down for information; she was truly a member of our friend group now.

"I'm sorry if it's hard for you to deal with Finlay," she said suddenly as we walked. I glanced at her, startled. Kipp noted the conversation start and paused, deliberately padding a good distance behind us for privacy.

"Why do you say that?" I asked, puzzled.

"I mean, I know he's ... difficult. Troubled." She paused, as if debating whether to continue. Unsure how to respond, I held my tongue and waited for her instead. Finally, she sighed and continued.

"He has a lot of demons, and he's taken to dancing with them, rather than overcoming them. It's been decades since he's truly been sober."

She pondered her own words for a moment before continuing. "Honestly, though – this is the best I've seen him in a long time. He's normally more impulsive, self-corrupt, and arrogant. But as you can see, he's insanely powerful. He's in line for the throne, you know. After the queen passes it on."

I blinked in surprise at that. "Is there no one else between him and the queen to take the throne?"

She winced gently, as if she had expected the question but was not prepared to answer.

"Both of his parents passed away when he was young. He was raised by our grandparents – the queen's son – in another land. Daersill, the same one my parents live in. But our grandfather passed away recently, too, and it's left our grandmother in a state. Not that she's in line for the throne herself anyway, without being a blood relative," she explained, wringing a piece of hair in her fingers as she recalled the experiences.

"That had to be so hard. For all of you," I responded softly. She tossed me a halfhearted smile, and after a beat, I ventured, "Does that happen often? Faerie parents – dying young?"

She shook her head emphatically. "Not at all. Especially not for the royal family. We always assumed they made some serious enemies because – well, they weren't natural deaths. The queen was devastated, especially considering how few of the Aes Sídhe there are left as it is."

I absorbed the information in silence, and Darrya cleared her throat. "I'm so sorry, this is nothing that needs to worry you! I only wanted you to understand Finlay a bit better. And hopefully give him a bit of grace, all things considered. He's had a rough go of it, and has a lot on his shoulders. All I can hope is that he finds his way in due time."

I nodded, giving her a distracted smile to assure her all was well. We arrived at Cas's home, and as everyone dissolved into conversation, I retreated into my own mind. Finlay's parents were gone, and so was one of mine. Though, for all intents and purposes, I reminded myself grimly, both of mine were.

Chapter 18

"By all the gods," Darrya breathed.

Another few days had passed, and thanks to peer pressure from the group, I had finally caved and agreed that we should tell Darrya the entire truth, then see what information she knew that could be helpful. She'd rapidly blended into our little family regardless, and I knew we could trust her.

The other silver lining I saw in dumping this information on her was that it seemed to have sufficiently distracted her from remembering it was my birthday.

"Well, unfortunately, I don't have much to add to the equation," she admitted. "There is some unrest because of how we are merged with the other Fae folk, and how close we are with the human world. There's always some disgruntlement with the low numbers of Aes Sídhe. But that's a bipartisan path we've been on for years."

The others nodded in solemn agreement. After some consideration, she added, "That being said, there have been more dark Faeries encroaching on the borders, just in the past week or two. The army has been incredibly busy tackling that."

So, that explained Blaise's absence in the evenings. I hadn't seen a hint of him outside of our training.

"What unrest? What's going on here?" I asked Darrya, but it was Kipp who responded.

"The queen and her court have welcomed all good Fae folk into their lands as equals for the better part of three centuries, despite varying power levels. They encouraged us all to intermingle with each other and with the human realm, and that has spread to all other lands, over time. But some believe that the Aes Sídhe are far superior and should be the only ones in any position of power and shouldn't...*breed* with other races, in order to replenish bloodlines and keep their powers pure."

His hands tightened almost imperceptibly into fists, but he continued.

"Furthermore, they believe that mingling with the human realm taints the purity of our powers. As you know, when you enter the realm, your power is dimmed, but it always comes back upon reentry."

I nodded, remembering the flood of power that washed over me the moment I returned, almost as if I were above water and breathing once again.

"I would argue it's nearly the opposite," Darrya added bitterly. "Faeries that stay here seem to lose their sense of compassion over time; their emotions and grudges run rampant until they can focus on nothing else, only knowing the negative emotions they let consume them."

"And it's those types of Faeries that have focused their hatred solely on these issues." I finished for her, understanding. She bobbed her head in agreement.

"But that's been an issue for a long time. I don't think that's our main culprit. I would recommend speaking with Blaise, to see if anything he's dealt with lately raises any questions. And I'd also check out the library, see what they have on Cú Chulainn. Something there might be the key to your role in this."

I agreed, making a mental note on both of those points for later, but I couldn't help the unease that rose in me, knowing how long I'd lived in the human realm. I wondered if some here would hold that against me. *Just another to add to the list,* I thought bitterly.

"Along those same lines, I had a few questions." Darrya propped her elbows on her knees as she stared me down from Cas's couch. "First off – you're telling me you have a demigod's horse, just chilling in the pasture?"

I grinned, exchanging a glance with Wren, and then nodded. "I call him Gray," I said fondly. Darrya let out a breath of laughter.

"Alright. And you're telling me your mom at home had no idea you're a Faerie?"

I shook my head, and noticed with surprise as Kipp shot Darrya a seething glare. Darrya was none the wiser, however, and let out a low whistle.

"Shit, girl. Well, you're a full Aes Sídhe if I've ever seen it, with your powers. Even your non-signature magic is stronger than most. I wonder who your real mother is."

My world came to a screeching halt, even as the pieces came together in my mind. Pieces I hadn't even bothered to assemble until now. Of course...she hadn't been able to see Kipp. No part of what was happening to me had registered with her. If I was fully Aes Sídhe, that meant – that meant –

A whoosh of breath escaped my lips, as though I'd been punched.

Darrya's grin faltered. "I'm so sorry, Kate. I thought somebody would have said something by now."

"I need a minute," I mumbled, and walked out. My feet took me back to the palace of their own accord. I pointedly ignored the shadow of Kipp and the blue flash of his concerned, wolfy eyes that appeared from the bushes every now and then.

Mindlessly, I darted into the palace and walked through the hallways. I found myself ambling down endless stairs, desperate to be alone with my own thoughts, though the plan was quickly foiled as I found most doors were locked.

I changed tactics, and this time found the room I searched for, opening the large wooden doors to find the library utterly abandoned.

The dead quiet lulled my mind, and I strode on soft feet, barely breathing for fear of upsetting the peace that hung over the space. The large, refined, floor-to-ceiling bookshelves stretched back into darkness with the now dimming light. The carved pillars separating each section were a work of sheer aristocratic splendor.

I trailed my fingers along the dark timber shelves and the spines of the books as I crossed the room, inhaling their intoxicating smell and wondering with a small ache how long it had been since I had last read. The first sets of books were sorted by historical dates rather than the organization of human library systems. I figured what I searched for must be in this first section.

My gaze snagged on a book with Cú Chulainn's name and, as I pulled it from the shelf, the sound of coughing had me springing up on full alert. I caught the sight of a small glow further down the corridor, and crept closer.

My eyes fell on a mass of tousled blond hair, illuminated by an orb of fire. It was Finlay, sprawled across a leather lounge chair, gazing intently at a book held in his free hand. He swished the palm currently creating his makeshift reading light lazily, and I took a moment to observe him without interruption.

He looked...peaceful. He wore no cocky, crooked grin, and his eyes were clear. Though I noticed his flask on the side table, he didn't seem keen on indulging. I wondered what he was reading. If he were perhaps escaping, as I intended to.

My foot scraped, and I paused. His eyes darted up in alarm.

"Little angel," he said, blinking. I detected only bewilderment in his tone – no arrogance – and relaxed my posture. "Happy twenty-first. What brings you here instead of celebrating?"

"Catching up on some light reading," I replied, choosing not to address his birthday comment, but also pleasantly surprised that he remembered. Instead, I gestured to the book in his hand. "Same for you?"

He hummed in response and closed the book. "I come here at night sometimes to get away from it all."

I nodded in understanding. "I can't think of a better place for that. Or a better way to pass the time than reading." I looked around at the stunning library once more, remembering all the escapes I'd found in books over the years in the human realm.

"That is true. Books don't ask anything of you, other than to try and understand them."

His observation made me feel like I had invaded something very private, and I turned on my heel to rush out, but his next words stopped me.

"No. Please, stay."

The soft tone he used, so unlike his normal commentary, gave me pause. Slowly, I turned back and moved to sit in the chair next to him. I wasn't entirely sure what made me do it, but the first words out of my mouth were, "I heard about your parents."

He stiffened, his eyes meeting mine. Whatever he saw in them, though, made him raise a brow.

"Usually that's followed by some sort of apology," he remarked carefully, and I simply shrugged.

"I hate when people say they are sorry for your loss. It feels so ... empty. And you're obligated to say that it's okay, as if it's you who needs to make the other person feel better. And it never really is okay."

He studied me for a moment. "You've lost someone, too."

"My dad. When I was ten." I paused. "And as of tonight, my mom."

He lurched in shock at that, and I had to admit, I wasn't entirely sure why I was telling him this, either.

"She's not really dead — well, not that I know of. But the mother I always thought I had, it turns out, isn't really my mother at all," I confessed.

Finlay sat quietly, letting me talk, his arms crossed. One palm remained facing up, casting a glow of fire. I watched it dance, soothing me as I spoke.

"It makes sense, really. I grew up in the human world, with a human mom and she...she fit in. Everyone loved her. She wanted that for me, and it just never happened. I already saw it when I visited home; the way she was moving on so happily with her life, without me in it. And honestly, I am happier here, too. But to hear it tonight, officially, it feels like the final nail in the coffin on that old life. Nothing at all holds me there anymore. It was a piece of me that never really fit, but still – it's a piece of me that's gone now."

The reality flooded out with those sentences and I wiped at my nose discreetly; it had started to run as though my emotions had let it loose. I kept my gaze down for a few moments, absorbing my own words. He allowed me the same and chose not to provide any empty words of solace. Instead, after a beat, he spoke in a hushed tone, offering his own story.

"They say it gets better with time, but the truth is that each milestone I reach without them gets more difficult." His words were raw, each one laced with pain. I glanced up to see him studying the fire in his own hand, expression shadowed. It was as though he was looking into the flames of hell, but had done it often enough that he saw it as a home.

"They should have seen me graduate, should have seen me master my elements. Over a century, and there are still days when I wonder what it would have been like if I had my mother to comfort me, or my father to turn to for advice. I had my grandparents, sure, but it still feels like a piece of my true identity that I'll never actually have. A piece of me that's gone, without ever knowing what it was like to have it in the first place."

His eyes turned to me, somber and shimmering even paler blue with the reflection of the flames. I offered a small smile of understanding in return, holding his gaze. We sat silently for a moment, letting the quiet of the library settle over us like a blanket as we took in what we'd shared – two souls, slightly lost, pieces missing. And yet finding a way, day by day, to act whole.

Chapter 19

My time in the library had calmed the rush of emotions warring inside me. I crept silently back to my room, still clutching the book I'd found, and paused as I saw the figure leaning against my door. Blaise.

He was still wearing his fighting leathers, now covered in dirt. He turned to me as I drew closer, and I realized traces of black blood were smattered across his cheeks. His expression was pained and desperate, a sight that caused the color to drain from my face.

"What the –" I started, before he cut me off.

"I can go if you ask. But I just needed to see you," he murmured, and it took me all of a heartbeat to nod. I pushed past him, opening my door and ushering him inside.

"You're going to need to clean up your face, though," I said as I put the book down and picked up a washcloth, running it under some water. Blaise perched obediently on the side of my bed, willing to let me clean him up. He hissed softly as I pressed the washcloth to his face, where a long gash was embedded in his skin.

"So, this explains your absences as of late," I muttered in an unspoken request for more information. He grunted, shifting slightly on the bed.

"I'm not entirely sure why it's happening, but it's almost as if the dark Faeries are answering some sort of call, some of them even gathering en masse. I figured the one you ran into at the festival had been a fluke, but it's only gotten worse since." He eyed me as I moved to the other side of his face. "Have you gotten your mark yet?"

I shook my head, and heard him curse under his breath.

"We'll go first thing tomorrow morning. It's more important than training," he insisted as I walked away. I dropped the washcloth in the basin of my tub and washed my hands. He removed his shoes and settled back onto the edge of the bed. I considered his words, my heart beating faster.

Dark Faeries, gathering in groups. Was this really the start of the war we'd been dreading? I suddenly yearned for the days I'd been impatiently waiting for information like this.

"Are you saying you don't trust me to defend myself? You must be a pretty shit teacher, in that case," I teased as I turned to face him, a feeble attempt to lighten the mood. He saw the attempt for what it was and went with it, a ghost of a smile playing across his lips.

"You're strong enough for one-on-one combat. One of the strongest I've trained, in fact. But if these Faeries continue to join forces, you're not trained like my troops. You're not prepared for a full-on battle."

"Are you saying you want me as one of your troops, then?"

He smirked deeply at the thought, dimples flashing. It was the kind of smile I'd only seen a handful of times, and only when we were alone. "No. I don't believe you were ever made to fall in line."

My breath hitched at his response, and I became acutely aware of the fact we were alone, with him seated expectantly on my bed. Slowly, I approached him, and he watched me with a carnal hunger shining in his eyes.

"Where should I get my mark?" I breathed.

His eyes slid from mine, down my body, and I clenched my thighs in desire at his intense gaze. He took his hand and raised it to my collarbone, visible in the oversized sweatshirt I wore, tracing it lightly with his fingertips. I moved my hand up his arm, feeling the muscles ripple beneath my touch.

"Here," he murmured, sliding his palm down my side and resting it on my waist. His thumb brushed my hip bone, right along the band of my leggings. Toying with the edge, dipping slightly underneath. "Or maybe here."

My body came alive at his exploring touch and I leaned into it. He took the invitation, grabbing my hips with both hands and pulling me into his lap. His lips claimed my own, and I threw both arms over his broad shoulders, feeling the warmth of his hands running up my back. His fingers snagged on my ponytail and he pulled my hair free, causing it to drape around us like a curtain.

My entire world narrowed into the moment, yielding to the rush of desire burning within me as he nipped his way gently down my neck. My fingers scrambled to unstrap his leathers and failed, distracted by his large, warm hands, exploring their way under my sweater, where I knew there was no other fabric to find.

I cursed as the straps slipped out of my fingers once more. Blaise released a low chuckle, deftly flipping us so I lay back onto the bed with him pinned over me. He leaned back, and in a few graceful moments, he wore nothing but his flowing white undershirt and soft fabric pants, all signs of leather gone. I stared at his gorgeous face above me, his smile wicked as he leaned back in to kiss me once more.

His fingers toyed with the edge of my pants again and paused in question, his eyes burning as he hesitated. I swallowed. After clumsily losing my virginity a few years back to a high school boyfriend, I'd only ever messed around with a guy here or there since. I'd never wanted to go further – until now. I desperately wanted to, now.

"I don't know any – tricks." I blurted suddenly, and then immediately flushed with embarrassment. Blaise's mouth opened and closed in surprise. Then, he grinned.

"We don't need any tricks, sunshine," he growled, and I practically trembled with yearning as he pulled my leggings down, kissing his way back up my legs, ankle to hip, as he made his way up to reclaim my mouth. A soft moan escaped my lips, and I tugged his shirt off, desperate to see and feel more of him.

The sound had him moving quicker, his hands slipping under my sweatshirt as he explored my mouth with his tongue. He ran his hands over my stomach, and I felt the smile on his lips as my body bucked in response to him brushing his thumbs over the peak of my nipples. I clawed at his back, sure I was leaving marks, but neither of us cared.

He broke our kiss just long enough to pull his pants completely off and tug my sweatshirt over my head. He took a long moment to lean back, eyeing my bare skin ravenously. I returned the favor, absorbing the perfection of his muscles that culminated in the perfect V I'd imagined time and time again.

I reached for him, aching to press my body against his, and he released a noise of satisfaction as I arched my breasts against his bare chest. I traced his jawline with my fingers, and his hands, large and warm against my bare back, gripped me as he gently lowered me back down on the bed.

My heart thundered and my breathing came unsteadily as his mouth brushed over my chest, marking the same spots his hands had been moments before, stubble grazing my skin. His fingers began an ascent up my thigh, landing at the thin barrier of my underwear. He groaned, finding the evidence of my desire there, and the sound had my skin positively tingling. I pressed into him as he circled his thumb against me, coming alive at his touch.

He looked up, slowly removing the fabric. His eyes were hooded with a dark need surely mirrored in my own. He slid his fingers into me, luring and coaxing, capturing my moan greedily with his mouth. I closed my eyes, falling into bliss. Just when I was sure I would shatter, his hand disappeared, and I felt him shift himself between my legs.

My eyes fluttered open and I saw his hazel gaze, burning voraciously. His jaw twitched with restraint as he held still, inspecting, the final silent question to ensure this was okay.

"Please," I panted, almost a whimper, and that was all the encouragement Blaise needed. He slid forward, taking a moment as we both sighed, basking in the feeling of our bodies merging. His movements were slow at first, but his grip on me tightened as we gradually chased our pleasure in unison.

My hips ground up to meet him, faster, my muscles beginning to tense around him. We kept going, each demanding more until I tipped over the edge with a cry of sheer ecstasy, which had Blaise groaning my name and following me over the same edge shortly after.

We rode the aftershock together, panting and slick with perspiration. After several long moments, Blaise pulled back from me, and I felt a pang of regret at losing contact. Almost as if reading my mind, he scooted close once more, and began trailing his fingers idly over the length of my leg. I shivered happily at his light touch.

"Why me?" I whispered, flipping over to study him. He thrummed his hand on my hip, contemplating his next words. Finally, a low laugh escaped him, startling me.

"You already know I find you beautiful," he started, "but more than that, I think I knew I'd fallen for you when you threatened to hit me. Even more so when you actually did it." He chuckled softly again and pulled me closer.

I stiffened in surprise, wondering if he was telling the truth, or simply saying what he thought I'd like to hear. Blaise lifted onto his elbows, eyeing me curiously.

"I find it hard to believe that my unladylike attitude is what drew you to me," I said haltingly, my voice riddled with doubt.

He merely grinned in response. "I've known very few people in my life who have the courage to stand up for what they believe in, especially if it's against me. I see that spirit in you, Katherine. And it's stunning."

Chapter 20

Blaise spent the night. I found that I slept peacefully, despite his presence being more than a little distracting, with us fooling around a second time at some point in the night when our touches became unbearably heated.

The next morning, he took me to get my mark. I had the artist put it on my collarbone, tossing Blaise a knowing grin as he bit his lip hungrily in response.

The prick of the needle felt like nothing more than a tiny scratch against my skin; like I'd been itching a little too hard, and before I knew it, it was over. The artist uttered some words in a gruff language I didn't understand with his hand placed over my mark, and I felt a swell of pulsating energy — the same energy I'd felt when touching Blaise's. In an instant, it faded, though if I touched the mark and focused, I could still feel it there, distantly.

"Is that it?" I asked Blaise, who nodded, visibly more relaxed. I thanked the artist as Blaise guided me out of the room and to the courtyard. He gave my hand a squeeze and winked, slipping away as I waited for my magical lessons. I sat on the bench, wringing the bracelet on my wrist, and brushing my fingers over the newly bandaged mark as I waited. Patience was never my strong suit.

"Kate. There you are, thank gods." Darrya rushed to embrace me. Finlay came to a stop a short distance behind her, flashing me a surprisingly shy smile.

"I am so sorry for what I said last night. I should have realized. It wasn't my news to bring to your attention." She shook her head. "I feel so terrible about it. Please tell me you'll forgive me?"

I looked into her pleading brown eyes and gave her a soft smile. "There's nothing to forgive, Darrya. I know you'd never intentionally do anything to hurt me."

She exhaled a deep breath, clearly relieved. "Good. Because last night, I was thinking about someone else who may have an idea of your heritage. But it involves a trip." She glanced over her shoulder at Finlay. "To Daersill."

I remembered the name from our conversation the other night – her homeland. Finlay's, too.

"What's there?" I asked, curious.

"The grand duke, Lachlan. He lives in their capital city, Leven. He is perhaps one of the oldest Fae alive, and he's a seanchaí like Kipp. If anyone would have information we won't find in books, it's him."

"Can we trust him?" I asked hesitantly. Darrya twirled a strand of hair in her hand thoughtfully.

"Lachlan, yes. As long as his sons aren't visiting."

At my raised brows, she explained further. "They're a different story – all they do is party and fuck. They're set to oversee Daersill and rule their original land, Brytham – if they can ever grow up enough for their father to relinquish his seat to them."

Finlay shook his head, taking a cigarette out and lighting it. Darrya shifted uncomfortably and continued. "I was technically set to marry one of them, to ensure the ties between Muiranvia and Brytham stay strong, but Lachlan told me himself he wouldn't subject me to that torture."

I let out a soft chuckle at the image of Darrya being told to do much of anything, much less agree to an arranged marriage. "They sound like pieces of work."

"They are. But really – Lachlan is great. Do you want me to arrange a meeting?"

I nodded emphatically, heart pounding. Perhaps I'd finally get some of the answers I'd desperately been hoping for. The news of the dark Faerie gathering flickered across my mind, and I wondered fleetingly where I'd find answers to that problem. *Nope – one issue at a time,* I reminded myself.

Darrya bounced on her feet, excited, and began rattling off what we should attempt to tackle in today's lessons. I tossed my hair over my shoulder as I settled in to listen, and Finlay caught sight of the bandage on my collarbone, going still.

"What happened?" He asked, a surprisingly angry rumble to his tone.

I traced the bandage and commented, "I had to get the Shield Knot marked on me."

Both Darrya and Finlay raised their eyebrows, and Darrya exclaimed, "Of course! I completely forgot to see if you needed that –

it's been so long since I've had to worry about it, I didn't even think you wouldn't have one."

She rolled up the sleeve of her dress to show me her mark, placed high on her forearm. "Who was it that remembered to tell you?"

"Umm...Blaise," I responded, feeling my body flush warmly as I recalled his hands and mouth on me last night. Darrya studied me, then beamed.

"Holy shit," she laughed. "You two totally did it."

My gaze traveled to Finlay first, even as I flushed further. His eyes jumped to mine in surprise, but other than a twitch of his jaw, he didn't react.

"What? What makes you say that?" I asked feebly, refocusing my attention on her.

"Oh, please. I'm like a bloodhound for these things. I can basically smell the sex on you," she teased, sniffing deeply with emphasis. She leaned in close, her eyes twinkling.

"So how was it?" She whispered mischievously.

Finlay cleared his throat and muttered something about excusing himself so the ladies could talk. Darrya didn't miss a beat though, pelting me with a barrage of questions. By the time I had sufficiently dodged them with vague answers and looked up, he had disappeared. I wasn't quite sure what to make of the twinge of guilt that panged in my chest.

We had a brief magical lesson, and then, with Darrya consumed by contacting the grand duke, I snuck off to take Gray for a nice long bareback run, leaving Kipp sunbathing near the barn. I found myself headed to town astride him, and as I approached Castille's house, an attractive Faerie I didn't recognize stumbled out the front door.

He was pulling on his boots as he left, his hair disheveled. He glanced at Gray and me, then said with a sneer, "What's this, Cas's next gods-damned bedroom guest already showing up?"

I frowned at his tone, and as if reading my emotion, Gray's ears pinned back. The Faerie stalked by, glaring up at me, but before I could react, Gray snapped his teeth at him. The Faerie jumped, scurrying down the road and letting out a stream of curses as he went.

Castille poked his head out the door curiously at the commotion, and then grinned as he saw me. "Katie-cat! It's you!"

His eyes traveled to Gray, widening with appreciation. "Ah, and this must be Gray. Well, I do see what all of the fuss is about."

"Speaking of," I said, sliding off him and motioning down the road. "What was *that* fuss about?"

Cas rolled his eyes and ushered me in. "A disgruntled suitor. We had differing ideas about our relationship."

"Like what?"

"He assumed we had one. I did not."

I snickered at the utterly Cas-like line and took the glass of wine he offered me.

"Speaking of, I did want to ask you a question, especially without Kipp around." I ventured, and Cas gave me an intrigued look. He sauntered to the couch and patted the seat next to him, encouraging me to sit and continue.

"So, I'm not sure if it works differently in the Faerie world, but..." I fiddled with my glass nervously. "I figured if anyone would know, you would. How does one...do what you do, regularly — but with a male and a female — and not..."

Cas's expression was blank. I tried again, the words rushing out.

"Is there a special way to sleep with someone and not worry about getting pregnant?"

His eyes went wide, then he tipped his head back and howled with laughter. I coughed in embarrassment, adding, "Well, I was on something before, in the human world, but it only lasts in your system for so long..."

He grabbed me and ruffled my hair affectionately. "Oh, Katie-cat, you are such a delight." With that, he pushed off the cushions and went into the kitchen, where he grabbed a bag of loose tea leaves. I frowned, puzzled.

"Enchanted tea," he explained, noting my confusion. "Steep a pinch and drink it once a month, and you'll be just fine. I don't need it – obviously – but as a healer, I like to keep certain things in stock."

He made to hand me the entire bag, but as I went to grab it, he whipped it back.

"I'll give this to you on one condition," he said, eyes glimmering with tomfoolery. "Who's the lucky guy?"

I huffed, but after a moment, replied.

"Blaise."

His eyes shot up in astonishment, and he handed me the bag with a low whistle.

"The commander-in-chief? Well, I have to say – he's *fine,* and he could get it." He grinned impishly. "Though he may not have the right sense of humor for my tastes, personally."

"You definitely require a certain sense of humor to be around, Cas," I responded playfully, relieved by his lack of judgement. He put a hand over his heart dramatically, as though I'd crushed his soul.

I tactfully avoided discussing Blaise further by turning the conversation towards Darrya's idea about the grand duke, to which Cas murmured his approval.

"I've heard good things about Lachlan, even if his sons leave something to be desired," he said. "He will help you if he can."

A piece of hope sprung in my chest at that, fluttering around eagerly. I stayed for a few more glasses of wine, and then thanked Cas for the tea and exited to take Gray home.

When I arrived back at the palace around sundown, I made a beeline for my room. I intended to read as much of the novel I'd discovered as possible. However, a pungent smell hit my nose as I crossed the courtyard — a rustic, ashy smell I was now familiar with.

I followed the scent, unsurprised as it led me straight to Finlay. I found him dozing off at the base of the large tree in the middle of the courtyard, his hair elevated from its usual perfectly imperfect tousle to complete disarray. A cigarette dangled from his lips.

I crossed my arms and looked around for a few moments, wondering if I should just leave him to sleep it off. Part of me felt sorry for him, knowing this was likely his way of drowning those long-standing demons of his — but the other part of me knew this was far from the best way for him to cope with his problems.

Just this once, I decided, I could at least offer some support. With a sigh, I grabbed him. He was surprisingly heavy, and I scrambled to find a place to grip him; his large chest and arms were more muscled than his loose-fitting clothes let on.

"Damn you," I hissed as I dragged him out of the courtyard and into the palace hallways. He muttered something unintelligible as I propped him against the stone wall, and called out for Corryn.

"Shhhhh," Finlay whispered, and the whoosh of smoke and vanilla whiskey hit me like a train. "Too loud."

He straightened slightly against the wall, now mostly holding his own weight, and gave me a pinched expression.

"Too bad," I responded and called once more. In a flash of red hair, Corryn appeared, eyeing us quizzically.

"Yes, ma'am?" She dipped her head to Finlay, acknowledging him. "Your Royal Highness."

I pressed a fist to my mouth, partially from annoyance at the situation, but also to avoid laughing at the royal acknowledgment for someone as completely faded as Finlay clearly was.

"I'm looking to get him safely back to his room. Can you tell me where that is?" I asked, attempting to keep my voice pleasant. Corryn nodded, explaining before deftly slipping away into the shadows. *Great. Thanks for the help.*

I struggled my way up the stairs with Finlay on my shoulder, still mostly useless. The palace had easily over forty bedrooms alone, not counting the great hall, library, or other entertainment chambers, and I had never been in this wing of the palace. We made our way slowly down the hallway – which now seemed far too long – and I halted at an intricately designed door.

"Keys?" I asked, and he fumbled in his pocket for a moment, eventually pulling another cigarette out. I slapped it out of his hand.

"No," I hissed. *"Keys."*

He looked at me, his pale eyes a touch clearer, and shrugged. After another moment of shuffling, he found them and passed them to me.

I unlocked his door and dragged him inside, stopping to observe his bedroom for a moment. I was struck by the lack of decoration and general cleanliness of it, as though he barely spent any time here. Compared to the chaotic and colorful personality he usually boasted, it was almost unnerving to see this as his home base.

He stumbled his way to his bed and flopped down, struggling to kick off his boots. I spied a glass of what I hoped was water – a quick sniff confirmed it wasn't more liquor – and handed it to him.

He drank obligingly and then dropped onto his back, sprawled across his bedspread.

"Oh, no," I chastised, rubbing my face and coming around to the side of his bed. I tugged the sheets out, forcing him to roll onto his side. "I'm guessing you've lived over a hundred years now; I won't have you dying tonight from choking on your own vomit."

He snorted in response to that and, with a pat and a roll of my eyes, I turned to leave.

"Good night, Finlay." I called over my shoulder, half-sarcastically, as I closed the door. I heard his voice call back, with a slight slur to it.

"Good night, little angel."

Chapter 21

Darrya secured a visit with Lachlan for us at the end of the week. I spent the days leading up to our trip training excitedly, and the nights devouring what I could from the library. Blaise had been out patrolling nights again, which helped me to avoid a conversation regarding my reading choices which I couldn't easily explain.

It turned out Cú Chulainn was indeed one of the greatest Celtic warriors, complete with all the hero tropes. Born a demigod, he was gifted with superhuman strength, powers bestowed by the gods, and was devastatingly handsome. He found the love of his life, Emer, whose father had trapped her in a tower until Cú Chulainn could prove himself.

In response, he had traveled to the Isle of Sky and trained for many years with the warrior goddess Scáthach. There he acquired Gáe Bolga, a terrible barbed spear that inflicted thirty wounds on its target from only a single strike. Finally, he grew strong enough to fight his way to Emer, and they ran away to marry.

He fought fiercely in many battles after that, earning such glory that the goddess Morrígan offered him immortality. He turned her down, continuing to fight as a demigod, until the battle with Gray that led to his ultimate demise. Gray was mentioned in all the ways Kipp and Wren had conveyed to me – even calling him the King of Steeds.

I was stunned to find that in his final moments, Cú Chulainn tied himself to a stone, to ensure he died standing with his sword raised to the heavens. His rage and reputation were such that no one attacked him until a raven – the Morrígan herself – landed on his shoulder, revealing he was dead.

What I found most curious, however, was his questionable heritage. He was originally named Sétanta and in some tellings, had two royal, but totally human parents. In others, he had both a divine and mortal parent: his mother was a human princess and his father, as Wren had mentioned, was Lugh, the sun and light god and king of the Tuatha Dé Danann.

I researched until my eyes burned, and while I now knew more than ever about Gray's previous master, none of it indicated why Gray had appeared to me. Cú Chulainn had only had one child, Connla, but the son was born out of an affair. In fact, he ultimately killed his own son in battle without realizing the relation. Which put me and my own questionable heritage back to where it was before – square one.

"Are you ready?" Blaise asked. I blinked, pulled out of my thoughts.

"Ready?" I echoed.

"To meet my friends?" He said patiently, a small smile on his lips.

"Oh. Yes. That. Yes!" I said, and his smile grew bigger. He leaned in to kiss me gently, then handed me his arm.

"Good. We've had a long week. We all deserve a night out."

"Well then, we better not waste another minute here."

We made our way into town and directly to a pub, nestled on a side street. The timber-framed structure, walls starkly white in contrast, stood lower than the other buildings. Though it was clearly older, I could tell it was lit with loud music and lively conversation before we'd even crossed the threshold.

The enticing smells of bar food mingled with smoke, and Fae folk of various shapes and sizes mingled in every nook. The pub was overflowing, packing the small space tightly. The crowd set the atmosphere abuzz with so much magic, and my own magic sparked in response, humming as if it drank in the energy, too. I wondered if that feeling was more reason for everyone to mingle in the bar than the drinks.

Blaise led me to a side room where several of his soldiers were already gathered, and within a moment, two had broken away to greet us. One was fair-skinned with piercing green eyes, the other, ebony-skinned with warm, dark eyes. They wore identical shit-eating grins as they approached.

"What took you so long?" The green-eyed Faerie demanded.

"Off...making friendship bracelets, no doubt." The other Faerie turned his grin on me, dark eyes twinkling. I took an immediate liking to him.

"These are my friends, Soren," Blaise pointed to the Faerie with the green eyes, "and Larke." Larke's grin widened as he shook my hand.

"Guys – this is Katherine." Blaise said.

"But you can call me Kate," I jumped in, offering my nickname with a friendly smile.

"The famous Kate. We haven't stopped hearing about you since you clocked him on the training field." Larke said with a note of humor.

"Larke is my second in command, and Soren is my third," Blaise explained. I expected his demeanor to sour at Larke's teasing, but he simply grinned, taking the jest on the chin. "They were...incredibly *amused* to hear where my bruise came from that day."

I snorted, muttering how he had deserved it and earning a volley of laughs. As I observed the two of them closer, I realized they were slightly different than Blaise – and exclaimed with surprise, "You're both Aes Sídhe!"

They nodded, and I felt the brush of magic tap against mine in silent question. I returned the favor, feeling them out. After a moment, it whispered to me in that way I still couldn't quite pinpoint – Soren's dominant magic was air and Larke's was water.

"What is your signature element? I can't seem to tell." Larke inquired, tapping his chin. Soren's curious look told me he had the same question. I bit my lip, disappointed the answers were still so out of reach.

"If you ever do, let me know, because I'm as in the dark as you." I countered, shrugging guiltily.

"Kate's still working on her magic," Blaise supplied, breezing over the moment, before turning to me.

"Larke and Soren are unique circumstances. They both took more interest in fighting than politics. Which led them to me when we were all young." He tossed a knowing grin at them, which they returned slyly.

"It also doesn't hurt to have their magic on our side. It makes fighting much easier when you have Soren supplying an air shield, or Larke using his water magic to...*coax* answers out of otherwise stubborn prisoners."

I turned a wide eye to Larke, who simply winked in return. I tried to imagine a cold side to him that involved interrogating and waterboarding prisoners, but couldn't.

"I've only had to do that once...or three times." He stated the dark fact easily, then raised his hand to beckon over a server.

We ordered a round of drinks and I settled in to get to know the two of them better. Larke's quick wit and humor grew on me as the night went on; Soren was more reticent, only opening up to talk about a mysterious woman he'd been seeing lately, Myriam, who was nowhere to be seen.

"Come on, man. I threw Katherine into the lion's den," Blaise complained. "You couldn't return the favor?"

Soren simply shrugged, a small smile on his face.

"Maybe she doesn't want to be drowned in liquor," I supplied, smirking into what was easily my third glass of cider.

"Oh, remember the first time we drank alcohol?" Larke asked, and I heard Blaise's groan as he rubbed a hand over his face. Pointedly ignoring him, Larke turned to me and continued his story.

"Soren's uncle thought it would be fun to bring some whiskey to the lake. He left early but left the bottle with us. Three poor bastards that had no idea where the line was supposed to be drawn."

For the first time that night, I saw Soren truly grin, eyes lighting up at the memory.

"I think that's the first and last time I ever saw Blaise *dance.*" Soren snickered, and Larke jumped in, roaring, "Especially with the only music being our terrible voices!"

"I'm pretty sure nobody ever paid the poor guy whose bakery we raided when we stumbled back home that night," Blaise added thoughtfully, chuckling.

"But it was the best cheese bread I think I've ever tasted." Larke rubbed his stomach in emphasis.

"Don't forget, you beat the shit out of that kid who was always bothering your sister." Soren snorted, though I immediately felt the mood shift.

"You have a sister?" I turned to Blaise in surprise and watched as Larke cast a wary look at him as well. Soren had the decency to look abashed, realizing he'd opened a sensitive line of discussion.

Blaise merely grunted, responding with a mumbled, "Not here, but back where I grew up."

"That's the night I knew you'd grow up to lead the army. They just don't make 'em like that place made you," Soren said softly.

I sipped my drink in silence, keeping my eyes averted. A few moments passed, then Larke changed the subject, leading us into less treacherous waters for the next hour or so. My mind remained somewhere else, wondering why Blaise had never mentioned his sister to me, and what the place was like where he had left her behind. Soren retreated to silence once more, his only communication being his reserved and analytical looks when I mistakenly caught his eye the remainder of the evening.

"Is Soren normally that ... distant?" I asked as we walked back to the palace later that night.

Blaise considered for a moment and replied, "Yes and no. He's typically more outgoing when it's just us men, but he's never been someone I would describe as extroverted."

"Well, my apologies for bringing my feminine energy into your bromance." I teased, and he eyed me with a smile.

"Never apologize for that. Like I said, I would gladly have you as a part of the army, if I thought you would ever listen to my orders."

I bumped his shoulder as we walked, laughing. We went a few more steps in silence, and then he spoke again.

"I wish there could be more nights like this." His voice was wistful. "Everything has been so strenuous lately. All of you deserve to be able to just relax and have a night off."

My heart tugged, realizing how he meant his army, me ... everyone under his protection.

"You deserve that, too," I reminded him gently, giving his hand a squeeze. He tossed me a grateful grin.

And when we returned to the palace, I pulled him into my room and reminded him exactly how deserving he was.

Chapter 22

The morning rolled around, and I stood at the entrance to the palace, buzzing with anticipation. I'd opted for a dark blue dress, borrowed from Darrya, who assured me it would be good enough for the grand duke. Regardless, I kept smoothing the fabric, as if it would calm my nervous energy.

"Hell hath frozen over." I heard an amused voice closing in on me. "I do believe this is one of the first times I've seen you in a true Faerie wardrobe. Barring the festival, of course."

I turned to see Finlay approach, looking more put together than I'd seen him – well, since the festival too — dressed in that same deep purple tunic and golden belt that clearly signified his royal lineage. I wondered briefly if he would be visiting his grandmother while we visited the grand duke.

"Not that I mind your human wardrobe," he continued, rolling a toothpick in his fingers before placing it in his mouth. "It hugs you in the best way."

Irritation coursed through me. "Hell really must have frozen over, if you're finally sober enough to try your pathetic lines on me," I ground out.

He flinched slightly at the blunt truth in my words. In the glimpses I'd seen of him this week, he hovered somewhere between his normal state of partial inebriation and the mess I'd helped into bed the other night. This was the clearest I'd seen him in quite some time.

"Takes one to know one," he responded, recovering his composure. "I bury my problems in activities of the medicinal sort. You bury yours in activities of the ... physical sort."

His eyes traveled pointedly to a small blemish near my new Shield Knot mark, where Blaise's mouth had been the night before. My cheeks blazed, and I tossed my hair to cover it.

"Blaise is a good man."

"I never said he wasn't," Finlay responded lightly.

We stood there for several long moments in silence, with only the harsh, raucous call of a crow above to break the tension.

Crunching footsteps indicated Darrya's approach. Her marigold ensemble was stunning, her stance regal, every bit the queen's envoy. She wore a large brooch on her sensible dress to indicate her status, and the friendly grin she donned belied the intimidating outfit.

She fondled the fabric of my dress with approval. "Well, look who came to play today! I told you that would look great on you."

I returned her grin as she pulled some Faerie dust from a small pouch. "Are we ready to go?" She asked, glancing between the two of us.

I nodded, locking arms with her and bracing myself. The rush that ensued was no easier to stomach than before: a pinch just behind my belly button and a head rush that felt a lot like standing up too quickly. I squeezed my eyes shut, and by the time I opened them again, we were there.

I gaped at the rolling expanses of green in front of us – a different feel than the forest Kipp and I had portaled into from the human realm, and different still from the quaint town of Sairas. The hills sloped gently, dotted with long stretches of gray penny walls. There were no trees in sight; instead, the emerald green of the fields met directly with the vibrant blue skies.

In one direction, the hills dipped down to a long expanse of deep blue water. Even at this distance, I could see the whitecaps crashing together. A part of me ached to dip my feet in the ocean, like I used to as a child.

We moved in the opposite direction of the ocean, on a gravel road that led upward to a spread of stone homes. As we crested the hill, more and more houses appeared below, and a massive stone fortress loomed in the distance, dominating the skyline. The capital, Leven: Lachlan's city, and Darrya and Finlay's hometown.

As we drew close to the castle, Finlay murmured something to Darrya and slipped away. She and I were left to approach as I truly inspected the dominating building looming before me. It was clearly built for defense as opposed to luxury, with a strategically high po-sition around the town and foreboding curtain walls surrounding the main stronghold. It was a contradiction to the palace I'd called home for the past few months, but it still had an elegance to it, with magnificent spiral towers and stone carvings adorning the outside of the structure.

Darrya painted on her professional face as we approached the gate, nodding stoically to the guards and striding through. She made her way through the castle without hesitation, chin held high as she acknowledged every Faerie who crossed our paths. I took the opportunity to admire how she juggled this composed, diplomatic side of hers with the relaxed, fun-loving one she showed her friends.

I was surprised when we passed through what was clearly the great hall, instead moving into a side room. The room was still extraordinary — rich red walls covered with portraits and the pale furniture arranged around a magnificent statement fireplace.

Darrya murmured to a young-looking Fae to let the grand duke know of our arrival. He bowed and closed the door behind him. As soon as the door closed, she flopped down on the sofa, grinning at me.

"This is an interesting place for a meeting," I observed, moving to sit beside her.

"Honestly? I asked for it to be more informal. I wanted to keep it as hush-hush as possible. There are too many snooping eyes and ears when it comes to meetings in the great hall."

As if to underscore her point, she flicked a hand, and a spark started in the fireplace. Soon, the loud roar of the fire filled the room.

"Should I be concerned about your impressive double life as a spy?" I teased, and she beamed at me in response.

The sound of the wooden door opening drew our attention and we watched as a tall, older gentleman strode into the room, followed by the younger Faerie. I followed Darrya's lead as she stood and curtsied with a "Your Grace."

"Come now, lass, how many times have I told ye?"

I looked up in surprise at the sound of his voice and his thick, heavily accented tone, which rumbled with warmth.

"Just call me Lachlan."

"If I ignore my manners too often, Lachlan, I fear I may slip up when it actually matters." Darrya quipped back gently. "How many times have I told *you* to quit being a bad influence on me?"

I gaped at her forwardness, but Lachlan simply boomed a laugh, so loud and friendly that I felt its reverberation in my chest. "And this is the wee friend ye spoke of?" He motioned toward me, and I gave a shy smile as I observed him.

He was older than any Fae I'd met, even the queen, though his age suited him well. His hair, long enough that it fell in waves down his neck, was streaked with gray, but pieces of its original coppery hue still shone through. He wore his facial hair short but smartly trimmed, and his soft blue eyes were clear and sharp, a mirror into the centuries of wisdom he clearly held.

"Yes, this is Katherine. Kate." Darrya amended, offering the informality on my behalf. I relaxed slightly and Lachlan grinned, flashing the dimples on his cheeks.

"I understand ye have quite a story to tell." He settled into a chair on the other side of the fireplace and motioned for us to sit. Darrya's eyes traveled to the Faerie behind Lachlan, and his gaze followed.

"Kimber," Lachlan said, waving his hand, "You may leave us." With a nod, Kimber left, and the duke turned back around with eyebrows raised. "This must be verra interesting, if it is for my ears only."

"If you consider the reappearance of Liath Macha interesting, then yes," Darrya stated bluntly, and Lachlan blinked, clearly expecting anything but that.

"To the lass?" He pointed the question at me, and I nodded, clearing my throat.

"I still don't know why, but yes. In the human realm, where I'd grown up." I said, keeping his gaze. I felt a soft brush against my magic as he explored curiously. My muscles tensed, but I waited patiently, putting my faith in Darrya's trust of the duke and the kindness I saw in his eyes.

"And yet here ye are, a full Aes Sídhe," he noted, and I nodded, expecting the comment.

"I have no idea who – who my real parents are. My father died when I was young, and the mother I knew is clearly human."

Darrya stiffened next to me, still feeling guilty for her part in my realization. Lachlan's eyes darted to her.

"And ye'll have been training her since her arrival? Have ye discovered anything about her lineage through her powers?" He asked, but Darrya shook her head in response.

"Not yet. Earth seems to be her strongest thus far. She has more power in each than I've ever seen before, but she hasn't mastered one particular one yet, and we still haven't tackled fire." Darrya replied, tossing me an affectionate look. "She's a quick study, though."

I returned her look with a grateful smile, and added, "I tried to research Cú Chulainn to see if I had some lineage there, but it seems his only son was killed early on."

"Aye," Lachlan said, nodding. "That is true." He gazed into the fire for several long moments as he absorbed our news.

"Apologies, lasses, but I have to be blunt." He turned his blue gaze back on us. "I dinna see what good is to come of this. Liath Macha is a horse meant to be ridden into war – a fearsome god of his own right. He wouldna return for no reason."

"We know," I replied softly. "And we are trying to get ahead of whatever it might mean."

He nodded, tapping his fingers. "Cú Chulainn made many enemies in his time. It could be any number of descendants or monsters who came to settle a debt, but I must imagine it would be someone powerful to cause Liath Macha to come to our aid." He shook his head, continuing.

"I canna say what kind of creature that might be, but I do know of a way for ye to learn more about yer heritage."

I leaned forward, heart leaping. Lachlan waved his hand lazily and the fire surged, crackling louder. He leaned in toward the both of us.

"A secret for a secret. Trust this with only those closest to ye." His eyes twinkled, and Darrya nodded emphatically. I barely dared to breathe.

"The Tuatha Dé Danann. We understand well enough that their supernatural powers run through our veins today. But where did they get them?"

My mind pondered his question as I sifted through what I had learned so far. Kipp had mentioned their ties to the goddess Danu, and how they had created the entire Faerie realm. As for their immense strength —

"They were ... fallen angels?" I ventured, my thoughts flickering briefly to Finlay's nickname for me.

"A widespread belief, but no. They garnered their skills and mastered their magic by progressing through four mythical cities." Lachlan tapped a finger as he recited them, the storyteller in him obvious.

"Four cities no mortal eye has seen, but the soul knows. Wind comes from the spring star in the East, sun from the summer star in the South, water from the autumn star in the West, and earthly wisdom from the winter star in the North."

I tipped my head as I listened, wondering where this was going. Lachlan caught my eye and smiled.

"Aye, that doesna mean much – it just sounds pretty. But I'm getting there. From those cities, they acquired four magic talismans. It is said that if all four talismans are gathered, and the magic of the lands is mastered, the hero will once again be able to lead a force into battle and become king, presiding over the seventh lifetime. I dinna ken the whole truth in that prophecy, but the four talismans do exist."

He leaned back and sighed. Darrya and I exchanged wide-eyed looks.

"How do you know?" Darrya asked.

"I found one of them. *Lia Fáil*. The Speaking Stone." Lachlan replied easily.

"And the others?" I breathed, to which he shook his head in disappointment.

"I have just the one. And that alone took me the past two hundred years, mind ye. I believe they were likely passed down generations, moved, and lost or forgotten over time." Lachlan ran a hand through his copper hair and down his jaw.

"But the stone is the only one that matters for yer purposes. As the story goes, it is a stone of destiny, said to cry out when touched by the rightful sovereign. To all others, it whispers validation of one's path."

"How do you know that?" Darrya asked quizzically, and he grinned.

"Why, lass, what do ye think the first thing I did was?" He boomed with laughter and rose, motioning for us to follow him. "I didna simply touch it. I added it to my throne."

Chapter 23

We made our way to his throne hall, my heart pounding the entire way. The corners of my eyes registered the sweeps of red and gold tapestry and the statues of soldiers lining the outskirts of the room, as if watching over us protectively as we moved forward.

But my sight was set solely on the stone throne, armrests clearly crafted from the Speaking Stone itself. Circular swirls arched their way down the front of the throne, perfectly positioned for each palm to rest on them. Lia Fáil, now upgraded by Lachlan into a throne of destiny.

My anticipation nearly pulled me onto the seat of its own volition, and it took some additional willpower to stop me from simply taking the grand duke's rightful place. Glancing at him, I waited for approval. He gave a low chuckle.

"By all means. Ye've piqued my curiosity as well here, lass." His eyes twinkled and his dimples flashed. I made a mental note to tell Darrya later that he reminded me of a rugged Faerie Santa.

I climbed the steps to the throne and faced Darrya and Lachlan as I sat. With a deep, trembling breath, I closed my eyes and placed my hands, palms down, on the stone armrests.

A cry shattered through my very being, thunderous and drawn out. It sounded like what I imagined a siren's song would bear resemblance to: low and piercing, but in a way that filled my head with wonder. My back stiffened, but I leaned into it, my closed eyes squeezing further with concentration.

The roaring noise grew and spread over every inch of my body until I couldn't bear it anymore, and I gasped, opening my eyes. I felt the cry expelled outward, pulsing away, and I expected to see Darrya and Lachlan standing in front of me in the throne hall.

Instead, images flashed over my vision, and I felt the landscape shift in my bones as if I were in the middle of a full-immersion movie theater. The images swirled and progressed rapidly, as though each was taken swiftly by the wind.

I envisioned a strong, tall man, standing over a hound – that same man, grasping the hand of a beautiful woman as they ran from enraged shouts – a baby, bundled tightly in blue in a dark nursery, and the same beautiful woman creeping backward out of the room, tears staining her eyes. I felt her despair rip through me.

I watched as a pale-faced woman with jet-black eyes and hair stalked forward. Shadows of prey and dark tendrils swirled around her like feathers, and my gut dropped with terror. This woman was a darkness to be feared.

The depictions of people shifted into a rushing river, and then a pair of glowing amber eyes. I felt myself choke as though close to drowning. The last image that seared into my vision as I emerged, gasping for air, was of a scorching, golden, white-hot light. It burned through my entire soul as I jerked back to the present.

I sat, panting, shaking my head as if I could shake away what had just ripped through me. Lifting my palms away from the enchanted rock, I vowed silently to never touch this throne again, and wrung my hands together. Darrya and Lachlan both stared at me, as if waiting for an answer. Darrya had moved a few steps closer, as if to catch me, should I fall.

"I-I don't know what any of this means." It came out as little more than a rasp, my throat constricted with frustration. "I expected a voice whispering in my ear, or maybe a conversation. But all I got were flashes of some story I didn't understand. None of it made any sense. And there was no whisper – if anything, it was a shriek." I shook my head and ran my hands through my hair.

"We heard it, too." Darrya said quietly, and I looked up at her in surprise. "The cry – and the light."

"What light?" I asked, puzzled.

"When the cry stopped – there was a light that pulsed out from you. It flashed outward and passed through us. Your eyes opened, but they...they were white. Almost like you were a seer for a moment. I've never seen anything like it."

Lachlan finally spoke. "There isna anything like it."

He turned to Darrya, and when he continued, his voice was clear and formal.

"The stories I hear are often marked with several shades of gray. The same story, told long ago by many mouths, will leave more questions than answers as time goes on."

"But us all witnessing this," he motioned to the throne, to me. "leaves no room for interpretation. That was the cry of fate. The stone has spoken of your destiny."

He looked me right in the eye, his own shimmering with awe. Then, he dropped to a knee, head bowed. "You are the true ruler."

Chapter 24

Our goodbyes were rushed, and I stared off in the distance as Darrya spoke in hushed tones with Lachlan — something about keeping it quiet and time to adjust. Sweat pricked my palms as I worked to quell my racing heart. I had barely begun to understand this realm, a place I'd called home for mere months — how could I be expected to rule it?

Absorbed in my own thoughts, I couldn't be bothered to mind any social etiquette as we walked down the streets of the town. Darrya allowed me my silence, calling to Finlay softly as we stopped before a quaint building. I simply blinked as he appeared. Finlay slowed and gave me a curious look, but a sharp "don't" from Darrya kept him quiet as we traveled home.

The twist and pull of the Faerie dust barely registered in me as we arrived back at the palace, and my feet took me in the direction of town the moment we touched down. Darrya followed behind, waving Finlay away, who merely shook his head and took out a cigarette. Despite my shock, a snide thought entered my head that

I was impressed by his willpower to have made it this long without one. I didn't have the energy to comment on it, though.

Kipp opened the door before we even knocked, clearly having heard our approach. His expression twisted into one of concern as he saw my face and glanced between Darrya and me.

"What happened?" He asked, opening the door wide for us to enter. Cas poked his head out of the bathroom and, seeing it was us, ducked back in, reemerging a moment later with a robe on.

"What were you doing in there without clothes?" Darrya asked curiously, a breath of laughter in her tone.

"Get your head out of the gutter, D. I was taking a midday bath. You should try it sometime," he teased, breezing into the room and flicking the belt of his robe at her.

I poured myself a glass of whiskey, gulping it down in one go, and repoured another glass. Kipp raised an inquisitive brow.

"I take it the meeting didn't go well?" He asked cautiously.

"Kate found out a little more than she bargained for," Darrya hedged, glancing my way.

Unsure how to act, I turned away uncomfortably, swirling the amber liquor in my glass with feigned intrigue.

"Like what?" Cas piped up, eyes gleaming with curiosity.

I didn't answer him; instead, I turned to Kipp and asked, "What do you know about the four talismans of the Tuatha Dé Danann?"

His lips parted in surprise, but he took a moment to think. "Bits and pieces. What comes to mind first is a quote:

'Four presents brought with them,
By the nobles of the Tuatha Dé Danann:

A sword, a stone, a cauldron of worth,
A spear for the death of noble champions.'"

He eyed me curiously while I absorbed the information.

"So, the rest is a spear, a cauldron, and a sword," I said to no one in particular, wheels turning in my mind. The three talismans that I now knew without a doubt, truly existed.

Darrya nodded, her conflicted look traveling between me and the rest of the group. I could tell how badly she wanted to fill them in, but held back, understanding it wasn't her news to tell. For her sake alone, I pushed my warring emotions aside and cleared my throat.

"I touched one of the four talismans today. The Speaking Stone. And it...cried out in response," I explained haltingly.

Kipp's eyes widened, putting the pieces together in his mind. He rubbed his hand over his jaw in astonishment. Cas frowned in confusion as he glanced between us.

"She's the true sovereign," Kipp murmured to him.

My muscles tensed as I waited for their reactions, anticipating our dynamic to be changed entirely. Since Lachlan's bow, so opposite to his relaxed and jovial nature before, I'd held a kernel of fear deep in my chest about what this news meant for those I cared about.

I hadn't dared to so much as exchange two words with Darrya on the way home in case her demeanor towards me had changed as well. I couldn't stand the thought of being treated differently, again, for something so outside of my control, when I had just now found a foothold here.

"Well, thank the gods," Cas said finally with flourish. "It was getting a little boring around here."

I jerked my head back in surprise to see him and Kipp grinning.

"I'm just glad we finally have an explanation for everything," Kipp added, and I found myself exhaling the deep breath I'd been holding. That wasn't entirely true — I found myself once again with more questions than answers — but at least it *was* a step in the right direction.

"So you're not...you're not going to treat me differently?" I asked cautiously.

"Do you want us to?" Darrya queried. I shook my head vehemently in response.

"Absolutely not. I would be horrified if you did," I answered earnestly, and their resounding laughs warmed my heart.

"Did you discover anything else about your heritage? Or what may be coming for us?" Kipp asked, and I shook my head.

"I received some visions, but they didn't make any sense," I replied and relayed what I recalled. Two parents running from something, the mother leaving her baby boy in the dark, a pale dark woman, a river, and a light. A cursory glance at the blank faces in the room told me the descriptions made as much sense to them as they did to me.

"But we did get more of an idea of how to prepare for whatever is coming." Darrya supplied. "The remaining magical talismans. If they're gathered, Lachlan said the ruler will once again be able to lead a force into battle. I imagine the combined power is unstoppable."

"The sword, cauldron, and spear," Kipp spoke thoughtfully.

"You're forgetting one piece," I said, nervously rubbing my palms together. "The magic from the four lands that I need to conquer."

Darrya shrugged dismissively. "To me, it just sounded like you need to be someone who has all four of the elements in your soul to wield magic with. Which you do, as an Aes Sídhe."

"But I've only managed three," I replied, my shoulders sagging.

Cas casually flicked his hand. "That'll be nothing for you. Look at how far you've come. You've already caught on to what takes us normal Fae decades to learn."

I gazed at him in surprise. "You really think I can master all four types of magic?"

He grinned back, eyes glinting. "I'm embarrassed for the both of us that you're even asking, Katie-cat."

A new type of determination buzzed through me as I walked home that evening. I made them all swear to secrecy, which they happily obliged. I had no desire to take any throne, and if the queen got so much as a whiff of this secret, I didn't doubt it would cause turmoil and place a target on my back. None of us wanted that.

Still, my friends had embraced my newfound fate without question, with nothing but support shining in their expressions. Even Wren, who had come home late after a shift at the stables, hadn't so much as flinched, instead throwing her arms around me.

"I can think of nobody better to lead us. Someone who flicks off men who violate her magic, and punches commanders who disrespect others," she had said, leaving us all in stitches.

I crossed my arms in satisfaction, grinning at the memory as I walked. I didn't even notice as the ground grew sparse, blackness swallowing the space around me while the light of the moon waned. The dry ground crunched beneath my footfalls, and I only slowed as a feeling of dread washed over me.

I squinted into the darkness, coming to a stop with a shiver. My gut whispered that something was terribly, terribly wrong. *Misery*, I thought, naming the feeling that entered the depths of my body, a split second before I saw it. The moving figure looked like a rider astride a horse, but I had to blink several times to make sense of what approached.

It was larger than a horse, and what rode it was larger than any Faerie; in fact, it was neither horse nor man. What approached was one entity, a merged monster that made my mouth go dry with fear and horror as I beheld it.

The large creature had what looked like fins at its hooves, with no mane and tail. Where its large horselike face extended from the neck, one lone eye centered on its face and was focused on me, burning red like a single hot ember.

The thing astride it was even more grotesque: a torso of a man's body attached to the creature. It had no legs, but arms stretched so far on either side that they grazed the ground. There were curled, black talons where the fingers should be, and a head perched atop the body, though the face was simply a dark shape, with no mouth or eyes.

Most terrifying was that neither hair nor skin covered the monster; instead, its entirety was covered in sinewy, crimson muscle and yellow veins, coursing with black blood. I watched as its muscles writhed and contracted, each movement toward me on full display.

Cold sweat broke out across my own skin, and I took a trembling step back. Its mouth yawned open and a foul, black reek spilled out as one of its arms stretched toward me. I felt my knees tremble and I stumbled onto them, trying to summon my magic. I had no idea what I would do with it, but I had to do something, *something* –

A reddish blur tore from the shadows, leaping for the outstretched claw. I blinked as Kipp latched onto the creature, dwarfed even in his massive wolf form. Still, his silent speed had caught it unawares, and the creature swung its arm around, bellowing with rage.

Kipp went flying, his grip broken by the swing, but landed on all four paws and spun to face the beast once more. His ears were flattened to his neck, and his muzzle formed a lethal snarl I'd never seen before.

I rose sharply as it turned its attention on Kipp, feeling a panicked energy flood through my body as I summoned my magic. The beast raised an arm to strike, but I willed my earth magic into being. A pillar of the ground shot up between the monster and Kipp. Its talons grazed the soil, leaving chillingly deep gouges, then it whirled on me, narrowing that burning red eye.

"Run!" I yelled to Kipp, turning to do the same. The palace loomed ahead, a small but present dot, and I knew our odds would be better if we reached the front guards. Possibly even Blaise.

I ran, arms pumping and legs instantly burning from the sudden increase in pace. I willed my air magic to propel me faster, but it proved futile as the four-legged creature galloped behind me. An outstretched talon snagged on my leg, scraping the skin of my calf before catching on my shoe. I screamed as I went down, and I heard Kipp's snarl as he skidded to a stop to defend me once again.

I twisted, dragged backwards toward the creature, whose mouth had opened wide, that vile smoke trickling out and consuming my senses. My mind raced as I thought of any way to use my magic to escape this — I had no use of my fire yet, which was the best option; using earth could break my own leg with its grip; water and air both seemed useless –

"Anything can be a weapon. Even a small weapon can do damage. Especially one an enemy does not expect."

Blaise's words rang in my head as I scrambled to reach the dagger. In a swift movement, I brought it down on the creature's arm, watching as blood, black as tar, spurted from the wound I'd inflicted. The roar that followed rattled my bones, but it released me, and I scrambled backward.

It only increased the beast's rage, and my gut dropped as Kipp stepped between us, a low growl rumbling in his throat. The two of us were no match for this thing, and we couldn't outrun it. The thunder of hooves came from behind us and, for a second, I feared we had stumbled upon a herd of these creatures. I crouched lower and dared a glance over my shoulder to see if I was right.

But it was Gray who came racing towards us. His eyes had turned golden, ears pinned as his nostrils flared in pure rage. It nearly looked as though sparks flew from his hooves.

Gray was on the horrid creature before I could so much as breathe, ramming into it with his powerful chest and burying his teeth into its side. The monster shrieked, a bloodcurdling sound that had me grabbing onto Kipp as if his fur could shield me from it.

Before its large talons could even make to wrap around him, Gray whipped around. His massive hind legs struck out and caught the creature in the head, the power of the kick sending it tumbling a few feet back. My hands flew to my mouth as he moved to where the beast lay, now writhing on the ground. Gray reared, his massive hooves coming down in one last fatal blow. The reverberation made the ground tremble.

After several long moments, Gray gave a final snort and turned to me. The glow had faded from his eyes, and he walked over to us, head lowered as he studied me intently.

"You saved my life, boy," I whispered, putting my forehead to his and stroking his neck.

"Our lives," I heard behind me, glancing to see Kipp back in his Fae form. He offered a tentative hand to Gray, who nuzzled it, and Kipp broke out into a grin.

"He knows you helped," I noted, scanning Kipp up and down. "Are you okay?"

Kipp nodded, returning the assessment. "Are you?"

I shifted slightly on my leg, feeling the damp patch where blood had soaked through my clothes. I was pretty sure other aches and bruises would appear in a few hours, but I could only feel the cut on my leg for now.

"Just a scratch," I said, offering him a smile that said not to worry.

"I wonder if he heard you scream, and knew to come help," Kipp mused out loud. I turned the idea over in my head, nodding.

"I can believe it. What was that, anyways?" I asked, braving a glance at the shape still laying on the ground a short distance from us. It was still as terrifying in death as in life, perhaps even moreso. I forced myself to look away.

"A Nuckelavee. A dark Faerie, basically a mutated hybrid of man and horse. Everywhere they go, they cause droughts, crop failures, and livestock deaths." Kipp frowned. "They usually stick around the sea, though, so I have no idea what brought one this way."

"Well, according to Blaise, they've been gathering more frequently, and coming closer to town." I shivered. "I wonder if it has anything to do with me."

"Well, if it does, maybe it means you're getting closer to the answers we need." Kipp said. "But in the meantime, let's get you back where it's safe. And make sure that this guy gets some extra love tomorrow, for all of his help."

I nodded, stroking Gray once more as we walked back to the palace. But Kipp's words had struck a chord, giving me an idea.

"Maybe it means that those creatures have the answers we need." I said, giving one final glance to the Nuckelavee.

Kipp shivered in response. "Let's hope we never get close enough to find out."

Chapter 25

"**I** need to learn offensive magic."

I stood in front of Larke, hands on my hips. I'd found him in the armory, sharpening weapons. He raised his eyebrows quizzically at my statement.

"Why not ask the queen's envoy?" He questioned. "I understand she's been the one training you in magic."

"She's great, but her magic is more defensive. And what she's taught me has been more … whimsical, used to grow my limits over time." I shrugged, then glanced down at my hands. "She hasn't seen battle and likely doesn't intend to."

"And *you* intend to?" He asked, lips curling into a curious smile. I remained silent, unsure how to answer. I hoped he'd see the part of me which mirrored his own desire to feel competent, protected, and able to fend for himself.

"Alright," he sighed, getting up and assessing me. "I'll stop by your lessons tomorrow morning, see where you stand with your magic, and we can go from there."

"Thank you," I said earnestly. Spinning to flee the armory, I ignored the burn as my injured calf, now clean and wrapped, complained against my movements. I hadn't visited town yet to have Cas take a look, and truthfully, I didn't mind the human reminder at the moment. I wanted it to fuel my training.

"Wait," Larke said, leaning over to the weapon he'd been sharpening. "I believe this belongs to you."

He extended his hand, and my mouth opened in surprise as I stared down at the dagger Blaise had given me. The one I'd rammed into the Nuckelavee last night.

"Kipp found me last night after it happened. I took one of my guys with me to dispose of the body," he explained. I tried not to wince, but failed terribly.

He noted the movement and continued, flipping the dagger in his hand thoughtfully. "You may feel helpless now, but this says differently. When it mattered, you didn't give in. You fought. And that's the important piece that can't be taught."

He offered me a soft smile and I realized that, as second in command, he probably had a large hand in training their army. If anyone could identify a fighting spirit, it was him. I smiled in return, grateful for his honest words.

I sheathed the dagger and walked out of the armory, coming to a sudden stop as I ran headfirst into Blaise. I bounced off his hard body, hissing a little as my calf gave out slightly from the unexpected jolt. He grabbed me in surprise, and his eyes narrowed as they traveled to my wrapped leg.

"Who did this to you?" He growled, his voice rough like sandpaper. His grip tightened slightly on my arms, and I felt a tingle at the protective fire that lit his glare. I swallowed.

"Umm...a Nuckelavee?" My voice rose in a near-question, and his eyes flashed at my answer. He cursed and let me go, stalking away. I watched in confusion while he ran his hands through his hair, a muscle in his cheek feathering as he paced angrily.

"I'm sorry," I started, "I was just walking back from town. I didn't think anything would happen."

He spun to face me, his expression one of disbelief. "You're sorry? I'm the one who should be sorry. For something that dreadful to be anywhere close to here; anywhere close to *you*..." Blaise gritted his teeth and ran a hand down his jaw. "It shouldn't have happened. Period."

I took the hand from his face and clasped his palm gently in my grip.

"Look," I murmured softly. His hazel eyes burned into mine, consumed by regret. "I'm okay. Everything is okay."

He took a breath, tracing his gaze across my body as if to assure himself that it was the truth, then brought his free hand to cup my cheek. The kiss that followed was rough, protective, and all-encompassing. When he pulled away, he picked me up, conscious of my wrapped calf as he carried me to his bedroom.

He laid me down on his bed with more gentleness than expected and began trailing kisses down my neck. As he reached lower, pulling my shirt up and kissing my stomach, I bucked my hips and reached for his shoulder. Blaise tsked and grabbed my hands, putting them above my head.

"No touching. Just enjoying," he demanded, and I couldn't help but shiver at his husky tone. In one deft movement, he had my shirt pulled up and my bra pulled down. He traced his fingertips over the curve of my breasts, following the trail shortly after with his warm, soft lips.

I groaned as he brushed a thumb over my exposed nipple and shot me a wicked grin. He captured my lips with his, moving his hand behind my back to unclasp my bra with minimal effort. My back arched as I pressed into his palm and bit down on his bottom lip, hard, on impulse.

He pulled back, eyes wide with surprise, and pressed his fingers to his mouth. "What was that?" He asked with a soft laugh.

I shrugged, suddenly self-conscious.

"I guess I got a little carried away," I muttered, my face flushing from embarrassment rather than desire. I pulled my shirt back down and Blaise studied me, but made no move to push the subject.

"How?" He asked instead. I threw him a puzzled look and saw his gaze fixed on my wrapped leg, fully on display as it draped across the bed.

"How what?"

"How did you get away from the Nuckelavee?"

I hesitated, and then reluctantly recited the story I'd prepped that morning: I'd been caught riding Gray, and he'd simply had a lucky kick that struck the creature down. When I finished, Blaise gave me a long, assessing look.

"Look," he said, brushing the hair back from my face and fixing me with a serious look. "I've known you were special for a long time now, Katherine. But even I think there's more to it than that. If there's a good reason you're keeping it from me, I respect that. But I feel like I can't help protect you properly if I don't know the full story."

"I –" I swallowed. That familiar fear of rejection bubbled inside me again; the worry that telling him would change things between us. As his eyes burned into mine, though, I felt my resolve falter. He knew me, I realized, and would not alter his perspective on something I had no control over.

And so, I told him. His face didn't change as I recounted my story, aside from a soft eye crinkling when I came to the part about the Nuckelavee. When I stopped, he simply pulled me close. I melted into his broad chest, breathing in his husky scent.

"You've certainly got a lot more on your shoulders than I thought," he murmured. "I'm sorry you've had to deal with this alone."

I squirmed in his embrace. "I'm not alone," I corrected him. "I have a lot of support. I just ... don't have a lot of answers."

He laughed, his warm breath feathering in my hair. "Well. I'm all for you conquering the world, sunshine. So, add me to your team. I'll look for answers first thing tomorrow."

I smiled up at him and placed a hand on his cheek. "And wish me luck. I start with my offensive magic first thing tomorrow."

Chapter 26

Offensive magic proved vastly more interesting than what I had done thus far. Gone were the attempts at persuading waves to roll and crash at my beck and call; instead, I bent the shape and temperature, creating scalding whips and frozen spears in turn. Darrya even joined in, dropping large orbs of water on objects, eventually including Larke's own head.

We had allotted an hour, but considering I had skipped Blaise's lessons for my leg to heal, I had the energy to spare; I was on a roll, and managed to squeeze out another thirty minutes of their time.

Larke was thoroughly impressed with how quickly I took to my lessons, stopping his guidance only to provide Darrya with brief explanations. Every now and then, his stares lingered on her golden hair, or her full, beaming smile whenever she threw back her head to laugh. He even joined in our merriment after he was utterly doused with water. I couldn't tell if it was because he was enthralled by her, or if he was simply trying to align this side of Darrya with the stone-faced portrayal of the queen's envoy. I had my money on the former.

"Alright. Tomorrow we'll work on earth magic – crafting vines, wooden spears, and manipulating the ground to unsteady the opponent. Things like that." Larke grinned, and with one last lingering look at Darrya, said goodbye.

"Oh, Darrya," I sighed the moment he was out of earshot. "He *so* has the hots for you."

She gave me a genuinely startled look. "What do you mean?"

"Oh, come off it, cousin. The poor man couldn't keep his eyes off you for longer than ten seconds." Finlay's voice sounded from beyond the tree. I started, wondering how I hadn't picked up on his ashy scent sooner.

"How long have you been there?" Darrya demanded, cheeks flushing pink. This was an interesting development – seeing Darrya rattled. Especially from a simple jest regarding a tall, dark, handsome something.

"Only about ten minutes," he replied, and then motioned to me. "That water whip was impressive. I might even let you try that on me sometime." His lips curled into a smirk around his cigarette, even as mine became a frown.

"I can water down your whiskey, if you'd like." I retorted, glancing pointedly at his flask. Darrya cleared her throat and looked away. Finlay feigned horror.

"Why would I need water in my apple juice?" He asked, clearly in the mood to taunt, but my leg had begun to ache and his self-deprecating ways were anything but amusing.

"Ah, yes. Because downing whiskey like it's juice is normal." My reply was curt and he sensed it, quieting as I limped by and tossed a goodbye to Darrya. A rustle and the scent of charred vanilla told me he followed, however, and I gritted my teeth.

"Don't you have anything better to do with your time than bother me?" I muttered when I paused at the steps of the palace.

"I heard what happened the other night," he said, voice low. "I just wanted to ensure you were alright. We have a palace healer, you know."

I sighed and shifted my weight, now acutely aware of the slight hobble of my footsteps. "I have a friend who will heal it later. I'll be just fine." I replied, turning to him. "But even better when I learn how to use my magic as a weapon."

"Yes, words aren't much of a weapon when wielded against a dark Faerie," he mused. "Though you'd be a force to reckon with, if that were the case."

I snorted and made to turn away before he added, "You don't have to feel helpless, you know. Your magic is incredibly strong already."

A dark part of me flared at his words, though they were well-intentioned.

"Do *not* presume to tell me what I feel." I snapped, and he blanched. That vulnerable piece tugged inside my chest, whispering that he was right — I *was* feeling helpless — but I pushed it down. Multiple reasons compelled me to train, even if helplessness was the chief one.

"I'm not training to defend myself against dark Faeries. I'm training to catch one. Interrogate it. Then kill it." I added for extra measure, arms crossing.

"Catch one?" He stiffened. I waited for him to react as if it were a joke, or at the very least, try to talk me out of it. But instead, he grinned and said, "Count me in."

I blinked. "What?"

"It sounds like an adventure." He shrugged. "I want in."

I was about to reply when I heard another voice.

"It looks like you have some trash stuck to your shoe again." Blaise drawled, appearing behind me. I felt his hand snake around my waist, tugging me closer.

A fire flared in Finlay's eyes momentarily, and then disappeared as he looked away, deflated. "Watch your tongue," was his only response. Glancing back at me, he mumbled, "I'll see you later."

"Bye, sweetheart." Blaise called after him, a sardonic lilt to his voice. I watched the prince walk away, the sun glinting off his golden flask as he retrieved it from his pocket, unscrewing it as he went. A tinge of guilt fluttered in my stomach, and I pushed away from Blaise.

"What the hell was that?" I demanded, turning to face him. He gave me a look of surprise.

"What do you mean?"

"That pissing match. It was like I was the dog, and you just decided to – to piss all over me, claiming your territory." I seethed, gesturing with my hands.

"I ran into Darrya on my way to find you, and she said you'd been bickering with her cousin and stormed off. I figured he'd upset you." Blaise at least had the decency to look somewhat ashamed.

I ran through what Finlay had said, the guilt intensifying as I realized my words had likely been far sharper than his. "Actually, I think it might have been the other way around." I admitted. "I'm just in a bad mood with this bum leg."

Blaise sidled back up to me. "Well, you know, it's your human touch that's making you deal with it, for whatever stubborn reason," he said gently, and I rolled my eyes at him. "But you are allowed to have bad days."

"So are you, apparently. I swear, sometimes I think if someone were to look at you wrong, you'd kill them." I muttered.

"Is that a bad thing?" Blaise asked, tossing me a Cheshire cat grin.

"I'd say that might make you a bad guy, especially if it's actually a good guy that you kill." I nudged him.

"Finlay might be the heir, but I don't know if I'd label him a good guy." Blaise ventured, tossing a glance down the path that Finlay had taken. I envisioned the wheels turning as he mentally recounted all the prince's indiscretions.

"Either way, I would kill anyone for you. Good or bad. That might make me the bad guy, but I'm surprisingly okay with it." He added, throwing a feral smile my way. My breath hitched at the intensity of his words as desire rushed deep in my belly. His eyes narrowed, noting the change in my breathing, and his expression turned ravenous.

"What did you come to find me for?" I whispered, and he cleared his throat.

"Right. I came to help you with your problem."

I glanced down at my leg in confusion.

"Not that one," he amended. "Though we can stop by Castille's place in town as well. But I found someone who might have answers for you."

My eyes widened and I grabbed his arm eagerly.

"Who? How?" I demanded, and he chuckled at my excitement.

"Easy there. It's not for certain. But my friend Ensley may be able to help." He smiled and motioned for me to follow.

Chapter 27

"Ensley is a Valkyrie." Blaise explained as we walked towards town. His long strides were an effort to keep pace with, especially with my limp, but I was spurred on by my own enthusiasm.

"Like – a female warrior?" I asked, furrowing my brow. When he nodded, I added, "Then is she in your army?"

"Yes and no," he replied. "She leads her own army of Valkyries. But we often train together, and if necessary, we fight together, too."

"I see. So, I'm not the first woman to defy your leadership." I teased, and he smiled at me fondly.

"Nope. You're both more than capable of forging your own path. But it's not her fighting skills we need today." At my curious look, he continued. "Valkyries are incredibly strong physically, but they possess no elemental powers. Instead, they are divine agents."

"What does that mean?" I blurted, now thoroughly confused. Blaise paused, nodding to a passerby who murmured their respects. The weather was divine, and plenty of Fae milled about the town, many of whom recognized the commander.

"They practice divination. It allows them to do all sorts of things – speak with animals, use telepathy, leverage precognition to focus on future events. Though what we need today is psychometry. She'll essentially use your touch to read your history."

"So, like palm reading, but with real power," I mused, and Blaise nodded. I shook my head in astonishment. This world would never cease to amaze me.

"Why did nobody else think of this?" I asked as we came to a stop. Blaise motioned for me to turn down a side street and lowered his voice, as if fearing being overheard.

"Valkyries tend to keep to themselves, and the extent of their divine powers vary with the individual. Ensley and I have a solid working relationship, which is the only reason I know the extent of her powers and felt comfortable asking a favor."

I nodded in understanding. If anyone could relate to wanting to keep to themselves, it was me.

Blaise located a back entrance to a building, concealed by a dark curtain draped across it. He pushed it aside cautiously, calling into the room to announce our arrival. A strong, clear female voice called back to enter. Blaise motioned to me and, tentatively, I crossed the threshold and peered beyond his solid body.

The room was dark, lit only by the numerous candles adorning the floor-to-ceiling shelves. Strange stones, plants, and ancient weapons that I couldn't quite place filled the shelves. It felt ominous but somehow inviting, just like its occupant who stood tall before us, separated only by a round, wooden table.

I ignored Blaise's introductions as I surveyed the warrior in front of me. She was incredibly well-toned; her black attire added to her already formidable physique, and golden armbands and bracelets gleamed against her light brown skin. Her face was as sharp as her muscles, with defined dark eyebrows and silken, dark hair to match, pulled back into a perfectly straight ponytail.

As she shifted to sit down across the table from us, motioning for us to do the same, I held back a gasp. Massive, feathered wings stretched out behind her — a grayish brown — and I watched as she allowed them to span fully, displaying a stunning striped underside. Whereas Cas's wings were delicate and beautiful, Ensley's were clearly designed for strength and speed, resembling a hawk's lethal wingspan.

Despite my best efforts, Ensley noticed my gaze and tucked in her wings, as if to be polite. I flushed and ducked my chin, murmuring my apologies.

"Do not apologize, child. Our wings are a point of pride for us," she said, her voice formal and low-pitched, yet soothing. My mouth twitched into a hesitant smile.

"They're beautiful," I insisted with sheer honesty. She returned my smile with an ethereal one of her own, deep chocolate brown eyes twinkling at me before she shifted her gaze to Blaise.

"What knowledge do you seek to gain from this meeting?" She asked.

Blaise motioned to me. "She's hoping to understand her heritage and learn how it plays into why she was brought here."

Ensley hummed, fixing me with another look. I squirmed slightly under her assessing gaze. "You are a curious one," she finally murmured, and extended her palms to me. "Give me your hands and think of your upbringing."

I obliged, and felt the connection between our palms take life. It wasn't like power-sharing, but I could feel the magic in it nonetheless – a soft probing, more like a whispering in the corners of my soul, rather than two separate forces joining in a dance of power.

Closing my eyes, I thought of my upbringing, flashing through my favorite times on the ranch, and the less favorable times spent in school. The happy moments of my parents together, and then the lost feeling that followed my father's funeral.

After several long minutes, Ensley pulled back. I opened my eyes once more, but any hopeful thoughts I had disappeared as I observed the look on her face. It was one of concern and bewilderment.

"I cannot access it," she said, lowering her head almost imperceptibly, the only sign she'd give of her defeat. "You've been blocked."

"What does that mean?" It was Blaise who voiced the question.

"It means one of my sisters already worked with her and put a wall up. Likely when she was first born," she explained. "but for the exact opposite purpose – to ensure nobody can learn who she is."

My mouth opened in surprise. "And you can't reverse it?" I asked in disbelief.

Ensley shook her head. "Only the one who used the magic to build that wall up can tear it down. I gleaned the magical signature, to find out who performed it, but – " she paused, "It is a sister of mine who was killed a long time ago."

Even Blaise jolted at that. "One of your sisters was murdered?"

"Yes. Many years ago, now." Ensley fixed her gaze on me. "I'm sorry. I am not sure who you are, but it seems that someone has gone to great lengths to ensure it stays that way."

My gut twisted uncomfortably as even Blaise fixed me with a curious stare. I peered down at my hands, and then another thought struck me.

"So, you can't uncover my past. But can you foresee the future?"

"To some extent, yes." She nodded, snapping her wings out as one would simply stretch their arms. I offered my palms once more.

"Can you tell me anything about the upcoming war?" I breathed, and felt Blaise stiffen beside me. Ensley raised her eyebrows softly, the only indication of her surprise, but took my hands willingly. After a moment, she dropped one of my hands and motioned for Blaise.

"If it is a war we are discussing, I can only assume you will be involved. Help me paint a better picture," she commanded. He obliged silently, offering a palm of his own.

She closed her eyes to focus, but I kept mine open, studying her face. She breathed calmly for a few moments, and then shuddered, her eyes flashing back open. Instead of her normal chocolate eyes peering back at us, they now swirled with glassy gray waves, almost like a dark storm at sea.

"I see it," she rasped hoarsely. "There will indeed be a war. It is already inevitable."

"Who will win?" I demanded, but she shook her head.

"Impossible to say. So many routes could be taken, so many decisions changed…the outcome is an ever-moving target." Her brow furrowed.

"It's more Fae than I've ever seen. Dark, light. All races. All sides. Red and black blood both. There will be indescribable losses for both sides."

I thought of the nightmares I'd had weeks ago and shivered. Perhaps I'd had premonitions of my own.

"Who? Who will die?" I asked, my throat constricting as I realized I wasn't prepared for the answer.

"Again, I cannot say. If a weapon moves left instead of right, everything changes. It depends on the move of every soldier."

"Do you see the leader on the other side?" Blaise asked, leaning forward.

"I see…shadows. Blackness. Feathers." Her hand went cold in my own, squeezing, and I could feel her mind push towards the image. "I believe it is female. Tall, pale. But whoever she is, she is hidden by an immense dark power. Stronger than my own."

I thought of what I'd seen while touching the stone throne, and suddenly knew exactly who Ensley pictured in her mind. The woman with jet-black eyes and hair, whose dark aura still hung fresh in my memory.

"Is there anything that we can do to change the tides?" I implored, desperate for more information.

Ensley remained quiet for several moments. "The dark Fae work for her. They have information you can access."

She paused. "There will also be a sword, a special sword. I cannot see where from...but it is one of great power. If you wield this sword, there may be hope."

Finally, she released our hands, squeezing her eyes shut and breathing heavily.

"I am sorry," she said. When she opened her eyes, they had returned to normal. "There are too many paths, too many possible outcomes. That is all I can see for certain."

"Please, don't apologize." I choked out, still reeling from the information. "You've been immensely helpful."

She smiled at me gently and Blaise stood, murmuring his thanks as well. I made to follow him out to the street, but Ensley's voice trailed after us.

"Blaise, may I speak with you privately for a moment?"

Blaise locked eyes with me and we exchanged a curious look. I parted my lips, ready to object — what did Ensley need to discuss with Blaise that I couldn't hear?

"Go – I'll catch up with you." Blaise said finally, giving me a small, reassuring smile. I closed my mouth and nodded, revisiting the information Ensley had given us as I continued walking. I hadn't learned what I'd hoped, but I had two new pieces of information — no, three.

One was the woman I had seen: tall, slender, pale, and covered in black feathers. The reason for this inevitable war. And I had likely been a piece of this puzzle for far longer than I'd realized — since I was born, perhaps.

The second was that I needed to obtain the sword, possibly kept in one of the mythical cities, to even have a chance of winning.

And the third was that I was now most certainly going to do everything in my power to catch a dark Faerie, to try and learn more about this powerful shadow-woman we were up against.

Two figures traipsed down the path where I waited for Blaise and I stiffened, relaxing only somewhat when I recognized Soren. On his arm was a beautiful woman, with hair so blonde it was nearly white. Her frame was slender, but she carried herself in a way that bespoke of power that didn't require brute force.

"Kate," Soren said, catching my eye and stopping in front of me. "What are you doing here?"

"I'm just waiting for Blaise. He had some business to attend to." I surprised even myself with how smoothly the lie came out. The woman on Soren's arm caught my eye, and I sucked in a breath at her awestriking eyes, a pale gray.

Soren caught my look and smiled — actually *smiled*, with a shy expression that caught me so off guard I nearly took a step back.

"This is Myriam," he offered, and her face flashed into a deadly beautiful grin as she extended her hand.

"I've heard so much about you, Kate," she replied, and I bit back a correction to my full name as I took her hand. Something about the female made me want to keep her at arm's length, though I wasn't sure if it was her appearance — stunning but lethal — or her connection to Soren, who remained a riddle to me.

"The girl with the mysterious heritage," she continued, assessing me with those pale gray eyes. "An Aes Sídhe, but with a...*human* upbringing."

She sneered as the word 'human' passed her lips, and I bristled. Suddenly, my aversion made more sense. She was part of the community that Kipp and the others had warned me about — those who looked down on intermingling with the human realm. Soren shifted, as if he sensed my tension, but made no move to address Myriam's tone. I marked his choice internally.

I was saved from a response by Blaise's reappearance. His face was almost perfectly arranged into his typical expression as comman-der-in-chief, which was intentionally devoid of emotion, but I noted the slight pallor to his skin. He noticed our new companions, and transformed his expression seamlessly, bowing his head to Myriam.

"You must be Soren's lady. I'd be mad at his lack of focus as of late if he hadn't been so honest about your beauty. Now I understand." His flattering words sounded genuine, but I noticed the flatness of his tone as he offered his hand. "I'm Blaise."

"Myriam." She extended her hand and batted her eyelashes. I nearly bared my teeth as jealousy reared its ugly head, but Blaise took no notice. Instead, he made an excuse for us to quickly leave and promised drinks soon to get all of us acquainted.

As we walked, the tension returned, and I stole a glance at his face. It looked pinched and pale once again.

"What happened?" I asked, concern sparking my every nerve. He studied me for a long moment, and then simply took my face, pulling me in to kiss him. It was both rough and tender, a kiss filled with need.

"I just can't stand the idea of you going into war, the possibility of losing you. I need to protect you. Her words, about how many we will lose...I only wish I could protect us all," he said as he pulled away, voice breaking slightly. I stared into his eyes, nodding.

"I wish I could, too. But every step like this one is a step closer for us." I tried to sound encouraging, but I knew my voice fell short. He gave me a smile that didn't quite meet his eyes, clearly feeling the same, and took my hand.

"Come on," he said. "Let's get you healed, and then straight home. Maybe there's something we've missed."

Chapter 28

I could tell I was the last person Finlay expected when he opened his door the following afternoon. In fact, he likely hadn't been expecting anyone, by the looks of his wardrobe – or lack thereof. He sported dark lounge pants and no shirt, golden hair flopped messily over his face in a manner that partially covered his surprised cerulean eyes.

Despite my best attempts, my eyes dragged down his stomach, astonished at the chiseled muscles I found there, ending in a sharpened V where his pants rode low on his hips. I forced my gaze back up, my mouth drying slightly as I paused at his shoulders, taking in the strong slope of them.

Finlay lifted his eyebrows at me, a toothpick hanging out of his mouth. He leaned against the doorway, inclining his head as a lazy grin spread across his face. "You like what you see?".

I swallowed, willing the disarming heat that spread at his words to leave my body. "You're not smoking." I commented instead.

He took the toothpick from his mouth and swirled it in his fingers. "Someone told me it was a bad habit," he remarked with a smirk. I gave him an incredulous stare and sniffed the air, realizing I didn't scent his normal vanilla whiskey.

"No apple juice, either." Finlay said, noting my expression.

"So did you just come here to experience my dreadfully boring sober side, or did you come here with another purpose?" He continued, shifting off the doorframe and heading back into his room. After a moment's hesitation, I followed, and noted the open book on his bed — the activity I'd clearly interrupted.

"I came to take you up on your offer," I began as he pulled a shirt on. His own Shield Knot, I noticed, was located on his right shoulder blade. The mark flexed with his muscles as he lifted the shirt over his head and turned back around with a puzzled expression.

"Which offer?" He asked hesitantly, eyes skirting over my body. My lower stomach clenched at his gaze, but I crossed my arms over the area and willed the suggestive heat away.

"The one where you help me catch a dark Faerie." I replied, lifting my chin.

I half expected him to change his tune or laugh me off, so I was stunned when he just grinned. "Oh, that one! Yes, that offer is still on the table. As are others, of course. But I do have one condition."

"What's that?"

"If we're seriously going to do this, I need to know why. No lies or excuses — the real reason."

He crossed his arms expectantly, his grin broadening as he waited. I bit my lip in contemplation. This was the queen's great-grandson, the next in line to rule. If anyone would have a reason to be upset with what I'd learned about myself, it would be him.

But I needed a safety net for my plan. Finlay wasn't going to talk me out of this, not the way my other friends would try to, Blaise included. *Especially* Blaise.

"Do you remember my horse?" I asked, shifting on my feet.

Finlay nodded.

"The one who scared the shit out of me the first time I met you? Yeah, I remember him," he quipped.

"So...he's not actually mine. He belonged to a demigod, ages ago. He just appeared to me one day in the human realm, and ever since, we've been doing research to figure out why. It turns out, we're likely on the brink of a war — a war between us and the dark Faeries. Blaise's army has been running itself ragged trying to keep them in line lately. Catching one would give us insight as to who is leading this on the other side."

Finlay pursed his lips, looking more serious than I'd ever seen him. Walking slowly to his bed, he ran his hands through his hair and then sat down upon the mattress, looking up at me.

"You've been in some heavy shit since you've been here, little angel. No wonder you've been practicing offensive magic."

He peered at me curiously. "So, why you in particular? Did you discover what your lineage is when we visited Leven?"

I bit the inside of my cheek, then sighed. "Not necessarily. Lachlan found an old talisman, the Speaking Stone. And apparently–"

"It utters a cry when the true sovereign touches it." Finlay murmured, cutting me off. I froze for an instant before nodding. Trying to gauge his feelings on the revelation, I explored his face for a moment. His jaw was tight, but his pale blue eyes remained unreadable.

"It did. I still don't have all the answers, but that...it seems to explain a lot. I also visited a Valkyrie but apparently, there's some sort of block preventing their divination from accessing that information, too. So, it goes back...well, as far as my birth."

I shrugged helplessly, then went silent and allowed him to absorb the information. I wondered, not for the first time, why I felt so willing to share all of this with him.

He said nothing, merely rubbed a hand over his mouth and then let it rest on his jaw for a minute. Eventually, he exhaled and glanced up at me with a chuckle.

"Well, I have to say, that's the best explanation I think I could've asked for," he muttered good-naturedly.

"You're – not mad?" I asked, apprehensive.

"Of course not." He gave me a lopsided, sympathetic smile. "In fact, I empathize with you. That's a lot to throw on you in such a short amount of time. I've had over a hundred years to prepare for my role in this world, and I still know I'm nowhere near ready for that kind of power."

"Oh, shit." I mused with a laugh. When Finlay tilted his head, I added, "I think you and I suddenly have something in common."

His lips curled from a smile of sympathy to a full grin, and he let out a bark of laughter. "Little angel, I think you may be right."

He slapped his knees and rose off the bed.

"So, what do you need me to do?"

I couldn't help but beam at his jovial attitude. "Alright, so, I'm going to need you to head down to the armory and grab us two swords, without letting anyone know what they're for – especially not Larke or Blaise."

Finlay raised his eyebrows at that, but didn't comment.

I continued, "I'll need to go pick out a dress and speak with Wren. And then you'll meet me at sundown in the courtyard. Does that work?"

He nodded, and I was grateful for his lack of questions. As I left, I felt a certain level of wonder over this upbeat, sober version of Finlay, and more than a little alarm at how much we may actually have in common.

Chapter 29

The dress I wore made me feel like I was a true Faerie of the forest. It was cream-colored and simple, yet hugged my figure nicely and billowed out at my legs, providing enough room for movement. I pulled at the hem as I eyed the setting sun, feeling self-conscious but begrudgingly accepting the necessity of it. I had done my research thoroughly, and even carried a pipe in my satchel to entice the creature.

I had spent a good two hours with Wren before cleaning up and changing, and I felt confident that I had mastered the magic needed to hold the Faerie captive. All that was left was –

"Well, aren't you just every bit the fallen angel of my dreams." Finlay drawled, coming up behind me. He wore dark leather pants and an oversized white long-sleeve shirt, looking nothing like the royalty he was. I often wondered if it was intentional: a statement to piss off the queen, perhaps.

"Though I have a feeling you're fixing to replace your halo with horns," he added slyly.

"Bite me." I retorted.

"Horns it is. Though, I *would* let you bite me. Any day. With great pleasure." He flashed me a feral grin.

I rolled my eyes and decided not to antagonize him further. "Did you bring what I asked?"

"A large feat, my lady, but alas, I succeeded in my noble task." He handed me a sheathed sword. I glanced around before belting it to ensure no one was around to witness the exchange, and motioned for him to follow me.

"Where are we heading off to?" He asked as I scrambled for the outskirts of the forest. The sun was just beginning to set, and soft beams slipped through the canopies of the trees — a beautiful white and orange contrast to the greenery on the ground.

"Somewhere far enough in the forest that we can make a fire without being noticed by the palace." I moved swiftly, only relaxing once we were hidden in the trees. I made a mental note of gratitude for Cas and his healing powers as both of my legs moved steadily through the forest, no sign of my previous injury remaining.

"So, you know about the four talismans," Finlay began conversationally. "And Lachlan has one?"

I nodded. "I'm not sure if that's supposed to be common knowledge, though." I cast him a worried glance. He crossed his heart with his finger.

"Secret stays with me," he reassured me lightly. "But does that mean you'll be hunting for the other three?"

"I guess so," I mused, thinking of my conversation with Ensley. "But I have no idea where to start."

"I have a few books," Finlay offered. "It's how I knew what you were referring to. I'll be sure to give them to you when we get back."

I smiled at him gratefully, and we walked a few steps in silence. Out of the corner of my eye, I admired the casual grace with which he navigated the forest, as if he were one with the quiet wilderness. I wondered if this was what sober Finlay spent his free time doing — wandering the forest and reading books. It honestly didn't sound like a bad way to spend a day.

"So, do you actually know how to use that thing?" I pointed at the sword around his waist.

"Absolutely. I was learning how to wield a sword the moment I could walk."

"Does everyone learn that young?" I asked in bewilderment, and he shook his head.

"Not that young, no. That was specific to me. But all the Aes Sídhe are starting to learn it at some point. We must learn to protect ourselves." He paused for a moment, and I realized he must have been thinking about his parents.

"Are there really so few left?" I questioned softly, and he nodded.

"Less and less every year. There are rumors that someone is purposefully picking off our race, but—" Finlay shrugged. "They're just rumors. My theory is simpler. Dark Faeries are drawn to the highest power source, which means they often specifically target us Aes Sídhe when possible. Especially the ones that gain their power from other Faeries, instead of producing their own."

I shivered, remembering our task, and wondered for a moment why Finlay had agreed to this. He was likely the most valuable of our race: someone to be protected at all costs. The queen would probably have my head for putting him in harm's way, if only she knew. I decided against voicing those thoughts, however, and instead stopped.

"I think we're far enough out." I said, and surveyed the land around us. "I'm going to need you to back up."

Finlay obliged and I stretched my arms, bracing my feet as I prepared. Squinting at the land in front of me, I willed my earth magic to cooperate. After a few moments, the earth began to shake and separate, creating a perfect hole. I concentrated harder, willing an impeccably thin layer of grass and twigs to cover the top, completely obscuring the abyss below.

Finally, I lowered my hands, my breathing slightly labored yet with a proud grin lighting my face. I sent a silent thanks to Wren's mischievous nieces for the excellent trap we had fallen into all those weeks ago, and added a prayer for this to work for good measure. Finlay let out a low whistle.

"Did you just learn that today?" He asked, admiring the intricate work. I nodded. "Your magic really is no joke."

"Well, now it's your turn. I'm going to need some fire," I said. The familiar twinge of defeat bubbled up inside me for not having summoned true fire yet. If Finlay saw it, he didn't acknowledge it; rather, he simply nodded and asked where I wanted it.

In response, I used some additional earth magic to create a pyre of wood a short distance from our trap, with us positioned in the middle. With a flick of the wrist, Finlay had it burning. I watched his face, sober and stoic, dancing in the flames he'd so easily summoned. The handsome orphaned fire prince.

I pushed down a slew of emotions that rose unexpectedly in my stomach, and pulled out the pipe from my satchel. Finlay eyed it quizzically.

"I realize I never asked this before," he said slowly, "but what kind of dark Faerie are we even luring here?"

I smiled, lighting the pipe on the fire. "The type that loves pipes, fires, darkness, and young, powerful women." I eyed the crackling fire, now bright against the nearly set sun. "A *Gean-Cánach*."

Finlay blinked. "That's what you want to lure here?" He asked uncertainly, and I shrugged.

"I did my research on them. Plus, I've had experience with one." I said, and with that, I settled back and waited for a Love Talker to take our bait.

I reminded myself, for at least the fifth time, that patience was not my strong suit as the minutes stretched on. It had only been ten minutes since I'd last asked Finlay the time, who likely regretted his choice of adventure at this point.

I sighed and shifted my seat, biting my tongue to ask how long it had been again. Finlay must have sensed the question burning on the tip of my tongue, though, and lobbed a different question my way.

"Are there any other ways to entice it that we may be missing?"

I looked at him curiously, and he merely shrugged. "It's only attracted to women. Maybe it's my presence."

I shook my head. "No, I was surrounded by men that night." But I pondered his question, wondering what else had triggered the Love Talker that night.

Unmet desire.

It popped into my head unbidden, and I stiffened as I realized what was missing. Finlay noticed the rigidity of my posture and straightened up, glancing around.

"What? What is it?" He asked, but I simply shook my head in disbelief.

"I can't believe I didn't think of this," I grumbled. Finlay looked at me inquiringly, and I shifted uncomfortably.

"I think...I think what's missing is my scent." I admitted.

"What?" Finlay chuckled softly. "What does that even mean?"

I bit my lip, considering for a moment how awkward this conversation would be. But we had already come this far, and I was determined to get the answers we needed. We'd waited too long and worked too hard to throw it away based on my discomfort.

"When I talked with it before, it mentioned how it had been observing me, and sensed my unmet desires." I said. "I think it scented my desire and sought me out from the crowd for that specific reason."

"Oh...*oh*." Finlay said in realization, and shifted on his feet awkwardly. "So, you'll probably need...Blaise."

I shook my head vehemently, even as a flash of guilt panged through me.

"No," I asserted. "I don't want him here. That would only result in a lecture, or him getting in the way trying to protect me, no matter how well-intentioned his actions are."

Finlay bit his lip, considering our next moves, and I eyed him curiously for a moment. An idea sparked in my mind, and I leaned forward.

"Talk to me," I commanded.

"Talk to you?"

"Talk to me. Tell me – tell me what you would do if we were flirting. *Actually* flirting, not the silly banter you've pulled on me before."

He raised an eyebrow, but I shot him an exasperated look in response. "Look, we're already here, everything is ready. It doesn't hurt to try."

He took a moment to think, and then sighed.

"Alright," he conceded, and came to sit cross-legged in front of me, our knees touching as we sat on the grass. I forced myself not to pull back, unsure if I felt uneasy from his closeness, or because of the way my mouth had dried in anticipation. The fire crackled behind him and lit his golden hair with sparks of orange as he assessed me.

"I would tell you," Finlay began, voice low, "how stunning you look, even in a dress as simple as this one. But no matter what you wear, you look most beautiful when you smile. The type of smile where you tip your whole head back, sometimes laughing, too, with your whole body."

His eyes darkened, as if the memory was taking him somewhere else. My mouth dropped open in surprise at his words, more romantic than sensual. Did I really smile like that? I hadn't ever noticed, and I wasn't sure what to make of the idea that he was studying how I smiled.

"I would tell you," he continued, his voice beginning to carry a slight rasp, "that when I see that smile of yours, all I want to do is grab your waist and kiss my way down your beautiful neck, and back up to claim your perfect lips."

My breathing stilled. Warmth crashed over me, even as a part of my brain warred against the image in my head, knowing I shouldn't be *this* tempted by the thought of Finlay's lips, crashing into mine. But Finlay sensed it, and leaned in, encouraged.

"And if that line worked," he added, spreading his hands across his knees. "I would take that kiss, and I wouldn't stop there."

My stomach tightened. "What would you do?" I whispered, and he grinned wickedly.

"I would kiss you so long and hard that your lips would bruise," he growled. "I would explore every inch of your mouth, and then I would move to bite your ear, and then your neck, leaving a mark so that everyone could see you were *mine.*"

His eyes narrowed, focused on my neck, where he'd spotted the mark from Blaise previously, as though he wanted to recreate it. To banish the previous memory from my mind entirely. My hands tightened into fists, as if that would control the heat pooling everywhere inside of me.

"And if you liked that," he continued in that low, throaty tone, "I would whisper in your ear and ask if you, little angel, wanted to fuck me."

I leaned in so close that our noses almost touched, and felt him let a breath loose, fanning across my cheeks.

"And what would that be like?" I breathed, my voice nearly a whimper. He brushed his nose against mine, the soft touch like static, as he moved to reach my ear with his lips.

"I already told you once," he whispered, his low tone holding sensual promise. "I would *worship* you." His teeth grazed my ear ever so slightly as he pulled back. My core turned molten as a soft, guttural moan slipped past my lips.

He sucked in a breath as his eyes met mine once more, and I saw the raw desire in his expression, surely mirroring my own.

I was about to close the mere hair's breadth between our mouths when I saw his eyes flick over my shoulder. His whole body tensed.

"What is it?" I murmured, blinking away the near delirium that plagued me. My awareness came flooding back as Finlay's hand touched the hilt of his sword. His voice was low as he responded, but no longer sensual; rather, it was dark with warning.

"We have company."

Chapter 30

Visually, the creature looked like the one I'd encountered at the festival, still attempting to play to my desires as a devastatingly handsome Faerie. I distinctly noticed how my emotional awareness remained sharp, despite the fog that surrounded the beast. My mark pulsed at my collarbone, working to dispel any possible attempts the Love Talker made at ensnaring me. I breathed a sigh of relief at the protection.

I could sense Finlay warring with his emotions beside me, torn between wanting to protect me yet understanding I had a plan of my own. I chose for him, stepping ahead and working to calm my racing pulse.

"Who are you?" I attempted to keep my voice airy and full of wonder, summoning snippets of my memory from the night at the festival.

"Whomever you want me to be," the creature purred. His image shuddered slightly, like an old movie tape that had been scratched. His eyes flashed between green, blue, and gold, his hair light, then dark. He frowned, noting my scrutiny.

"You're indecisive," he said, stepping closer. My eyes flickered to the ground briefly before I met his gaze again. Just a few more steps.

I licked my lips and watched as his ever-changing eyes tracked the movement.

"Indecisive?" I breathed, making a show of taking another step forward, only to freeze in feigned awe. "What – what do you mean?"

The creature's gaze flashed to Finlay for a moment. "Your desires are undecided," he crooned. "I can give you them both."

I cocked my head, but my surprise was genuine. "Both?"

"The light and the dark. The soldier and the prince. Your innermost fantasies are filled with thoughts of both," he murmured.

I realized his features were struggling to settle on one image, solely for that reason. He was working to pick which I desired, but there lay the truth – I desired more than one.

I blinked away the revelation and prayed Finlay would disregard it too. More important things were at stake than a silly game of hearts and desires. And I came to play the real game.

"How can I have both?" I murmured, leaning forward and suppressing a victorious grin as the creature took the bait. The fog thickened and swirled to encompass us both. He moved to close the gap as I refused to leave my spot – one step, two –

And collapsed into the trap.

In a flash, I was at the edge, working to layer the top with a thick air shield. His fog danced along the barriers of the shield, trapped inside as if an invisible glass wall lay there. The beast screamed in rage as it realized what had happened, and the fog disappeared, leaving him seething at the base of the pit.

I grinned with pride at my accomplishment, but it was short-lived as the dark Faerie bared its teeth up at me. In response, I unsheathed my sword, pointing it down at him.

"Tell me about your master," I demanded, but he simply sneered.

"I have no master," he replied darkly, and I gritted my teeth in frustration.

"I know you have a master. And I know she's organizing something much bigger than a few one-off Faerie attacks." I snarled. "So, you can either tell me now, and I'll consider releasing you to bring a message back to her alive. Or I will leave you here to rot, for however long it takes a semi-immortal Faerie to either starve to death or go mad in isolation."

Silence fell as he considered my words, the sneer abandoning his face for a moment as he squinted up at me. Then, he snorted.

"You wouldn't," he scoffed. "You're just a nice young girl. You haven't lived long enough to see a dark day in your life. I've been through worse than you could ever dole out."

A whoosh of heat flared behind me, and I glanced back to see flames in Finlay's hands, mirrored in his eyes with an anger I'd never seen before. But I shook my head and raised a hand, silently telling him to hold off. After a moment, he reluctantly dulled the fire, but didn't douse it completely.

Turning back to the Love Talker, I willed water into my own hands. I wouldn't resort to torturing him the way Larke tortured prisoners. But I could get damn close. The water extended into a long thin rope which I sent down into the pit. The air shield recognized my magical signature and allowed it to pass through. Slowly,

I guided the rope to wrap around the creature's neck, whose eyes widened in alarm.

"Are you sure you want to test that theory?" I hissed and tightened the rope, the water forming a strong torrent within the confines of its shape. "Your kind wants to start a war against my friends, my *family?* You will see how dark your days can get."

I transferred all the heat I could muster into the rope, remembering Finlay's lessons as I urged it on. My blood boiled with the intensity of my own defensive rage, as if this moment alone could halt the storm I knew was coming. My hands began to glow a golden white, and the liquid rope I held started to shine as well. It sizzled as the water began to steam. I pressed harder.

"Kate."

I jerked my head, surprised at Finlay's use of my real name for the first time. His eyes caught mine, and a look of shock spread across his face at whatever he found there.

A yelp from below dragged my attention back to the creature. He writhed and pulled on the rope at his neck, which now singed his skin.

"All right!" He cried out. "I'll tell you; I'll tell you!"

I let the rope drop, and the water faded into the earth as if the weapon had never existed. The Love Talker gasped, crawling to the furthest corner of the pit. Thunder rumbled above as he began to speak, as if even beginning the conversation was a bad omen. Flecks of rain pelted my cheeks as I waited with bated breath.

"We've been under her leadership for twenty, maybe thirty years?" He started, still panting as he glared at me out of the corner of his eyes.

"She provides protection and power that we do not normally have. It has taken a long time for her to gather us all together, to trust each other; we normally keep to ourselves –"

"We know you've formed an army." I interrupted. "Is she one of you? Or is she an Aes Sídhe?"

"Neither," he replied, picking nervously at the dirt. "She is more powerful than us, than you — than all of you. And even so, she is not yet at full power. Right now, she works mostly with spells and incantations as her weapons. But with her sisters, she will be unstoppable."

My stomach sank, and I exchanged a quick glance with Finlay. Rain had begun falling heavily around us, extinguishing the fire and covering the surrounding space in a cloud of dark smoke.

"Who? Who is she?" Finlay demanded, turning back to the Love Talker.

The dark Faerie opened his mouth, but nothing came out. He tried once more, but produced nothing except a croak. Finlay cursed.

"He's been spelled," he muttered angrily. "He can't say her name." He kicked the ground in frustration.

"The ravens," the creature finally choked out. "She is the queen – the queen of ravens."

I nodded eagerly, leaning forward in the now-soaking ground. "Can you write it?" I asked. "Can you write it in the mud?"

He hesitated, then turned and pressed a finger to the wall. The second he finished the first letter, however, he released a bloodcurdling scream. I dropped to my knees, gripping the edge of the pit as Finlay held me back by the shoulder gently. I looked on in horror.

The creature doubled over. His screams of pain evolved to coughing, and then full-fledged choking. I watched as black blood spilled slowly from his mouth, and he collapsed to his knees. His eyes met mine, conveying sheer agony and terror as he gagged on his own blood.

Despite my own hesitations at leaving him alive after our exchange and the fact I'd subjected him to torture just minutes before, I felt the roiling in my gut at watching this – a slow death that I wouldn't wish on anyone.

A final cough sent splatters of blood flying across the ground and he slumped over, eyes now glazed. I squeezed mine shut as if it would dispel the image, but I knew it would haunt my dreams tonight, and for many nights to come.

I allowed the rain to envelop me completely, letting the sound fill my ears and the feel of it wash over my face and body. I couldn't help but see the image of my father, over ten years ago. It had been storming that day, too.

My mother had told me to stay in the car, but it only spurred my curiosity, so I snuck out to explore – and came face to face with the same blank, lifeless expression I'd just witnessed. It had only taken moments for the first responders to cover my father's face as they carried him away, but I had seen enough. Back then, it took much longer to understand what an unblinking stare like that meant; now, the realization of death stared me blatantly in the face.

I shuddered and felt a soft, warm hand grasp my shoulder. I didn't open my eyes, but I allowed Finlay to lift me off my knees as I took a deep breath. After a moment, I exhaled and opened my eyes. He watched me with concern.

"I'm sorry you had to see that," he said.

"It's not the first dead body I've seen." I whispered absentmindedly.

"It doesn't mean it gets any easier," he told me gently, and I turned to him, surprised.

"How many have *you* seen?"

"More than I can count," he responded, shifting on his feet. "The queen only sends messengers with her condolences when royal families lose a member. I try to make a point to visit any family I've known when they lose a loved one, which has unfortunately been many over the years. Oftentimes, I'm the first they hear from."

I nodded in understanding. For him, it was personal: a way to regain control of the narrative. The chance to deliver the news in a way I'm sure he would have wanted with his own parents.

I glanced back over to the pit.

"Hey," I said with a start, and knelt back down. "Do you see that?"

Finlay came to kneel beside me. "What?"

"That." I replied, pointing just above the dead Faerie's body. "He wrote the first letter."

Finlay squinted, the last slivers of sun making it difficult to see. "Well, would you look at that? His master's name starts with an N."

I glanced at the letter, then the body, and then away. I couldn't think of what it meant while we were here, surrounded by death.

"I'll get Blaise to dispose of the body," I murmured. I pushed up to start back, needing to get away from the site.

Finlay followed silently for a while, leaving me alone with my thoughts. I walked briskly, hoping to alleviate some of the cold that was spreading through my body from the rain.

Finally, he broke the silence. "How did you do that, back there?"

"Do what?"

"That magic with your eyes."

"My eyes?" I echoed, bewildered. Finlay paused and studied me.

"Your eyes. They were glowing. Golden."

I frowned and absentmindedly rubbed my eyes, as though that would provide some answers.

"I didn't feel anything different." I replied. "I was just trying to do offensive magic. Maybe finally summon some fire."

"So you've never had that happen before?" He asked. His voice was hesitant, almost astounded. I shook my head.

"Add it to the list of things I don't understand, I suppose," I muttered. Another question I was sure no one had an answer for. I quickened my pace, brooding over the fact. Finlay left it at that, seeming to sense my frustration.

I stopped as we approached the edge of the forest, panting slightly. The sun was now fully set, but the lights and fires from town illuminated the path. I shivered, wondering idly if Castille would be opposed to me taking a hot bath at his place. I bet he had all sorts of fun bath salts and luxurious oils.

Suddenly, my entire body warmed, and I nearly sighed with relief. It was almost as if by –

"Was that you?" I turned to Finlay, surprised.

"Fire does more than destroy," he offered by way of explanation. He shot me a small smile, but I noticed how his eyes dipped briefly down my dress, now hugging my body tightly from the rain.

I chose the moment to study him unabashedly in return. His hair fell in messy strings over his eyes, now a dark brown as they dripped with rain, drops trailing down his piercing jaw and over his lips.

I thought back to his words earlier in the night; the dangerous game we'd played as we waited for our trap to work.

"Why did you come with me tonight?" I asked suddenly. He tilted his head and raised an eyebrow.

"I mean, it wasn't because you thought I needed protecting, was it?" I inquired. Finlay shook his head forcefully, sending droplets of water flying.

"I'm well aware you can hold your own," he said mildly. "It wasn't for you. It was for me."

He brushed his hair back, now positively drenched, and continued.

"I spend so much of my life learning politics, talking politics. Preparing for more of the same. My adventure usually lies in books. But you, little angel?" He offered me a smirk. "You are a new adventure every day. And this seemed like a particularly exciting one."

I let out a soft laugh. "Surely this wasn't the adventure you were expecting."

"No," he grinned in response. "But somehow, it was better."

Chapter 31

The next afternoon all but dissolved into a massive research party, if you could call it that. I invited Cas, Wren, Darrya, and Kipp to the palace library. Given their propensity to argue, I didn't mention it to Blaise or Finlay, which proved to be just fine, as five was already plenty.

Mostly, we searched for answers to the clues provided by the dark Faerie last night. I also kept an eye out for any books regarding unique magical powers — particularly magic that could make eyes glow. I hadn't mentioned it to anyone else, and prayed Finlay would be discreet. Somehow, despite all his other bad habits, I knew he could be trusted with my secret.

I sipped my coffee as I scanned the pages in front of me, groaning softly at the delightful taste. As I'd suspected, it tasted far better than coffee in the human realm.

"I've never known anyone to be so addicted to caffeine," Wren commented with a dry smile.

"Well, you've never had a biochem lab at seven in the morning," I replied, flipping a page and glancing up at her. She blinked in confusion, and I laughed. "Never mind."

"I think I found something," Kipp spoke suddenly. We all leaned in while he turned the book around to face us. There was a drawing of a tall, slender woman, facing forward, arms outstretched to ravens circling above. Two other women stood slightly behind her, their arms reaching out to either side, expressions somber and down-turned.

"This is a text on the triple goddesses. There are a handful of triple goddesses; sisters that, together, have formidable power. Mostly, I think of our mother goddesses – they aided with wonderful things like fertility, culture, and poetry – but we have dark goddesses, too. These triple goddesses are chief among them. And you'll never guess what their names are."

He tapped a finger to a specific portion of text, and I read it out loud.

"These triple goddesses were named as such: Badb, a goddess of courage in battle. Her symbol is a crow. She is known to prophesize outcomes of war and change the tide with fear and confusion. Macha – " At this name, I paused and exchanged a look with Kipp, who nodded, and Wren, who leaned in closer.

"Macha, a goddess of sovereignty. Her symbol is a horse. She is known to battle against injustices to women and children. And lastly, Nemain, a goddess of fate and death. Her symbol is the raven. She is not known for fighting in battle; rather, finding other ways to influence the outcomes by causing madness, insanity, and frenzy with her battle cry."

I cleared my throat and shivered slightly as I continued.

"Together, these sisters would fight alongside the Tuatha Dé Danann, and are known as the three *Morrígna* – or the triple goddess, the Morrígan."

We sat silently for a moment, before Darrya finally spoke.

"I don't get it. If they fought to protect the Tuatha Dé Danann, why are we preparing for a war against them now?"

I shrugged. "It sounds like it's only one of the sisters. Nemain. And if the Faerie we captured last night was correct, she's trying to get her sisters back."

"It sounds like she's the worst of them." Cas murmured. "With her sisters, perhaps she had voices of reason – some sort of balance between the light and the dark linking the three."

"It makes more sense now with Kate as the sovereign, that Gray would seek you out. Especially seeing that he was originally a gift from Macha." Kipp said. He gave me a supportive smile, though it did nothing to reassure me.

I exchanged a glance with the others, feeling the uncomfortable tension radiating from them. Suddenly, by putting a name and a story to this mysterious threat, it was all becoming far too real.

"But I know for a fact Macha was slain in battle long ago," Wren said, scratching her head in confusion. "Cas – is there a way to bring someone back from the dead?"

Cas shook his head. "Not at all. No healer I know can do it, with any type of power or spells. But perhaps it's different for goddesses.

There used to be whispers of necromancy as a power among the gods."

"If any god would have it, it would be a goddess of death," I added uneasily.

"Alright, well, it's a good starting point. We have her name, and we have her next step. Let's see if we can do some research on how to cut her off before she does more damage." Wren said hopefully, attempting to inject some positivity into our souring moods.

"And see if we can find any more information on those remaining three talismans, or at least the cities they came from," I added. "We'll need more weapons, and more power."

We spent the next few hours in the library, bantering and researching. The main takeaways were how interchangeable Nemain's actions were with the Morrígan name – she was essentially known as the raven of death, swooping over battlefields and prophesizing the fatalities of the soldiers. The stories were intermittent regarding her powers in necromancy, and chilled me to the bone each time they were mentioned.

Her sisters had indeed both been slain, but the most confusing part was a brief mention of Nemain's death as well.

"Do you think they got it wrong?" Wren asked, and Kipp shrugged.

"There's always a chance. But if she is the goddess of death, maybe..."

"Maybe she was able to bring herself back." I finished for him, a shiver running up my arms. How did you kill someone who could simply...come back to life?

Cas groaned. "But how could she bring herself back, and not her sisters? This makes no sense."

I bit my lip, considering. It seemed like every time we found new answers, it only led to more questions.

"Well, the only way to find out is to do some more searching," I said with a sigh. "Let's keep at it."

The four talismans were like finding a needle in the haystack. Ancient stories were much more focused on whimsical sayings and poems, rather than strategic mentions of how to find or wield the treasures.

We'd been able to narrow down the sword as the magical sword of Nuada. It was also known as "The Answerer" or "The Whisperer", its power being that it always swung a fatal blow.

It was forged in the blistering heat that only metalworking shops in Fionnias were capable of, and as a result, withstood blazing temperatures. As for where it now lay, our research didn't say, but Kipp had an answer.

"I remember a story about a blazing sword, one that seared at the touch and shone with light. It might be the same," he insisted. "The story says that it was plunged into the chest of a supernatural demon, and it fell with him into the depths of Annwn."

Cas let out a low whistle. "You're saying that to retrieve it, she'll have to go to the Otherworld?"

Before I could ask, Darrya cut in. "He's saying *we'll* have to go to the Otherworld." She lifted her chin defiantly, and Cas gave her a startled look.

"Can someone explain what Annwn is?" I interjected.

"It's a realm where the souls of the dead gather. Like a parallel world, with a heaven and a hell." Wren explained, her voice steady even though her face had slightly paled.

"And it's safe to assume our demon friend didn't float his way into heaven." Cas added, his sarcasm falling flat. I wasn't sure if this was a common place to visit – even possible to *visit* at all – but I had to assume there weren't many places lower on the bucket list than the hell of an Otherworld.

I rolled my shoulders, shaking the jitters from my hands. "Well, I'll do more research later, but it sounds like I'll need to do more training with Larke if I'm going to plan a visit to hell."

Darrya nodded emphatically, agreeing, and I smirked at the blush that tinged her cheeks at the mention of Larke's name. I was surprised, however, when Wren piped up.

"I'll train with you," she said, soft but confident. "I want to be prepared as well."

"Well, I'm sure he won't mind a few more trainees," I said, reaching for her shoulder and giving it a soft squeeze.

Kipp grabbed my wrist as I began gathering up the books we'd spread out across the tables, and I glanced up at him. His eyes swam with concern.

"Are you sure this is what you want to do?" He asked. "We're working off little more than hunches here."

I placed my other hand over his. "I came here with you on nothing more than a hunch, you know," I reminded him. "It's led me this far. And most importantly, it led me to all of you."

Kipp smiled hesitantly at that and then nodded, helping me gather our books. Just as we finished putting them away, Finlay burst into the library.

"Hey," I said excitedly, "You'll never guess what we all figured out today –"

"Thank gods you're here," Finlay cut me off, glancing between his cousin and me with relief. It was only then that I noticed the sheen of sweat gathered on his forehead and the panic in his eyes.

"What is it?" Darrya asked with alarm, stepping forward. He worked to catch his breath, likely having run through the whole palace to locate us.

"Dark Faeries," he said breathlessly. "They're everywhere. Invading the palace."

I felt a whoosh of air as Kipp transformed beside us, a soft snarl erupting in his chest. My hand located the dagger at my waist, vividly remembering our encounter with the Nuckelavee. I wondered how many of them were outside at this very moment.

"Is this it?" Wren asked, shooting a panicked look between us all. "Is this the start of the war?"

Finlay shook his head. "It's not nearly enough for a war." He caught my eye and added, "Just enough to send us a message."

I bit my lip and voiced the message grimly. "She knows we know."

Chapter 32

I tried my hardest to send Castille and Wren home with Darrya and Kipp to guide them, but they all stood firm. Finally, I sighed in frustration and led them to the armory, at least convincing Cas and Wren to stay there. Cas insisted he would wait until it was over to heal anyone who needed it.

Blaise's weapons were missing, and a flash of panic coursed through my veins. Rationally, I knew there was nowhere else he would be, but I still sent a silent prayer to the gods begging to keep him safe. My sword was untouched – likely due to its lighter and shorter stature; it was a poor choice for most of our soldiers. I seized it, turning to size Darrya up for a sword that fit her build. She caught my look and shook her head.

"Not my weapon of choice." Instead, she stalked over and pulled a full-sized bow and a quiver of arrows off the wall. I watched, openmouthed, as she located a leather arm guard and an archery finger tab, deftly pulling them on. She grinned as she noticed my stunned expression.

"I didn't realize you were trained with weapons," I said, surprised.

"When they told me that as a female, I didn't *need* to learn with weapons, it only served to inspire me more." Darrya explained with a wry smile, slinging the quiver over her back.

"She's underselling herself. She's the best markswoman I know," Finlay chimed in, the affection toward his cousin apparent in his voice. It made me smile, despite my dread at our current situation.

He grabbed a sword himself and sheathed it in one swift movement. Holding the door open, he looked both ways before turning back to us.

"Are you ready?" He asked, glancing down at Kipp, then up at us both. A flicker of concern danced in his expression, but he hadn't breathed a word about us staying behind. I wasn't sure if it was because he grew up with Darrya and knew a lost argument when he saw one, or if he had faith in us from watching our training. Either way, he seemed to think we could hold our own – or at least, understood that we would do what we could to protect whomever we could.

I nodded to him, but as we slipped out and approached the courtyard, the bell in the tower began chiming, indicating the danger that had befallen the palace. I gripped my sword with apprehension, knuckles turning white. I had never used it outside of my training with Blaise, so I had no idea where that put me in terms of skill.

Finlay seemed to sense it, leaning over to me as we paused at a corner.

"You're more than capable with that weapon, little angel. I've seen you disarm Blaise, and he's the best we've got. Trust yourself."

My eyes widened at the compliment, but before I could think of a reply, he had tucked his head around the corner, only to jerk it back with force. My breath caught and my heart raced as I saw shadows approach.

Palace workers I only knew by face barreled around the corner. Corryn was among them, and I caught her eye, but she was panicked past the point of recognizing me. Someone in their group choked out "Run!" as they flew past, and as quickly as they'd come, they left us to our own silence.

"I need a higher vantage point," Darrya finally breathed, motioning skyward. Finlay nodded, and we curled our way around the corner of the bell tower, heading for the stairs. Darrya let out a low hiss as she worked to open the first available window, surveying the view below us.

The courtyard swarmed with dark figures of various shapes and sizes. The sun had set, but even with the night sky, the space was unnaturally grim, covered in a murky haze. My heart thundered as I felt the ominous energy radiating from the courtyard.

The creatures varied from the grotesque Nuckelavee I'd encountered days earlier to Faeries that almost appeared normal. When I peered closer, however, there were sickening differences. Their magic looked tainted, summoning black weeds out of the earth or producing purple flames, distorting nature's order. My fear dissolved into anger as I witnessed helpless Faeries I'd seen around the palace, cornered and crying, or running for fast-dwindling exits.

"Come on," I said, tugging on Finlay with newfound vigor. "We need to get down to help them."

"Go," Darrya said, an arrow already notched. A ripple warped the air as she shielded the window, allowing her to loose her arrows on the monsters below, but none to return. Her expression changed to one of serious determination and, in the most fluid motion, she exhaled and loosed another arrow. An animalistic scream pealed from below, and as Darrya's mouth curled ever so slightly, I knew she'd hit her target.

"Kipp. Please stay here." I turned to him and watched as his ears flicked back. "Finlay and I will be fine. Darrya needs someone here to watch her back. She has to keep her eyes on us below."

I watched as it registered with him, but he emitted a soft whine regardless. I reached down and put a hand on his head, running his thick, coarse fur through my fingers. "I'll head straight for Blaise. He'll protect us from down there as well."

Kipp's ears flickered a few times, but he accepted and padded over to Darrya, placing himself by her feet. I straightened and met Finlay's eyes, surprised to see the same heated expression I'm sure was reflected in my own. He jerked his head, and we were back on the move.

We flew down the steps on silent feet, but as we rounded the corner leading to the courtyard, I was suddenly thrown back against the wall.

Before I could manage a cry of complaint, Finlay raised his finger to his lips, and I stilled. A long claw stretched from the other side of the bend, curling around the wall. Finlay didn't hesitate. Grabbing the thin, ashen arm attached, he yanked it forward while using his other hand to spin the sword, sliding it into the beast's chest in one rapid movement. It sputtered in surprise, a rattle emerging from its throat before it collapsed.

I exchanged a look with Finlay as we silently communicated to move forward. I didn't allow myself to look down and feel an ounce of sympathy for the slain beast as we stepped over it. This wasn't like the Love Talker we'd trapped and tortured, that had suffered a slow death by someone else's hand. These Faeries had made the choice to bring death and suffering here. And they would pay.

We rushed into the courtyard with furious purpose, and I willed myself to slow my breathing, practicing everything I could muster from my training to propel me forward. The first Faerie I made contact with was an easy target, facing a soldier I didn't recognize from Blaise's army. I rammed my sword through its back, following it to the ground before stepping on its body and yanking the weapon back out.

I didn't dwell on how easy it was — how I had already compartmentalized this death as something else. I surrendered to the only emotions I left room for: preservation, rage, and vengeance.

Every move and kill thereafter became easier and I stopped only briefly as I searched for my friends, ensuring they still held their own.

Arrows hit their mark with seamless precision, telling me Darrya still held her position above without fail. Finlay's fire, blazing crimson and orange against the abnormal purple flames of the dark Fae, told me he remained upright and fighting as well.

I paused in fascination, watching Larke and Soren as a unit, back-to-back. Larke swung his sword and beheaded a winged dark Faerie with ease, while in the same movement kicking another that approached. The kick sent the beast back into Soren, who waited with his sword to drive it through the creature, as if they had done this a million times before. Their unhinged smirks told me how little they minded shedding this blood.

Blaise was more difficult to spot. He moved like a silent shadow, and his bloodied face bore an expression of grim determination. He didn't like this, not in the same way that Larke and Soren did. He would kill without hesitation, but I knew that after tonight, he would be devastated if even a single life on our side was lost.

To my surprise, he worked without even drawing the broadsword from his side. Instead, his fighting was much more physical, leveraging mostly his fists and a curved dagger. The Faeries had noticed his skill and clearly pegged him as their top threat, jumping on him in groups of two or three. This didn't deter Blaise in the slightest.

His fighting was a beautiful, lethal dance as he took them on. He'd hold a dagger to one while throwing an elbow at another, or flash a fist out to smash the neck of a beast, scoring a perfect hit to send it collapsing to the ground. Even those with magic weren't fast enough for him as he grabbed their arms, twisting before any magic was summoned, then plunging the dagger into their throats.

A scream tore my eyes from Blaise's fighting, and I started forward as I saw someone being dragged from the courtyard on their back. The creature hauled them by their tunic with a long talon. A Nuckelavee.

I hesitated, cursing at the sight of the creature this close. For a moment, I wondered if I should call out for Gray and allow the illusion we'd held onto for so long to be shattered in the face of this bloodshed. Before I could make the call, however, the sound of large wings erupted from above, and I glanced up to see several brown wingspans covering the air.

The Valkyries had arrived.

Ensley herself landed in front of the Nuckelavee, and I watched as the creature dropped the soldier it had been dragging, who crawled frantically out of the way. Tucking her wings in close, she drew her sword and, even from a distance, I could see that her fighting stance was immaculate. The Nuckelavee lowered its horselike head, monstrous muscles rippling as it pawed the earth, preparing to charge.

I narrowed my eyes and strode forward, stretching out my hand in a final decision. I would not fear this creature anymore. I would prove that my magic could help defeat it. I needed this for myself.

Before it began charging toward Ensley, earth magic shot from my palms, and I wrapped the creature's head within the confines of a halter. I yanked down, bringing its head crashing to the earth.

The sudden restraint, paired with its attempt to charge, caused the torso on the Nuckelavee's back to lurch forward. Ensley didn't hesitate, driving her blade into its chest before those long arms could so much as lift in retaliation. In the same movement, she pulled the sword back and beheaded the creature entirely while it remained confined.

I released a breath — it was well and truly dead. I met Ensley's eyes as she gave me an approving look before spinning to face the courtyard. The arrival of the Valkyries had noticeably changed the tune of the battle, and dark Faeries had already begun to flee, either taking off in flight or charging back out of the courtyard.

In an unspoken agreement, we all remained to pick off those we could catch, and by the end, I was shaking with fatigue. I glanced down at my sword, now positively dripping with black blood, and only then did I allow my emotions to swell. The shaking turned more violent, and I dropped my sword entirely.

A figure appeared behind me, and I turned to see Blaise standing there, face heavily smeared with black blood.

"You shouldn't have been here," he said darkly, and my face contorted in disdain at his words. I was about to reply when he cut me off.

"You shouldn't have been here, but I am so glad you were." He gathered me in an embrace and I collapsed into it, allowing my trembling to be absorbed by his solid figure. Despite the carnage surrounding us, everything seemed to disappear for a few fleeting moments as I took any scraps of strength I could from him, physical and otherwise.

"You were incredible out there. Truly," he muttered into my hair. "I was so worried when I saw you. Afraid I would need to break off and drag you back to your room in a bid to protect you. But you held your own."

I choked out a laugh. "Somebody trained me well." Then a thought struck me, and I disentangled myself from him reluctantly. "Why didn't you fight with your sword?"

I watched a muscle in his jaw jump, and realized it was a sore subject. I was about to take the question back when he replied.

"Larke and Soren, and most of my other soldiers, grew up learning how to use a broadsword before any other weapon. It's the way it's supposed to be taught." He hesitated for a moment, considering his next words.

"I grew up...very poor. My family and I had nothing. For many years, my weapons only included my fists, then finally a dagger, when I could afford it. You become very good at using the resources you have, when winning a fight with them means the difference of having dinner that night."

I opened and shut my mouth, unsure of how to respond. Instead of words, I opted to simply touch his cheek, ignoring the blood — the sign of our hard-fought win tonight. I stroked his cheek with my thumb, and he leaned into it for a moment before pulling away.

"Go find your friends and clean up. Get a good night's rest. We will deal with this." His order was gentle as he turned away.

Glancing over my shoulder, I glimpsed Cas, already out of the armory and helping tend to the wounded. The warm glow of his palms was a bright beacon as he poised them above a soldier's particularly ghastly chest wound. He wore an unnervingly somber expression and as I watched, he bit his lip in frustration, his healing magic sputtering slightly. I moved to aid him, thinking back to our power-sharing, but hesitated for a brief moment.

"Blaise?" I called, looking back. He turned. "Come find me tonight?"

It was a hopeful request, one I would understand if he couldn't fulfill, given what had happened. But he simply smiled and nodded.

"Always, sunshine."

Chapter 33

The knock on my door the next morning was tentative, but my sleep had been relatively fitful, so I was up in seconds. Wrapping a blanket around myself, I strode across the room and cracked the door open.

Finlay stood on the other side, shuffling nervously. Had it not been for what transpired the other night, I probably would have laughed at him standing there, looking like he was about to pick me up for the high school prom. However, I knew his normal cocky demeanor, and even last night hadn't rattled him to this point of nervousness.

I pulled the door open wider, standing straight. "What's wrong?"

Finlay looked up from the ground, but his eyes snagged on something behind me, and he stiffened. I knew without looking that it was Blaise, and I heard as he rose off the bed behind me. My chin lifted as I watched Finlay, daring him to shame me, and then I turned the same gaze back to Blaise as he approached, shirtless, in a silent warning to play nice.

Blaise's gaze flicked away from mine as he came to a halt next to me in the doorway, and I wasn't sure if the message had been received.

"Finlay," he said, in a nonchalant manner, looking him up and down. I held my breath. Then, he outstretched his hand.

"I can't thank you enough for your help last night. I'm sure it went against your royal orders, but it made a huge difference. I'm in your debt."

Finlay blinked in surprise, but took his hand and shook it.

"Against royal orders?" I blurted, glancing between the two of them.

"As the next in line for the throne, I'm under strict orders to keep myself out of harm's way. I should have been with my great-grand-mother and her special guard last night. Essentially, I'm to stay pro-tected at all costs." Finlay murmured, eyes downcast. I couldn't help but snort.

"Well, if that's the case, we both royally fucked up last night." I teased. When I received a stern look from Blaise, I added, "Oh, you both know my story. Don't worry, Finlay would be thrilled if I took his place."

I wasn't entirely sure that was true, but it seemed like the right thing to say to lighten the mood. Finlay's tentative grin confirmed my suspicions.

"Well then, I guess we're lucky you both remained unharmed last night." Blaise grumbled. I analyzed the taut expression he now wore, and pondered whether it was the way I bantered with Finlay that made him uncomfortable, or the fact that I'd trusted the prince enough to share such private information.

"I can think of no better way to help our people than to do what's in my power to protect them," Finlay replied easily. "Even if it results in my injury or death."

Blaise gave him a long, assessing look, and then hummed in approval. As he turned back into my room to get dressed, I fixed Finlay with a small smile.

"So, why are you here?" I asked, and watched as his face darkened.

"I spoke with my great-grandmother this morning. Aside from the tongue-lashing for my participation last night, she also requested that you come and see her today."

He let the words sink in. His great-grandmother, the queen, had specifically requested me. I clutched my arm, a sense of dread spreading in the pit of my stomach.

"Do you – do you think she knows that I have something to do with last night's attack?" I whispered, and Finlay shrugged, rubbing the back of his neck.

"If she did, she didn't let on," he replied, but the words held little comfort. Blaise reappeared beside me, fully dressed.

"When does the queen want to see her?" He asked, evidently having overheard our conversation.

Finlay fixed me with an apologetic look. "As soon as you're dressed. I'm to escort you."

I bit my lip but nodded. "Okay."

I turned to Blaise, giving him a soft kiss and sending him on his way. As I closed the door on Finlay to change, there was a swirl of emotions in his eyes, but he said nothing.

I chose to wear the same dress I donned the first time I met the queen, all those months ago. Brushing my hair, I examined myself. I wasn't much older, but I had tanned from my time training in the courtyard and gained considerable muscle, too. Most importantly, I noticed the increase in my confidence. I'd found my place here – my family. And last night, I discovered I would fight to the ends of the earth to protect that. I could only pray that it wasn't about to be ripped away from me.

I sighed as I rose and opened the door once more. Finlay surveyed me and nodded.

"Perfect," he said, and extended a hand. I took it, admiring the warmth and the perfect balance of calloused and soft.

My heart and head both raced as we walked. Would the queen kill me? No, unlikely. I hadn't heard any stories of her cruelty. Surely, she would just banish me back to the human realm and forbid me from returning. Perhaps the others could visit – perhaps I could even convince Kipp to return with me – but how could I take him from the others, now that they had become so close again?

I swallowed, turning to Finlay as we approached the final staircase before the queen's throne room. "Finlay, if I'm not allowed back here, can you give the others a message for me?"

He fixed his gaze on me, those pale blue eyes gleaming with intensity. "No."

"No?" I echoed.

"No," he returned coolly. "Because I won't allow it to happen."

"Finlay, you can't –" I started, but he cut me off, taking my other hand in his and facing me completely.

"I can, and I will. I won't allow you to take the fall for this. I will explain it all and explain my own involvement. I'll renounce my claim, if need be, if it will spare you." He spoke with a fierceness that left me slightly breathless.

"Why?" I shook my head, confused. He moved one hand to slide around my waist, the other brushing a piece of hair away from my face and resting on my cheek.

"Because this world needs you much more than it needs me, little angel," he murmured, his thumb tracing my lips for the briefest of moments. My breath hitched, and his eyes narrowed at the sound, both hands dropping to my waist and pulling me closer.

I allowed his body to mold into mine, and each point where our bodies made contact swelled with heat. I squeezed my eyes shut and took a deep breath, drinking in his smoky vanilla scent. I wondered if I could stay in this moment forever instead of facing the unpleasantries that were sure to follow.

After a long moment, I opened my eyes and looked up at Finlay. The expression he wore was pained, almost as if he'd heard my thoughts. He glanced up the staircase, then back at me.

"Come on," he said softly, "Let's see what awaits us."

Finlay dropped my hand moments before we entered the room, giving me one last reassuring look, and strode ahead as the doors opened. He took a position behind the queen and her throne, hands behind his back and gaze forward, but slightly downturned. He and Darrya had a similar professional, near-emotionless expression when it came to their royal masks. I wondered if they'd trained together in front of a mirror.

"Katherine." The queen rose from her throne. Her hound sat up from where it was laying dutifully by her side, eyes bright and alert. I dropped awkwardly into a curtsey, praying that it sufficed. As I raised my eyes, I noticed her expression: calculating and unreadable. My body went cold in anticipation.

"You have been holding onto a very large secret," she continued flatly. I risked a glance at Finlay. His face remained emotionless, but I noted the slight drain of color. Returning my gaze to the queen, I opened and closed my mouth, but no words found their way out.

When I didn't respond, she motioned to the large doors behind her. Two guards nodded simultaneously and opened it. As soon as they did, a man burst through. He was tall with dark, unruly hair in desperate need of a trim. He appeared thin and disheveled, and part of me wondered how he was allowed in this court looking like that.

As the man's gaze focused on me, however, I inhaled sharply. Finlay took a step forward in alarm, but my eyes were only for the man that approached.

His eyes had tormented my dreams for years, had graced photos that I had looked at, time and time again, until the edges were tufted and worn and white crinkles betrayed where I had folded them so I could carry them with me, always. Amber eyes that matched my very own.

"Dad?" I breathed incredulously.

Chapter 34

I stared into my father's eyes, so much like my own, bearing the same stunned expression. The entire throne room had narrowed into just the two of us, and suddenly, everything felt surreal. My mind struggled to keep up, continuing to dispel reality as fallacy.

"Katie, baby, is it really you?" He breathed, extending his palms to me. All I could do was nod, dumbfounded, and that single movement had him rushing forward and crushing me in an embrace. I was surprised to find that his arms felt exactly how I remembered, despite it being over a decade since I'd last felt them.

"I take it this is news to you as well, child." The unwaveringly calm voice of the queen rang out, and I lifted my head to examine her face. It displayed only the faintest sign of surprise. Clearly, my father wasn't someone she knew or expected to see, either.

"I —" My voice caught, and I cleared my throat, trying to collect the thoughts and emotions shattered to pieces at the sight of my father. "Yes," I replied finally. "As far as I knew, he died when I was ten."

My father moved to my side, grasping my hand as if he would never let it go again. This allowed me to see Finlay once more, whose impassive expression had broken, his pale eyes now wide and moving between my father and me.

"Your Majesty," my dad said, bowing. "I cannot express enough thanks for your willingness to unite me with my daughter once more. I would be happy to provide you with any answers you seek. I'm sure your questions are plentiful."

"Indeed," she murmured, and her pale blue eyes — startlingly similar to Finlay's, I realized — flicked to me for a moment. "I imagine they are quite similar to the questions your daughter now has."

He nodded, then smiled down at me. I merely stared back, drinking in his features. He looked haggard, and his expression betrayed his weariness, but he appeared no older than the last time I had seen him. I, on the other hand, had lived more than half of my existence now without him, and had fully grown into an adult.

"It is true," he began, facing the queen once more. "I was living in the human realm, with a human wife, attempting to live as normally as possible. I'd made it ages without discovery. But somehow, about ten years ago, Nemain and her folk caught wind of my existence, and I was forced to make a decision."

I shuffled back a step at hearing her name from his mouth, and stifled a gasp of surprise. *Nemain? She'd been hunting my own father?* He glanced my way, expression regretful as he continued.

"I needed them to think they'd simply found a human man, especially now that I had a family. The stakes were too high. I used my water magic and an enchantment to ensure I looked well and tru-ly...gone." He lowered his head in shame, but the queen just nodded. I peered at her closely, noting her lack of curiosity. I wondered what she knew about Nemain.

"It seems it worked well, until your daughter found herself mixed up in our world." Her eyes flashed as she mentioned me, and the blood drained from my face. I knew without asking that she had tied me to last night's attack — and worst of all, she was right.

Blaise had lost a few members of his army, and there had been civilians in the palace who had lost their lives too. That blood was directly on my hands. Blaise's presence was the only thing that en-abled me to sleep last night at all, even if it had still been fitful.

"I wasn't sure how much ability she'd possess, if any at all. I'd hoped her life in the human realm would be completely normal," my dad admitted. I shifted uncomfortably, the room suddenly feeling unbearably hot. After his passing, growing up in the human realm had been anything but that.

"You thought a life without her father would be *normal?*" The question was posed by Finlay, laced with venom. His jaw was set, and his eyes narrowed as he stared down the bridge of his nose at my father. I felt the judgment radiating off him. We'd discussed how it felt without our parents — the pieces that left us feeling less than whole. As I caught his gaze, I knew he was thinking of that, too.

"Finlay," the queen said sharply, reminding him of his place. He shifted and lowered his gaze, but I watched a muscle in his neck twitch, as if he had to physically swallow his remaining displeasure. I wondered absently if part of the heat in the room came from him.

"I couldn't think of a better alternative to keep them both safe," my dad replied quietly.

"So...she *is* my mom?" I ventured. Hope flickered in my heart like a barely lit match. My dad nodded emphatically as he turned to me, brushing my hair behind my ear in a gesture he used to do almost daily. I shivered slightly at the flood of emotions that followed — familiarity and love, but also, in a deeper, more sinister part of my soul, confusion and betrayal.

"Yes, she is. And she loves you so, so much. Genetic bloodlines can be strange, but I would bet my bottom dollar that you're as powerful as you are because of my grandfather," he said seriously, and glanced back at the queen. She leaned forward intently, eyes shining, a clear indication that she would be privy to whatever he said next.

Of course. Her bloodline was as pure and powerful as they come, designed by centuries of royal matchmaking. For me — a half-breed, a *Faeling,* I now realized — to be at my power level, was a curious thing indeed.

"Who?" I asked, my heart beating faster. Finally, I was about to understand everything. "Who is my great grandfather?"

"Cú Chulainn," he replied in a low tone.

"And I know," he continued, this time addressing the queen, who for the first time, wore an expression of genuine surprise. "His only known son was killed. But he had others. Three others, in fact. Nemain never forgot how Cú Chulainn spurned her as the Morrígan, and she vowed to destroy every drop of his bloodline. No matter how well he concealed them."

"Two were hunted and killed by Nemain as they tried to escape. My father was the only one able to fully disappear. He waited centuries before he felt safe enough to venture out, find love, and have me. He taught me to do the same. But she found him eventually, and me as well. She will never quit hunting."

"And she's finally making her move again." I cut in as realization dawned on me. Nemain was a goddess scorned. She'd hunted my grandfather and his children. Now, she was searching for me, just as I was searching for her. Last night's battle was just the beginning.

My dad gave me a questioning look, and I asked, "Were you not here last night?"

He shook his head. "I arrived this morning. I only knew that you were here when I felt the call from the Speaking Stone." At my bewildered look, he added, "I knew it was you. Blood calls to blood. That's when I started looking for you."

"My apologies, but I've heard quite enough," the queen interrupted, her voice adopting a cold edge that I'd never heard before. She rose from her throne and glanced between the two of us. The hound looked sharply at her, ears swiveling curiously, as if this callousness was a new experience for it as well.

"I am, of course, glad to have a family reunited. The gods know we need more of that every day." She stole a glance at Finlay, who purposefully fixed his gaze on the floor, remaining impassive. Despite her abrasiveness, I realized, she did have a soft spot reserved for her great-grandson.

"That being said, Nemain has already made enemies of the royal family. We cannot risk adding fuel to that fire by harboring two more from another bloodline that she desires to kill. You may stay in Muiranvia, but under no circumstances may you continue to stay here. I trust you understand."

My father nodded and made to bow, but was cut off by a simple word.

"No."

We all started, looking toward Finlay, who had risen to face his great-grandmother. The queen. She blinked in response, and I wondered for a moment if she'd had this many surprises in the past century, let alone in the past hour.

"I beg your pardon?" She inquired, clutching the side of her throne, though if it was to steady herself or to quell her anger, I wasn't sure. The room seemed to rise in temperature, and I shrunk back a step. A show of fire power between the two emotional royals was not something I wanted to experience.

"No." Finlay's response was firm. "If Nemain is after the royal family and after Katherine's, we share a common enemy. I don't see the sense in separating us and making us weaker. We should be standing together."

He straightened, and for a moment, I saw the confident, diplomatic prince he was intended to be.

"Pushing us into defensive positions and into hiding is exactly what she wants. It's allowed her to pick us off, one by one, over the centuries. Katherine has experienced more than one instance being here which indicates she is the key to winning this, once and for all. We will only make it more difficult for her to fulfill that fate if we ostracize her instead."

At this point, he came down to where I stood and placed himself beside me, so that I was placed between him and my father. We shared a look for a moment, and then his eyes returned to the queen.

"I say they stay, and that they fight. I say *we* fight."

The queen scoffed. "We do not fight, Finlay dear. We rule. There is an order to these things."

"They can be one and the same. How can we expect our people to respect our rule if we do not fight alongside them for peace?" He retorted.

I stayed silent, finding it wiser to allow this argument to remain within the family. I knew it revolved at least partially around me, but I also realized it ran deeper than the immediate issue. I recalled both Finlay and Darrya's extensive suppressed activities list. This was perhaps a long overdue conversation between the two Fae.

The queen didn't sit back down, but rapped her fingers on the throne thoughtfully for several long moments. Finlay's attention remained glued on his great-grandmother, and I glanced nervously between the two. The only sound came from my father, who shifted on his feet uncomfortably as we awaited her response. Finally, she sighed.

"I suppose if we do nothing to end the fight, the fight is bound to someday end us. You two may stay and prepare to strike against Nemain. Do *not* —" her voice rose with emphasis, resounding loud and clear, "—mistake this as my blessing. But...I will not stand in your way."

We sagged in relief, and I shared a grateful look with Finlay. He beamed back at me with pride, and we turned to face the queen as she moved to make her exit, all bowing respectfully. The queen paused one last time as she exited, fixing Finlay with a final look. I glimpsed a note of sadness pass over in her eyes.

"Be safe, Finlay dear," she said, then vanished through the doors.

Chapter 35

I was overcome with a strange sense of shyness as Finlay and I walked away with my father. We all basked in the heavy silence, which lasted several long minutes as we approached the courtyard.

"I'll have Corryn make sure there is an extra room prepared." Finlay eventually spoke, though his voice was once again flat, as it had been when he had addressed my father earlier. My dad bowed his head respectfully.

"Thank you. For that, and for advocating for my family as well. I cannot thank you enough." He spoke earnestly, placing a firm hand on my shoulder. Finlay's eyes followed the movement as he came to a halt. He pulled a cigarette from his pocket, lighting it with his fingers and inhaling leisurely.

"I didn't do it for you. I did it for her." He gestured to me, and I felt my cheeks redden. "You have an amazing daughter. It's a shame you weren't there to see her grow into who she is now."

It was my dad's turn to flush, though if it was from shame or anger, I wasn't entirely sure. Before he could respond, however,

Finlay turned on his heel and strode away dismissively into a cloud of smoke, playing true to his part as the prince of fire.

"He's quite a piece of work," my dad commented.

I gritted my teeth and, without looking at him, replied with more than a little bite to my tone, "He lost both of his parents when he was young. He knows for certain his aren't coming back. But I imagine they'd do everything they could to find him, if they had been able to."

My dad went quiet, absorbing the information and the obvious message laced within.

Why did you never come to find me?

It was dangerous territory for us to head into, though, and I wasn't sure I was emotionally ready to address it just yet.

"Come on," I said instead, changing the subject as I spotted Kipp's cinnamon-colored hair in the distance. "I'd like you to come meet my friends."

I had always been grateful for the upbeat personalities of my friends, but never more so than now. They descended on my father, their animated questions and stories saving me from offering up too much myself. Those were emotional conversations I wasn't ready to broach, but I was happy to sit back and experience it all from the sidelines.

My father had followed his father's footsteps and moved in and out of different lands, laying low and hoping never to attract much attention. He'd worked menial jobs, never quite allowing the full force of his powers to show or develop. Eventually, he decided the safest place to escape was into the human realm, where he fell in love with my mother.

"So, Patrick, is your signature element fire? Since Cú Chulainn's dad was Lugh, and Lugh was considered a sun god?" Kipp asked, to which my father shook his head. I felt a tinge of relief blossom in my chest, and then dug deep, trying to summon the fire that evaded me. Turning my hand over, I watched a brief spark play across my palm, only to disappear a moment later. I clenched my jaw in frustration and returned my focus to my dad, who continued with his story.

"He was a master of many talents, but most prominently, he's known for blessing the harvests — hence our festival in his name. My signature element is earth."

He flicked his hand, and an impressive field of strawberries blossomed outside in Cas's yard. Wren squealed excitedly, scrambling from her seat to go and pick them. Darrya followed, exclaiming over her shoulder about how she'd known earth would be my signature element.

I tried to mirror the grin she wore, but the smile didn't fully form. I felt emotionally drained and unsure of how I *should* feel, much less how I *actually* felt. Cas made a sound in the back of his throat, causing me to glance his way. He analyzed my face carefully for a moment, and then stood abruptly.

"If you don't mind, I'll join you both on your way back to the palace," he said cordially. "I'd like to make sure everyone who was injured last night is taken care of."

This time my smile was real and one of relief. He'd taken care of everyone he could the day prior and the palace had their own healer, so I knew it was only for my benefit — sparing me the alone time I wasn't ready for with my father. Cas gave me the subtlest of winks and returned my grin.

Kipp joined us as we began the walk back to the palace, but remained in his Fae form, clearly looking to be a part of the conversation as well. His eyes kept wandering to Cas, as if waiting to take his cues from the Pixie, unsure of what to do or say next. The air held a slight chill, but as the agonizing silence stretched on, my accompanying shiver had nothing to do with the weather.

"That reminds me," my dad murmured finally, wringing his hands as we walked. "You said something about Nemain making her move with this battle. What did you mean?"

I took a moment to think about how to explain all that had happened in as few words as possible. "Blaise and I visited a Valkyrie to learn more about my heritage. She said I was blocked," I started carefully.

My dad nodded. "That's true. I had a Valkyrie friend who owed me a favor. I had to make sure no one inadvertently discovered who you were, in case it got back to Nemain." He looked between Kipp and Cas curiously, mentally tallying the names he'd learned tonight. "Who is Blaise?"

I swallowed. Who was Blaise to me? We had never discussed our relationship perimeters; rather, we'd simply...been. I wondered what Blaise would say, if I asked him. Would he want more? Did I? I figured my answer would depend on his.

"A friend." I said eventually, and cleared my throat. Cas tucked his head, trying — and failing — to hide a smirk. I tried my best to shoot him a seething glare.

"But the main thing," I pressed on before my father could comment. "is that she told us war was coming, and it was already inevitable. I went looking for answers and discovered Nemain is trying to raise her three sisters, which will give her unparalleled power."

My dad nodded as understanding blossomed in his eyes. "Macha and Badb."

"Do you think it's possible? Could she really resurrect them?" Cas inquired, expression painted with apprehension.

"Unfortunately, yes," my dad admitted. "I have reason to believe many of her attacks over the years have been tests for necromancy. But just as she's been working for centuries to gain that power, I've been working to gain enough to defeat her."

"The four talismans," I blurted, realization dawning on me. Of course — he'd known and felt the Speaking Stone. My father dipped his head in affirmation.

"Do you have any leads?" I asked, feeling the sense of ambition rekindle in me for the first time since last night's battle. My father glanced around carefully before answering.

"Yes," he said, so low I could barely hear him. "I was incredibly close to locating the cauldron when I felt your call from the Speaking Stone."

Excitement coursed through my veins, and I couldn't help but clap my hands together, startling our group and scattering a few birds from nearby trees. I practically skipped the next few steps as we approached the palace, and fixed my gaze on Kipp and Castille.

"What do you say? Are you both in on this?" I asked, and they both grinned, white teeth gleaming against the moon's reflection.

"Always, Katie-cat." Cas responded. "But we'll need to wait a few days. We have to regroup and make a real plan."

I made a small noise of complaint, suddenly impatient. Every day wasted was another day gifted to Nemain to continue her own hunt.

"Not to mention, we should be here for the Last Honors Ceremony," Kipp reminded me gently, resting a hand on my shoulder. I bit my lip as I considered his words, accepting the truth in them.

The Last Honors Ceremony was a remembrance ceremony to honor those who had fallen in battle. Though the battle last night had not been as large or as bloody as we feared, we'd still lost nine people — two Fae that had worked at the palace, one distant relative of the queen, and six from Blaise's army.

It was enough to warrant a large local ceremony, and all were invited to pay their respects. Seeing as I was pretty much the main cause of it, I was torn between my duty to pay tribute to the fallen, and my desire to disappear altogether. My only solace was the fact we had managed to kill more than three times as many dark Fae before they retreated.

Finally, I faced Kipp. "You're right. We'll stay and go to the ceremony tomorrow. But then," I added, turning to Cas and my father, "we prep for the next talisman. We *cannot* let Nemain win."

Chapter 36

The ceremony was a grander affair than I anticipated. It seemed nearly everyone had come to the palace from town and, though the place was spacious, I wasn't entirely sure where everyone would go as I watched more families flow through the gates. The flowers — white lilies that covered nearly every surface not meant for seating — were a stunning contrast to the dark, muted colors worn by every grieving Fae.

Absentmindedly, I peered down at my own black dress, simple but elegant with its lacey keyhole back, and toyed with my hair. Every mirror in the palace had been veiled for the funeral, so I wasn't able to check my own appearance. Darrya explained this was an important part of the ceremony; it allowed the souls safe passage to Annwn, the Otherworld, so I dared not touch the sheets over any mirror.

The thought of the Otherworld made my skin itch, as I knew the part it played in our next stop after the cauldron — a deep dive into the hell where souls of dark Faeries went after death. My eyes wandered to the intricate, floral-covered wooden coffins that held the poor souls we lost in the battle, and I wondered briefly if they were going to Annwn's version of heaven or hell.

Footsteps approached behind me, and I turned to see Blaise, looking every bit the commander-in-chief that he was. Standing tall and regal, his dark hair was perfectly swept to one side, with not a strand out of place. He wore the same fighting leathers and golden, embellished buckle he'd donned for the festival of Lugh earlier this summer, highlighting his status in the army.

His hazel eyes were bright and alert, but I noted the slightest of shadows underneath. That and the tension in his jaw were the only indications of how personally he'd taken the events of the battle. Just as I had.

Tentatively, I reached my fingers out to touch his leather belt, tracing the band gently. He grabbed my hand and turned it over in his, brushing his lips against my knuckles. My heart fluttered at the soft touch of his mouth on my skin.

"You look beautiful, sunshine." There was a slight rasp to his voice, likely from barking countless orders during the battle.

"You don't look so bad yourself," I responded with a gentle smile. His bright eyes met mine, and he considered his next words carefully.

"I heard...about your father, I mean," he said softly. I blinked in surprise, and then squeezed his hand as I recovered.

"Yes, that. Um, I'll introduce you two later. I want you to be able to focus on this first," I said, hoping I sounded upbeat as I plastered a smile on to match.

I had avoided my father all morning and he hadn't sought me out either, which told me that he understood and respected that I needed some time. Instead, I spent all morning in the tub, trying to piece together the feelings and memories from my childhood with what I knew now.

I was still unable to reconcile the relief and joy of having one of my favorite people back in my life with the new, more acute sense of betrayal, knowing he'd purposefully left and withheld the truth of his life from me. The life that was now mine as well.

Blaise smiled, seeming to buy my act. "I'd really enjoy that," he said earnestly, and my heart squeezed at his eager face. I nodded, and he leaned in for a quick kiss before heading off, presumably to find Larke and Soren. As his second and third in command, I expected they would have a large part to play in today's events too.

I wandered, pushing my way through the murmuring crowd until I stumbled upon Darrya. She wore a beautiful black dress, with lace trailing up her collarbone and down her arms. She talked quietly with Finlay, twirling a strand of hair that fell from her blonde bun. They both turned to me, and Darrya immediately gathered me into a small hug. I smiled, now accustomed to her need for friendly touch, a stark contrast to my usual standoffish nature.

"I'm so happy you're able to stay," she whispered in my ear, squeezing me tighter. "I've never known Finlay to stand up to his great-grandmother. But I'm so glad he chose this moment to do it."

I smiled, and my eyes moved to Finlay, who was feigning interest in a floral arrangement nearby. He wore a black suit jacket, one of the most modern things I'd seen since coming here, and my eyes trailed down to the waistcoat tucked underneath his blazer. It was tailored to fit him perfectly and yet, both the bottom and top two buttons of his undershirt were undone, staying true to his devil-may-care attitude I'd come to know. Somehow, he had a way of making it look perfectly imperfect.

"Yes, well, she looked quite stressed about the whole ordeal," he commented airily, and faced us both with a lopsided smile. "Though, you know what the best fix for that really is?"

Darrya let me go, and we both gave him quizzical looks.

"An orgasm," he purred, and Darrya smacked him.

Before either of us could respond to his smart mouth, however, the music picked up to announce the queen's arrival. We stood at attention as she made her entrance, her dress tailored into a long curtain of black that mirrored everyone else. *An homage,* I thought, *to the fact that death unifies all classes and races of Fae.*

"We have gathered today to say farewell," she began, and all chatter dulled to silence. The queen's voice faded into the background as I watched Blaise move. Larke and Soren trailed like shadows after him and placed themselves in a line behind the coffins. They drew their swords, Blaise first, and then others followed. Lowering to their knees, they rested their foreheads on the hilts of their weapons. It was both a beautiful and ominous sight, and my breath caught, taking it all in.

It was eerie to see, after putting together the pieces I'd learned about Faerie life. We could live for centuries and, though our magic would fade and we would age, it would all happen slowly. And yet, despite our magical lifespans, our lives could still end so young, just as I'd anticipated for most of my life in the human world.

"...our first breaths are celebrated, and our last breaths are mourned. But rest assured — our love for them does not end with their lives. From the depths of our grief, our memories of these loved ones will surface. Until we meet again," the queen finished with authority.

"Until we meet again," the crowd responded in unison, an unearthly sound as the blessing chorused through the palace. As if the echo were a cue, servants appeared with trays and began moving throughout the crowd.

I peered at a passing tray, startled to see they contained small shot glasses of whiskey and tobacco packed in clay pipes. Before I could react, something pressed into my palm. I glanced up at Finlay, smirking down at me and gestured to my hand. Turning it over, I saw it was a pipe, which Finlay promptly lit with his fingers.

"It's tradition," he said, and winked. "Time for you to engage in some bad habits of your own, little angel."

My eyes traveled to Darrya for confirmation, and she returned my look with a wink of her own, lighting her pipe with a small burst of fire magic.

"It's customary. One last party to honor the deceased." She passed me a shot of whiskey and raised hers in a salute. Following suit, all three of us clinked our glasses and swallowed the liquid down. I crinkled my nose at the burn as they both took puffs from their pipes. I took a long, deep inhale from my own, holding the smoke for a lengthy moment before hearing Darrya hiss.

"Shit, girl, you're gonna feel that in a few minutes," she said, and my eyes widened in alarm.

"What is it?" I exclaimed, the smoke whooshing from between my lips. I felt no urge to cough, though, and the smell coming from it was surprisingly sweet, not at all tobacco-like.

"It's *voitín*. It's essentially — magical tobacco?" Darrya turned to Finlay for confirmation, and he nodded.

"Don't worry. You'll feel amazing for an hour or so. You can't overdose on it." He grinned and took another inhale of his. The music began again, though with a livelier tune. Darrya rolled her eyes and walked away, waving her hand in dismissal as she spotted our other friends across the room.

I made to move with her but was suddenly hit with a wave of lightheadedness that started at the top, and then rushed down my entire body. I blinked rapidly to clear it and, when it did, I was left open-mouthed as I took in the room.

Everything had a sparkling tinge, colors even more saturated than before, including shades I wasn't entirely sure there was a name for. The music began physically dancing in my ears and stayed in my head, as if the tunes settled there to play only for me. I shifted my feet, my body suddenly begging to dance as it felt featherlight.

I turned to look at Finlay, and my mouth dried as he grinned back at me, his white teeth gleaming and blue eyes piercing into my soul. My eyes dragged over the gold embroidery on his jacket and down to the form-fitting waistcoat, both of which followed the curves of his body. I wondered briefly if my mouth was still hanging open, and the thought made me giggle. Finlay's eyes crinkled at the corners as he chuckled at the sight of me, which made me laugh even harder.

"Alright, you lightweight, let's go dancing."

He extended a hand and I took it, flushing as warmth spread where our hands connected. I guessed he was purposefully shooting some warmth down his palm, as he had when we'd interrogated the Love Talker. He guided me to the dance floor and my eyes searched for Blaise, finding him preoccupied as he talked to families — likely those of the deceased.

The smile faded from my lips as I recalled the horrors from a few nights prior. Perhaps I should be providing condolences to these families too — though, I didn't have the faintest idea what I would say. I ran a hand through my hair in distress, frowning as I battled the physical urge to dance with the thoughts of how to speak to the families — to apologize for my involvement. My heart rate increased rapidly as the musings barraged my mind, too quick to keep up with.

Finlay made to pull me closer, but one look at my face had his expression turning from one of amusement to something remarkably serious.

"Come on," he murmured, interlacing his fingers with mine. "Let's get some fresh air."

I let him tug me from the room and we escaped outside, where he led me silently to the creek. The music slowly faded, replaced by the sounds of water spilling over stone. My eyes trained on the rushing creek, the sound of it calling to me more strongly than the previous music had. I kicked my shoes off and dipped my toes in.

It was cold, but I welcomed the shock, tipping my head back as I wiggled my toes and embraced the water that streamed over the tops of my feet. My eyes closed, and I sighed as every other sense felt instantly heightened — though I wasn't sure how much I could chalk up to my closed eyes or the high from the *voitín*. Emotions flooded through me as my thoughts continued racing.

"My mother hated water." I said suddenly. I felt the urge to voice my thoughts, as if that would release the burden of emotions that weighed on my shoulders. Finlay jerked slightly in surprise, clearly not expecting our conversation to head in this direction. The words continued to tumble off my tongue and I went with it, rambling on.

"She was the one who found my father after he drowned, and ever since, she's avoided the water. It's funny, though — I've always been drawn to it. I guess I thought someday, it would provide me with the answers I needed." I laughed softly. "I suppose my answers came from somewhere completely different, in the end."

Finlay didn't respond. When I finally rolled my head to face him and opened my eyes, he was watching me intently. His pale eyes simmered as they met my own.

"I don't agree with what he did, you know." The roughness of his voice startled me. "I don't blame you for avoiding him."

I looked away, unable to stand the intensity of his stare.

"I'm avoiding him because I don't know *how* to feel," I admitted. "Part of me knows I should just be happy that he's back. But the other part hates what he did to me and to my mom. He left us broken for a decade. I understand he was trying to save us, but that doesn't make it feel okay." I wrapped my hands around my body, allowing the vulnerability of my words to seep through me.

"Even villains are the heroes in their own eyes," Finlay said softly, and shifted to sit beside me. I felt the heat radiating off of him and, before I could think, I inched closer, resting my head on his shoulder. He stiffened somewhat, and I jerked back, alarmed.

"I'm sorry, I —" I started, but he shook his head, wrapping his arm around me and pulling me back against him.

"You just caught me off guard, that's all," he replied, his lopsided grin returning. "I never thought I'd see the day when you'd touch me and it wasn't to smack me for something I did."

"Well, the night is still young."

He snorted, but instead of pulling back, I snuggled in closer, enjoying the sensation of cold water at my feet mixing with the warm strength of Finlay against my side. After a slight hesitation, he rested his chin on my head in a move that felt surprisingly tender.

"He has a lead on another talisman," I said softly after a few long moments. Finlay shifted marginally, lifting his head off mine.

"Your father?" He inquired. I pulled back far enough to face him and nodded.

"He thinks he knows where the cauldron is. We're going to start planning the best way to retrieve it first thing tomorrow."

"Are you sure you trust him?" Finlay asked carefully. I pulled my feet from the water and crossed my legs, turning my body to face him directly as I considered his words. Finlay's hands lay softly at my side, eyes studying me intently as he awaited my answer.

"He may have left me," I started slowly, "but he's still my father. And I trust that he'll do whatever he can to get rid of Nemain. So, we have the same goal."

Finlay gripped my waist tighter, and my mind flitted back to how it felt when we power-shared. How it had turned me on, despite not fully understanding it. I remembered Cas's words about our souls, and how they had merged in that moment — a very different feeling than the friendly exchanges I shared with Cas.

My mouth went dry as I imagined how it would feel to physically be with Finlay, if our power-sharing had already been that intense. I pressed back into his warm touch, craving it in the moment. A low growl escaped him at my movement, and his hands shifted to splay across my back, touching the bare skin exposed by my dress. All the emotions that had been swirling chaotically in my head just minutes prior evaporated at his touch.

I arched my back closer to him, and he responded in turn, his fingertips tracing light circles on my skin. A hot, pleasant sensation flooded my veins, like my body was on fire in the most delicious way.

Despite the heat burning inside of me, I shivered as his fingers played their way softly across the open plane of my back and trailed down my spine. I pushed my chest closer and watched as his eyes fixed on the sight, the soft fabric of the dress doing nothing to hide the obvious peaked signs of my arousal. Finlay's jaw twitched, his gaze suddenly ravenous, and he tugged me into his lap in a swift movement.

"I'm coming with you tomorrow," he muttered through clenched teeth. "You may trust your father, but I want to be there. I need to be sure you're safe."

I put tentative hands on his chest as he spoke, curling my fingers around his blazer. He responded by running a hand up from my back to gently grasp my hair, and my head dipped back to give him full access to my neck.

"I can take care of myself, you know." I tried to speak with confidence, but the breathlessness with which I delivered the words didn't help my case. A low whimper slipped from my lips as Finlay trailed his nose down my throat, his fingers digging in tighter at my waist and the back of my neck, as if he was on the brink of losing control. I had to admit I was too, the wave of pleasure leaving me nearly lightheaded.

His mouth came back up to my ear, and he whispered, "I know you can, little angel. But that won't stop me from joining the fight to help you."

I let out a small, breathy laugh. "At this rate, we won't need Blaise's army. We'll just need our own little special operations unit."

At the mention of Blaise, Finlay's hands dropped like stones from my body. I felt an immediate chill, and my heart plummeted at the loss of his touch. He didn't remove me from his lap, but his pained expression had me scrambling back on my own.

"I'm sorry," he muttered, shoving his hand through his hair and sending those golden strands into immediate disarray. "I shouldn't have —"

"I wanted to," I insisted. I felt disoriented, but I was certain of that one thing. Finlay offered me a small smile, one that didn't quite reach his eyes.

"That's just the *voitín* talking. It would have felt incredible —" Finlay's voice cracked. "— but you would have regretted it later."

"You don't know that," I replied softly, though I blinked in confusion. Did I want him, or was I really that intoxicated? What about Blaise?

"Maybe. Maybe not." His hand reached for my face, and I leaned forward unconsciously, allowing his hand to brush my cheek lightly. "But if we do go there sometime, little angel, I want it to be different. Not like this."

What was that supposed to mean?

He straightened and brushed off his suit. "Let's get you to bed."

He beckoned, and after locating my shoes, I followed behind. Struggling to keep up with his large paces as I attempted to put them back on, I eventually gave up and jogged after him barefoot.

"What are you planning to do the rest of the night?" I asked, panting, as we approached the palace entrance. Finlay retrieved his flask from his jacket pocket and unscrewed it. He noted my frown with a light smirk.

"Ah, there she is again. Disapproving once more." He took a long swig and screwed the lid back on. "I'll probably keep doing this. Maybe wake up hungover in someone else's bed. The usual."

My mouth dropped open at his words, and I spun sharply to hide my disbelief. Why had I expected anything different, if even for a moment? Where did that reckless desire come from? Embarrassed and enraged, I stormed away, with him calling goodnight in my direction. I whipped around, flicking him off, and felt my anger hit new levels as he merely grinned in response.

A long bath was needed before I climbed into bed, and there I gave myself an internal assessment. I was surely no longer high. And yet, as I thought of Finlay's large, warm hands trailing over my body, I found myself desiring that with the same voracity as I had in the moment.

My hand moved over my lips as I envisioned what it would be like to kiss him, and I trailed the hand under my blanket as I kept the image in my mind. It stilled, however, as another scene came into my mind unbidden — Finlay, golden hair sweaty as he towered over another woman in her bed, with that ravenous, pale blue gaze fixated on her body. Lips on her neck instead of my own.

My hand shot back up and I snatched my blanket up to my nose, flopping over in frustration. I squeezed my eyes shut and willed myself to imagine nothing, until I finally fell into a fitful sleep.

Chapter 37

It was almost scary how well Blaise and my father got along. I'd passed along my father's information, and Blaise had insisted — as adamantly as Finlay had the night prior — that he would be a part of this.

I was currently sitting in my father's new room in the palace, alternating between waves of guilt over what had transpired last night with Finlay, and flashes of irritation at seeing how easily Blaise laughed with my father. He was incredibly handsome when he laughed — the lines of tension on his sharp face loosening, hazel eyes sparkling, and full lips quirking into a delightful grin. However, the way he so easily embraced my father without question scratched against that wound inside of me. A wound that still festered with the reminder of my father's abandonment.

"Should we include Larke and Soren in this?" I asked as we waited for the others to join. Blaise shook his head.

"I need Larke focused on getting the army ready for more situations like these. And Soren has only had eyes for Myriam as of late. I'm not sure I could get him to focus on much else."

I made a small grumble of disdain, remembering my only encounter with Myriam. She'd made her distaste for the human realm obvious. Despite presenting as a full Aes Sídhe, I could only imagine what she'd think of me now, knowing I was only half Fae.

Kipp, Castille, and Wren all appeared through the door. I arched my brows, surprised to see Wren, but she caught my eyes and set her lips in a determined line, raising her chin defiantly. I had to smile in admiration at that. In the time I'd known her, she'd gone from someone who was easily intimidated to an aspiring warrior, demanding to be a part of everything we faced.

I still had to admit, a little part of me was relieved to know that both she and Cas were more behind-the-scenes types with their help. It meant two less of my friends to worry about. Cas and I would both draw the line at allowing her into physical combat until she had real training — as we had during this last battle — but I loved the fire in her soul nonetheless.

Kipp never had any intention of leaving me to fight this battle alone, and while I loved and understood his reasons, I still recalled how easily he'd been tossed aside by the Nuckelavee when he last tried to protect me. I was still learning how to wield my power, but growing stronger every day. So, I'd be damned if I wouldn't work just as hard to protect him as he did me.

Darrya and Finlay were the last to arrive, and Blaise shot up from his seated position. "I didn't know you were a part of this," he said, eyeing Finlay.

"I knew you would be." Finlay replied lazily, raising a brow. His eyes were slightly glazed, indicating either fresh intoxication or lingering effects from the night prior. "And yet, I still showed up."

"The queen would have my head if she knew I allowed this," Blaise seethed, but Finlay only shrugged.

"Alright, you two." Darrya interjected, stepping between them. "As much as I'd love to take bets in this fight, that energy is misplaced. We have better things to focus on."

As they muttered and moved to find seating, I took the moment to study Finlay. I was hoping that seeing him this morning would dismiss the confusing images from last night, but my stomach still flipped at the sight of him, even as irritation flared alongside it. His eyes wandered to meet mine, as if he knew what I was thinking, and he offered me a half-cocked grin.

Cut it out. He spent the night with someone else. And you have your person.

I turned to grab Blaise's hand firmly. He sat down and dragged me into his lap, his hands moving possessively onto my waist. Finlay's eyes tracked the movement, but I pointedly disregarded him, snuggling further into Blaise's comforting embrace. My father wore a strange expression, but clearly decided not to voice whatever he was thinking.

"The cauldron of Dagda. It's what I've been attempting to locate this whole time. I even found the sunken city of Muirias, where it was meant to be," my father began.

"Meant to be?" Cas echoed, picking up on the phrase. My dad gave a wry smile.

"Exactly. Meant to be there, but it wasn't."

"So, someone stole it?" I put in, and he nodded, leaning forward.

"It's the Cauldron of Abundance. Legend has it that nobody can walk away from it unsatisfied, and some rumors suggest it can heal all wounds. Which means," he continued with a sigh, "that pretty much everyone has a reason to steal it, and the opportunities for where it could be are nearly endless."

"Hold on. I might know." Darrya spoke suddenly, her deep brown eyes glinting. We all leaned forward in anticipation. "You said it's Dagda's cauldron, right?"

At my father's nod, she continued. "Well, I've heard stories in passing from Dagda's familial bloodline about a treasure that was stolen. The whispers were that a monster stole it but lends it to those who complete three tasks for him."

We absorbed the information for several moments in silence.

"It makes sense," Finlay said slowly. "But Darrya...that's not much to go on. What monster? And where?"

"I'm not sure. I guess that's something you'll have to find out for us, cousin," she responded, giving his shoulder a flick.

"We'll all work on it. It's a great lead," Wren said emphatically, ever the optimist. We murmured our agreement and launched into logistics, discussing everyone's connections and who might be best informed.

Once everyone had a game plan, we stood and I gasped as Blaise spun me back toward him, catching me in a smoldering kiss. I stiffened, though only for a moment, before melting into it and enjoying the now-familiar shape of his firm lips against mine. He pulled me flush against him, and my body responded instantly, the warmth of desire pooling low in my stomach.

A low cough jolted me back to reality, and I pulled back to see my dad, his arms crossed and eyes narrowed.

"Just friends," he commented, his gaze assessing.

Anger flared inside me as Blaise jerked back as though he'd been burned. He muttered an apology to my father, but I stepped in front of him.

"What is it to you?" I asked, my voice rising angrily. Wren straightened, picking up on the tension and making an excuse to leave. She was quickly followed by Cas, Kipp, and Darrya and, after a fiery look from me, Finlay and Blaise too. I glowered at my father.

"You realize how old I am now, yes?" I ground out. Before my dad could answer, I continued, the words tumbling out with abandon.

"I'm not the child you last knew. I haven't been for a *very* long time. In fact, I probably haven't been that child since the day I saw what I thought was your dead body."

My words were laced with venom, meant to cut deep, and they hit their mark. I watched as he winced, but all I could think was, *good.*

"Have you even considered reaching back out to Mom? Do you know what she's been going through? Because believe it or not, I'm pretty sure I'm better off mentally than she is. No thanks to you."

I stalked toward the door, and my dad grabbed my arm as I passed by. I whirled, eyebrows raised, daring him to speak. His mouth opened and closed, but no words came out.

Dropping his hand from my arm, he finally ventured, "I know no number of apologies can make up for the time we lost. But I hope I can spend the rest of our time together making it up to you."

"You know what the worst part is?" I continued with my fists clenched, completely dismissing his apology. A part of me wanted to fall into his arms and let him be the father I needed once more but I pushed it away, replacing it with rage — needing to let him know what it was doing to me.

"It's how much I missed you. There was a piece of me that went missing with you, a hole you left that never went away. But you came back, and that hole hasn't filled in the way I thought it would. Now all that's there is anger. And disappointment." I spat the last word at him and shoved the door open. My dad made no move to follow, thankfully.

Once I closed the door, I ran straight into Blaise's sturdy frame. He peered down at me, those greenish-brown eyes brimming with concern. I folded into his arms without hesitation, selfishly taking all the comfort from them that I had wanted from my dad moments prior.

His arms wound solidly around me, and I breathed in the scent of him as I nestled closer, squeezing my eyes shut to will the tears away. Blaise was steadfast, honest, loyal. I could trust him in all the ways I couldn't trust my father.

"Do you want to get out of here, sunshine?" He murmured in my ear, and I felt his fingertips play softly with my hair. I nodded and took a deep, steadying breath.

"Absolutely," I responded, looking up at him. I knew my eyes were likely pink, betraying the tears I was fighting, but I attempted a smile regardless. "As long as it involves alcohol."

Blaise chuckled lightly. "I think that can be arranged."

Chapter 38

The bar in Sairas allowed me a much-needed moment to breathe. Blaise and I tucked ourselves in a corner with Soren and Larke, weaving and ducking to avoid the heavy crowd. The sound of glasses clinking played like the bar's personal soundtrack and magical energy buzzed as happily as the chatter. It lifted my mood considerably, just by proximity.

"So, I hear your father came back from the dead?" Soren asked, leaning forward as he munched on a piece of bread. Larke ran a hand over his face with a sigh, embarrassed at Soren's brazenness, and my eyes snapped over to Blaise.

"You told them?" I asked. His abashed shrug told me he absolutely did, though he knew I wouldn't approve.

"We all would have found out eventually," Soren asserted. With an irritated twinge, I had to admit he was right. "How do you feel about it?"

I paused, surprised at the level of gentle imploring in his tone.

"Pretty mad," I admitted honestly, and swigged a long gulp of cider as I considered what to say next. "I want to just go back to whatever relationship we had before, but I don't even know what that would mean. And now, I just keep thinking about what life would have been like if he hadn't been gone all this time."

Soren and Larke both made sounds of either sympathy or agreement, but Blaise was the one who spoke. "I think you should give him a chance."

I stiffened and shot him a piercing glare. "Why?" I demanded.

He returned my glare steadily with a fierce one of his own. It held no hostility; rather, it burned with emotion that simmered just beneath the surface.

"Your dad loved you enough to leave. My dad loved me too little to stay. There's a difference."

I blinked, caught off guard.

He had never spoken with me about his family or his past, other than what I'd gleaned from his friends and the brief conversation we'd had after the battle. I stayed silent, waiting to see if this was an opening to learn more. After a moment, Blaise carried on.

"Leyteras. That's where my family is from," he began haltingly, and glanced over at his friends. To my surprise, Soren was the one who leaned in to continue.

"It's the poorest land in Muiranvia," he added quietly. "Even so, Larke and I grew up in one of the better areas. Blaise grew up in one of the worst."

"Then how did you all meet?" I asked quizzically, my eyes drifting over the three men. Larke gave a small snort, grinning at them in turn.

"We all met in a local fighting ring. Soren and I had to take our combative natures to 'healthier outlets' than our local school." He made air quotes to emphasize the irony of his point. "And Blaise always kicked our asses."

"I needed to." Blaise cut in softly, and glanced at me with a sad smile. "My dad was never in the picture, so I became a good fighter. It was the only thing that won me money and food. Anything my mother and sister needed, really."

I took his hand and gave it a gentle squeeze. He looked me in the eye, and I took in his demeanor carefully. I glimpsed the pain, usually hidden deep within his guarded expression; now, his eyebrows were pinched and his shoulders sagged. I realized how much deeper his trauma went than mine, and how silly my vendetta against my father suddenly felt. How much different would Blaise's life have been, had his father cared?

I snuggled closer to him, resting my head on his shoulder. His arm wound around me instantaneously, and there was no trace of Finlay in my mind as I said the next words. "You're exactly the family I wish I'd had."

He squeezed tighter, giving my forehead a kiss. "Same to you, sunshine." Even though I knew he couldn't see it, I smiled against his shoulder, and as I scanned the crowd, I noticed two familiar faces.

"Cas! Kipp!" I waved, grateful for the natural break in conversation. They ambled over and I smirked at their completely opposite appearances. Cas's teal velvet jacket was a stark contrast to the plain dark leather jacket worn by Kipp. The Urisk had on a basic tan tunic underneath, whereas Cas wore nothing beneath his jacket except a thin gold chain necklace. They both grinned in greeting.

"Bold choice on the wardrobe, Cas," I observed, nodding at his bare chest. "I didn't realize this was your scene."

I repositioned myself as they took the chairs next to me, nestling closer to Kipp and his natural wolfish heat. He noted the move and offered me his jacket. The chill in the air had settled in, choosing to stay for the fall, and I still hadn't attempted to change out my summer wardrobe.

As he handed the jacket over, he exchanged a welcoming nod with Blaise. I was grateful to see that whatever animosity they'd held when we first met had resolved itself over the last few weeks. Working towards a common goal seemed to have that effect on us all.

"Cas is working on his first lead tonight," Kipp answered my question with a surprisingly strained smirk. "One of his...*acquaintances* has a habit of getting drunk and telling stories about monsters."

Cas turned mischievously towards me, flashing a wink. "It's his favorite activity. He loves any story about things that go bump in the night. It's a good thing I'm a sucker for his dark side."

"Funny. I used to consider all of *you* the scary stories told in the dark," I commented, earning chuckles from the entire table.

Soren perked up swiftly, his whole body standing to attention. "Myriam made it!" He exclaimed, sounding more cheerful than I think I'd ever heard him.

Larke laughed at his giddy demeanor, smacking his back.

"Come on, man. You go get your lady and I'll get the next round." He took everyone's orders and left for the bar. Cas's eyes followed his movements and I pinched his arm, causing him to yelp.

"Hands — and other body parts — off of that one," I reprimanded with a sly smile. "There's definitely something brewing between him and Darrya."

He settled back with an exaggerated sigh. "Fine. But only because those two need to get laid more than I do."

"How gallant." I grinned.

"Speaking of," he continued, turning his attention to Kipp. "How long has it been for you?"

Kipp shifted awkwardly, and Blaise pretended to be immensely interested in a coaster on the table, but Cas simply leaned back and crossed his arms, his expression expectant.

"Long enough," was Kipp's gruff reply, causing Cas to let out a startled laugh.

"Kipp! We need to find you someone. Perhaps someone of the...lupine persuasion?" His eyebrow cocked and he leaned forward, grin widening as he watched Kipp's hand swipe over his face uncomfortably.

"So, tell me..." Cas goaded in a low whisper. "Have you ever done it doggy style?"

At the choruses of disapproval from all of us, Cas lifted his hands and feigned innocence. "What? At some point, if you're not at least doing it *like* dogs, you're just doing it wrong."

Kipp turned positively crimson, and I laughed so hard I had to wipe tears from my eyes. My breath only returned to normal when Cas caught sight of his friend and excused himself.

As he walked away, he passed Soren, Larke, and Myriam, the former two carrying all the beverages while Myriam sauntered in front. Though it was a minor thing, my lips curled in distaste at her entitlement.

She sat down gracefully, perching with impeccable posture, and I watched as Kipp tilted his head and studied her curiously. She didn't even bother to spare him a glance; instead, her eyes trained directly on me.

"I heard your father is back," she said in a measured tone, and my skin prickled.

I took a long drink of my cider, smiling in thanks to Larke, then nodded in Myriam's direction as a response. Her pale gray eyes never left my face, and after a heartbeat, I chose to simply return the stare.

Kipp hadn't even blinked since her arrival, and my fist clenched in anger at his attention — not out of jealousy; rather, that her appearance alone could distract anyone enough from her awful personality. Blaise's hand skimmed over mine, a subtle reminder to relax.

Myriam let the long pause settle pointedly before she continued. "Intriguing. What bloodline?"

Panic shocked my veins, and I hoped the flush remained internal as I took a breath, responding with the first name that came to mind. "Dagda."

My eyes darted to Cas, still engaged in his conversation across the bar in his effort to hunt down the god's cauldron.

I could only hope it was a popular enough bloodline to be plausible, and high enough in rank that it satiated her curiosity. Aside from the obvious danger of my actual answer, I didn't want this woman to know any more about me than necessary.

She raised her eyebrows and leaned forward, resting her chin on her palm. Her fingers tapped against her cheek as she smiled. It was a lethal kind of smile, one that provided no comfort or joy.

"Really? I never would have guessed." Her voice was both bored and skeptical, and it urged me to continue.

"Um, yeah. So now I'm trying to learn as much about him as I can. I heard he had some sort of crazy mythical cauldron." *Slow down. Too much information is a sure indication of a lie.*

I closed my mouth, pressing my lips into a thin line, but Myriam's eyebrows only twitched before she continued, voice as monotone as ever.

"Yes. I've heard of that as well. He was also a chief of the Tuatha Dé Danann, which explains your power." Her smile broadened, and this time, I could almost believe it was intended solely to make me happy. The beauty of it was truly — and frustratingly — stunning. I glanced at Kipp to see if he still watched her, but he now studied his glass intently.

"Well, Katherine," Myriam continued, and my eyes flew back to her own. "If you ever feel like spending more time with us, I know a lot about Dagda, and the other powerful bloodlines, too. We could tell you anything you'd like to know. You'd be in good company."

I slipped my hand under the table to keep it from curling into a fist, grabbing Blaise's hand once more and squeezing hard. He choked on his drink.

A tempting offer. But I'd have to be on my last lead to even think about joining your biased Faerie power cult.

I tucked those thoughts away and curled my mouth into what felt like a grimace, but I hope presented as a grin. "Yeah. I'll definitely think about it."

Chapter 39

"She's insufferable!" I groaned as Kipp, Blaise, and I walked to Cas's house after saying goodbye to Larke, Soren, and Myriam. "Why does Soren put up with her?"

"Because she's hot," Blaise stated simply, and Kipp grunted in agreement. I gaped at both of them.

"Ugh. Men. You are so simple," I said, rolling my eyes and shoving Blaise good-naturedly. He grabbed me back, lifting me off my feet and causing me to squeal. A bird skittered off in the distance as my squeal dissolved into laughter.

"It is curious, though," Kipp ventured as we approached Cas's house. Blaise set me down, and we both looked at him. "Myriam," he continued. "She's an Aes Sídhe, right?"

I exchanged a glance with Blaise, who just shrugged and nodded. "The way she goes on about us, I assumed so, yes." I said to Kipp. "Not that I've ever attempted to read her magical signature. She gives me the creeps." Goosebumps flared on my arms as a breeze passed by, as if to prove my point. Kipp rubbed the back of his neck, brows furrowed in confusion.

"I could have sworn by her presence that she's an Urisk like me. She had the same type of energy around her." He flushed slightly as I choked out a laugh.

"I'm sorry, I just —" I stopped to suck in a breath, halting my laughter. "I genuinely think she would kill you if she heard you say that."

"You're probably right," he said, giving me a small smile. "So, this better not leave our circle."

We agreed, and as we burst through the door at Cas's, he jumped up instantly from the couch. The sly Pixie couldn't have beaten us to his home by more than a few minutes, but he'd already changed into a silken robe and had a glass of whiskey in his hands.

"A *beithir*," he said with an air of finality. "That has to be what it is." He slammed the glass of whiskey down on the table with emphasis.

He had clearly anticipated this moment and wanted to leverage it to the fullest. Kipp gave a slow clap, obligingly feeding Cas's ego, even as he laughed. I grinned at his dramatic flair as well, even as I looked to Wren for more information.

"They live in caves, which narrows it down...slightly," Wren said from her position on the couch, noting our startled expressions.

"But," Cas butted in, pointing at her and then us with triumphant flourish. "What narrows it down even further is the fact that all of the stories he told me about the beithir have taken place in Daersill."

"Shit." Kipp loosed a quick laugh. "So, the grand duke has been looking far and wide for the talismans, with one right under his nose?"

"In all fairness, you'd have to know exactly what you're looking for. His story in particular, well —" Cas took a sip, and shrugged abashedly. "Honestly, I may have lost track a bit in our conversation, but what I did glean was a story about a queen's son, who had an enchanted scarf that was really a beithir. There was a brief mention of a princess who gave the gift of a cauldron to that prince for their marriage."

Blaise nodded in understanding. "And just like that, two plus two equals four."

"Okay. So. What is a — beether?" I tried to pronounce it and tucked my head in embarrassment.

"A serpent," Wren replied with a tight smile. "An enormous, venomous reptile."

"Like a dragon?" I asked as panic flashed through me. I considered every story and movie I'd seen growing up that had fearsome, fire-breathing beasts. Blaise shook his head and shifted to my side.

"They don't have wings or breathe fire. They mostly travel by land and water." He took a moment, considering. "Though I suppose, everything else kind of makes it dragon-like. It's massive and scaly. Giant teeth, sharp wit. Loves treasure."

I nodded, my heart pounding. "Okay, okay. And are they...vicious?"

"They can be. But if this one follows the legend, I doubt it will be. They seem to get their kicks from games rather than savagery." Cas mused, swirling the brown liquid in his glass thoughtfully.

"And if not?" My voice held a slight shake.

"I cut its head off." Blaise said firmly, turning his smoldering, protective gaze to me. "We're getting you to that cauldron one way or another."

Two days later, the plan was set. I'd asked only Blaise to accompany me. Cas, Wren, and Darrya heeded my plea to stay put; however, I'd been unable to dissuade Kipp or my father from joining. They had spent the last two days together as three inseparable shadows, scouring over maps and crossing out any caves in Daersill that made no sense geographically.

They'd argued over bodies of water, cross-referencing stories of similar monsters until they'd finally narrowed it down to four possible areas. Blaise had been able to procure enough Faerie dust to transport us to all four, if need be, and ensured my father was outfitted with the proper weaponry. Kipp remained adamant that his shapeshifting abilities would suffice, much to my unease.

My dreams had been rife with uneasy iterations of everything my mind could construe as a monstrous serpent. Sometimes it had no legs, other times it had four sets, complete with claws longer than its fangs. Sometimes it was pitch black; others, it was bloodred. What my imagination couldn't decipher were the tasks expected of us in order to pass this beast. It felt like a test that I couldn't study for, but was completely unprepared to undertake.

I sat on a staircase in the palace, staring at my breakfast plate with a battle warring in my head. My mind told me I needed strength for the day ahead, but my stomach had been unreliable over the past two days. There was a rumble in my stomach which solidified my decision, and I took a disinterested bite of toast, forcing it down.

"Not even going to try for butter? Damn, you're hardcore." The voice behind me made me stiffen, and my stomach churned once more. I turned as Finlay sauntered down the steps and plopped down onto the same stair where I sat.

He wore more clothing than usual; his normally loose-flowing tunic was confined under a maroon leather vest, belted at the waist with a leather belt that shimmered with gold at the buckle. His dark breeches were tucked into shin-high leather boots, and his tousled hair was combed back out of his face. I would have been impressed by how handsomely put-together the ensemble made him look, if it didn't reek of ulterior motives.

I swallowed the bite of toast forcefully and kept my gaze pointedly on my plate. "What do you want, Finlay?"

"At the moment? For you to finish that mundane piece of toast. It's disgusting me." His tone was goading, but I rolled my eyes, refusing to take the bait.

"But I also came to ask to join your adventure today," he continued, his voice surprisingly hesitant.

My eyes whipped to his with alarm, and I was filled with a sudden self-loathing as my body reacted to our proximity, especially as I took in the fierce expression in his light cerulean eyes. We had almost done something truly terrible to Blaise a few nights ago, and *Finlay* had to be the one to stop it. I hated myself for it.

I set my jaw firmly, shaking my head.

"No. We don't need you for this." I willed my response to be as flat and emotionless as possible. I gripped my plate tighter and stood to return it. Finlay scrambled up with me.

"You don't know that. More manpower couldn't hurt, especially with my magic. And I'm just as good with a broadsword as Blaise." He kept pace with me as I traveled down the stairs, turning abruptly into the kitchen.

"Why do you care? Have things gotten too boring since the last battle?" I sniped, my words intentionally harsh. I felt his wince at my side, but he continued.

"It has nothing to do with that. I told you I would help in this fight, and I intend to keep that promise," he insisted, and then followed it up a beat later. "I want to ensure you're safe."

I slammed the plate down on a counter, flinching at the loud crash. Leaning in, I lowered my voice to a whisper, yet kept the ferocity in my words.

"I don't need you to keep me safe. I have Blaise, Kipp, and my father. And quite frankly, I can keep *myself* safe, thank you very much." I turned to leave and felt his hand grab my arm, gently but almost feverish in its heat.

"Look, I know. I know that. But —" he pushed his free hand through his hair in that now-familiar sign of distress. "I'll go crazy if I sit here, wondering what happened. I won't be a hindrance. Just please, let me come with you."

I considered him for a long moment. He distracted me to an unnerving degree and was unpredictable at the best of times. That being said...he *was* excellent with a broadsword, and his fire power was unbeatable. Especially considering I still had none of my own.

"Okay," I began slowly, "But this means nothing between us. The other night was nothing. And it will continue to mean nothing."

Finlay's eyes flickered, and he withdrew his hand quickly. I thought he was about to argue, but instead, he crossed his heart with his fingers.

"I swear it," he said solemnly, and then raised both palms. "I'll behave." Just as I thought he was being surprisingly serious, he gave a quick wink. I rolled my eyes and let out a frustrated sigh, turning to leave.

"Don't make me regret this!" I called.

"I would never!" His voice rang out in response, and I glanced back in time to catch his smirk.

My heart rate continued climbing as I changed back in my room, strapping weapons to my leg and across my back. I willed my palms to stop sweating as I made my way down to the courtyard to wait for the others, wiping them repetitively against my pants.

I nodded silently as they all arrived, their faces either expressionless or as somber as my own. The others were slightly surprised to see Finlay, and I noticed a flicker of disdain darken Blaise's face, but nobody made any comment. After one final check, Blaise pulled the

Faerie dust from his pocket, and in a flick of his hand, we were off to hunt the beithir.

Chapter 40

It only took two jumps with the dust to locate the right cave, much to my stomach's relief. I picked my way carefully along the path deeper into the abyss, following Blaise's lead. My muscles strained slightly as I focused on not slipping on the fractured, moss-covered rocks. It was hard to ignore the carved lines etched in them, looking like broad talons had dragged their way across.

A small stream wound deep into the cave, the soft rushing of the water a natural melody as it emptied out into the emerald lake outside. The chill radiating off the columned basalt walls made me shiver, and I tugged my jacket tighter against my body.

The stream eventually emptied into a small, still pool at the back of the cave, and I squinted to make out the clearance. The light was faint, but my eyes identified piles of broken rock amassed beyond the green-blue water. I glanced over at the others, who had stopped as well.

"Does this look right?" I whispered, willing my voice not to echo in the chamber. I saw Blaise nod, unsheathing his sword while my dad did the same.

"Finlay, do you mind hitting the lights?" Kipp murmured. Before I could ask what Kipp meant, Finlay's body nearly exploded. I stumbled back with a curse, and Finlay laughed.

"Relax, little angel." He chuckled. "It won't hurt you. Unless I tell it to."

Blaise growled in warning at Finlay's suggestive words and nickname. He shot a long glare at the heir before lifting his sword high, stalking off to inspect another corner of the cave with my father.

"Gods, Finlay, you're irritating," I muttered, though I couldn't take my eyes off him. I'd seen the magnificence of Darrya's signature air element in jest, but it was something else entirely to see Finlay's fire in action. He'd used it in the battle, but I'd been too preoccupied with my own fight to take much notice of the power he truly held.

Heat radiated off him, immediately fixing the chill that had plagued me moments before, but he was right; it didn't snake out to burn me. The fire tumbled in contained waves down his body, licking at his clothes without burning them. It lit up his golden hair and danced in his eyes, his lopsided grin now whiter than before. In fact, he looked relaxed, almost bored, and I realized that this took barely any effort for him. Perhaps he was a more valuable asset than I'd understood.

"So, what do we do now?" I asked, dragging my eyes from him and looking back to Blaise as he came to stand beside me.

"If our presence alone wasn't enough, Fireboy's heat will have alerted it that we're here. All we have to do is wait," he replied, settling onto a rock with his sword over his knees. I moved to sit next to him, and my father tentatively placed himself on my other side. I sensed his tension and could only imagine what thoughts were racing through his head. My mind wandered back to Blaise's comments at the bar and, after a moment, I turned to him and spoke.

"I'm sorry for what I said the other day."

My dad's golden eyes, so similar to my own, widened in surprise. My heart wrenched, seeing that speaking kindly to him had such an effect. I broke his gaze, turning my eyes to the floor.

"I understand why you left. I do. It just —" I paused, wringing my hands as I considered what to say next. "It's a lot of time and hurt to reconcile with."

"I know," he replied faintly, voice hoarse. "And I'll never be able to take that back. It haunts me every day. But I needed you to have a chance."

"Was it easy? For you to leave?" I asked, closing my eyes as they began to fill with tears. After a beat, I felt his arms circle around me. I didn't lean into the embrace, but I didn't push away either. When he replied, his voice was gruff.

"It was the hardest thing I've ever had to do."

I took a deep breath, feeling a weight lift off my chest that I hadn't even realized was there. I pressed into him slightly, and his arm tightened protectively at the motion.

"To be honest, Katie, I think you might have turned out better without me," he murmured, and I looked up to see a grim smile on his face. "You're amazing, you know that?"

I offered a small smile in return, quite possibly the first genuine one I'd given him since he came back. "I hear it runs in the family."

My father's grin widened, and he chuckled lightly. Blaise, who had remained purposefully silent and still throughout our interaction, stood abruptly, his sword at attention.

"Get ready," he ordered, and I heard every bit of the commander's voice in his tone. I wasted no time following his direction, scrambling up to attention. I gripped the hilt of my sword, feeling the prickle of sweat in my palms.

My eyes fell to the water as I glimpsed a ripple across the surface. It began in one small area, but slowly, more of the water was disrupted — at least the length of a school bus. My breath caught in my throat as the sheer size of the monster became apparent before I even saw its full form.

Suddenly, the entire surface of the cave pool burst, and I used my free arm to cover my face as waves cascaded around us, drenching us in water. I heard a hissing sound and smelled smoke, glancing over to see Finlay's fire partially doused. He unsheathed his sword and relit his flames, gaze trained in front of him. As I peered at him, I noticed something I'd never seen before in his expression. Fear.

I turned back to the water and found that we were finally face-to-face with the serpent.

The beithir was nothing like what my dreams had concocted. My heart pounded erratically, and my brain tried to keep up with the rush of emotions as it attempted to make sense of the implausible beast that rose above my head.

It was equal parts terrifying and beautiful. Fully scaled, it had spines along its back like an alligator, though its color was not at all dull. In fact, it radiated a dark navy blue, like it had captured the color straight from the depths of the lake. A long, scaly tail curled around its two sets of legs, which it leaned back on as if it were about to pounce, like a cat. It tapped a long, webbed talon as it observed us.

The flutter of my heart reminded me that I needed to breathe. I sucked in a panicked breath as my eyes traveled upward, all the way to where the monster's head tipped down from the ceiling of the cave to inspect us. It was truly massive; larger than anything I'd ever witnessed in the human realm. The size alone was enough to make me cower, wincing as if the slight movement put a safe distance between me and the creature. But it was the creature's face that made my breath catch in my throat once more.

Two large horns spiraled back from its head toward its shoulders and while I watched, a dangerous, spike-boned neck frill extended and retracted as it tilted its head to gaze directly at me. I met its eyes, pure gold and ablaze, punctuated with black slits for pupils. I tried to remember our next move, but any thoughts immediately tumbled out of my head as it opened its jaws. Rows of pointed, needle-like fangs gleamed, and a long, forked tongue darted out, tasting the air. The beast hissed, and my entire body went taut, ready to run.

What a curious group of Fae folk we have here.

A deep, gravelly voice resounded in my head; the 's' was elongated in a distinctly serpent-like manner. My mouth opened and

I whipped around to the others. The alarm that showed in their expressions told me they'd heard the same.

Yes, the voice murmured once more, and a rumble gathered in the beast's large chest, punctuating the point. The cave trembled. *This is how I communicate.*

My father's voice rang out. "We are here for the cauldron. We heard an exchange could be arranged." If he was afraid, his tone boasted no trace. He stepped forward, making a point to move slightly in front of me as he did so. The beithir's head whipped to view him, but he didn't flinch.

The cauldron of Dagda, the creature mused. *Yes. You heard correctly.* Its head reached further toward my father, its tongue flicking out once more. *Descendent of Cú Chulainn. The bravery of your line is not lost on you.*

Its head rose sharply, taking in the rest of our group. Kipp had shifted into his wolf form but, despite his massive size, he was positively dwarfed by the dragon-like creature.

An Urisk, a Daoine Sídhe, and an Aes Sídhe have joined you. How...collaborative. It paused, turning its head to look at me behind my father. Its frills flared, and my pulse quickened. *And your daughter, of course.*

Its head wound around my father to flick its tongue out, inspecting me. Out of the corner of my eye, I glimpsed my father's hand gripping his sword tighter.

I mean no harm, the creature purred in our heads calmly. *You are simply fascinating to me. I so rarely receive guests.*

It tilted its massive head to better view me, its golden eyes shining almost yellow-white. The glow flashed down its scales, lighting intriguing designs across its body. It opened its mouth, and my hair stood on end as an orb of light danced between its fangs. I didn't pull away; rather, I felt myself lean forward.

They failed to mention you were...so similar to me.

I glanced at the others, wondering if they'd heard that comment too, but it seemed this intriguing statement was meant for my head alone. Before I could respond, it snapped its mouth closed again and lifted its head back up, quick enough that Kipp growled in alarm.

Three riddles. It spoke, this time to all of us. *That is what I ask of you.*

A wave of unease rippled through our group as we absorbed the request wordlessly. I glanced around; my father's eyes had narrowed and Blaise's jaw had tightened. The bewilderment I felt was reflected openly on Finlay's face, his flames flickering uncertainly, and Kipp loosed a low, barely audible whine.

Finally, Blaise voiced what we were all thinking. "No tasks?"

I want for nothing, the beithir replied easily, *save for entertainment. Will you play?*

"Yes," I stepped forward, answering for us all. "Give us your first riddle."

I felt the shifting of the others to stand behind me, echoing their support. The beast snorted and assessed me for a long moment before speaking once more.

You live beneath a roof

that is upheld by me.
You seldom walk abroad,
but my fair form you see.
I close you in on every side,
your very dwelling pave,
and probably I'll go with you
at last into the grave.

I looked around at the others helplessly, hoping that our numbers meant at least one of us would have the answer. A spike of fear shot through me as I realized: we'd decided on a prize if we got the riddles right, but what was the punishment if we got one wrong? My breath caught in my throat, and I didn't release it until my father spoke.

"Wood," he said confidently, raising an eyebrow at the serpent. The creature bowed its head, acknowledging the answer as correct. "What's next?"

What is so fragile that even saying its name breaks it?

The question hung in the air. We looked around at each other for a moment, until the resounding nothingness sparked the answer from me.

"Silence," I blurted, surprising even myself at the beast's approving nod. It flared its frills once more, contemplating for a moment as it chose its last riddle carefully.

I hurt the most when lost,

yet also when not had at all.
I'm sometimes the hardest to express,
but the easiest to ignore.
I can be given to many, or just one.
What am I?

A low, steady dripping of water was the only sound for some time, echoing from far off in the cave as we scoured our minds for the answer. My chest tightened again at the prospect of answering incorrectly, or not having an answer at all. What would the beithir do? It *could* do quite a lot, if the fancy struck.

Suddenly, Blaise and Finlay both spoke, their answers coming in tandem.

"Love," they both replied, gazing directly at me.

My lips parted in shock at the heated intensity of their stares, but they quickly broke eye contact to exchange startled looks with one other, which promptly dissolved into scowls. I tilted my head curiously at their interaction, my heart urging me to demand explanations from them both, though my head screamed that it wasn't the time. The beast breathed a rumble of curiosity, tearing us all from the moment.

Very well. You have solved the three riddles. You may pass.

A light shimmered on a new path behind the beithir, and it began its descent back into the water with a grace that didn't match its gigantic size. I stumbled a few steps forward.

"Wait!" I yelled breathlessly, and it paused.

"Do you have a name?" I asked. The others gave me bewildered looks, which I ignored. For whatever reason, I felt a desperate urge to form a connection with this creature. It was dangerous, but enticing, and I'd felt the similarity it had mentioned.

Gorm, it replied, in what I now understood to be my mind only. I dipped my head in thanks.

"Katherine," I said with a small smile, and I swore Gorm's eyes softened, the onyx slits rounding slightly.

May we meet again, Katherine. Its voice resounded pleasantly in my head and, with that, Gorm slipped into the water and disappeared.

The others surrounded the new light, which emanated from a different source than the beithir. I peered around them to see the cauldron, fully aglow in dark gold and green waves. It sat atop a stone, surprisingly small in stature, though smoke formed a large ring around it.

"Making friends there?" Finlay asked as I moved to join them. He had extinguished his fire, the cave now lit from the light of the cauldron. I gave him a weak smile, nodding, and turned my attention back to the cauldron. Before I could reach it, however, a hand shot out to block me.

"Wait," Kipp said, now back in human form. He fixed me with a look, his bright blue eyes piercing into mine with a level of seriousness I had rarely seen. "Does nobody else think this is just a bit ... too easy?"

Blaise nodded slowly. "I was prepared for tasks. Not some silly riddles."

"They were easy riddles, too. Ones I've heard around campfires countless times." Kipp's tone carried a sense of urgency. His eyes wandered between my father and me. "I'd be careful if I were you."

"Okay, so we don't use it yet. We bring it back and have it inspected," I offered, but Kipp shook his head, then looked at Finlay and my father.

"Can you two use your powers to see if you sense anything? You're the most adept with your magic."

My father and Finlay exchanged glances, and I felt the unease between them. It lasted only seconds, however, before they both agreed. I sensed their energy pass through me toward the cauldron and, after several long moments, they glanced back at each other.

"Anything?" Blaise asked. They both shook their heads.

"I feel its power, but nothing...dark," Finlay said, and my father murmured his agreement.

Kipp loosed a deep breath and stepped away, motioning me forward. "Okay. Let's take it home."

I studied it intently as I approached. The sides had several figures and faces chiseled into them, dancing their way around the cauldron as if to tell a story — though what that story was, I had no idea. It almost spoke to me as I approached, stirring the earth power in me awake. I smiled, letting the smoke dance around me as I peered at the steaming water inside the cauldron.

"Remember. Don't drink from it, just grab it," Kipp called nervously from behind. I nodded, facing him and the others and taking a brief moment to survey them. They looked on intently, faces etched with concern and bodies tense, as if ready to spring into action. It made my heart twist as I recalled how, less than a year ago, I'd had barely anyone to call a friend or family and now, my life was brimming full of both, more caring and doting than I'd ever imagined possible.

I still wasn't sure why fate had chosen me to hunt down these talismans; to summon this power when I had barely grasped how to use it. But I did know that I would do anything in my power to protect my loved ones and, with this cauldron, we were halfway there.

My resolve solidified, and I clenched my jaw as I clasped my hands around both sides of the cauldron, bracing for whatever was in store. I felt a familiar twist in my stomach — the same jerking sensation as using Faerie dust. I squeezed my eyes shut, bracing myself, but when they reopened, I was greeted by darkness.

A voice rang out, one I'd never heard before, its tone low and ominous.

"So, it's the girl. How curious."

A breeze passed over my cheeks as a strange flapping sound grew closer. Some type of winged creature landed next to me, and I sidled away uneasily, but my feet tripped over something I couldn't see. From another direction, a low laugh sounded, disorienting me further.

"Let's get started," the voice hissed. Before I could move again, strong, rough hands grabbed me, and I cried out in pain as the burning began.

More From Jayme Hunt

Marked by Gods, the sequel to *Marked by Fate,* is coming mid-2023. Please follow the author for more updates!

Acknowledgments

When I was younger, I devoured every book I could get my hands on. I wrote, too – poetry, short stories, full-on novels. But as the demands of school and work grew, the time I had for reading and writing dwindled. It wasn't until I was 26, and on my honeymoon, that I picked up a novel again. I was instantly hooked. I read dozens of books in the span of a few months, and then opened my laptop to begin writing once more. It took a few tries, but when I finally refocused on what I know and love, this story came pouring out.

To my readers – especially my beta and ARC readers – who took a leap of faith in joining me with this initial journey. I am forever grateful to you all, and I can only hope you aren't so aggravated by this book's ending that you don't continue the journey with Kate and her friends and family. She has plenty more in store.

To my editor, Eden Northover, who made the process of shaping this story into a coherent novel surprisingly easy. I am so grateful for your kind, constructive feedback, as it kept me motivated and optimistic.

To my mother, whose passion for books rubbed off on me before I could even read, and whose incessant correction of my grammar growing up made my editor ecstatic. I'm sorry I routinely scar you with my wild book recommendations...but to be fair, you started this.

To my friend Dakota, who took the plunge and was one of the first to read my rough drafts. I hope you were able to wash your eyes out sufficiently enough to give this final draft a go.

To my friend Kara, who had just as ridiculous of an imagination as I did when we were young. Reading and writing with you gave me some of my best memories growing up, and I'm glad to be your friend to this day. Your Breyer collection remains unparalleled, and I'm sure the scratches we left on them as we made our stories come to life are the main reason they can't be sold (not that you should sell them, anyways).

To my husband, who watched our joint bank account dwindle without complaint as I pursued this wild dream. Thanks for being my ride-or-die. I know I can count on you to be interested in this story...as long as you can watch it on the TV someday.

To all authors who have written stories and worlds so grand I'm left dreaming of them for weeks (or months) afterward – thank you for putting the magical in the mundane. You inspire me daily.

And to everyone with a story brewing inside them, just waiting to be written: Go for it!

About The Author

Jayme Hunt studied marketing and data analytics in college, and continues working a full-time job in the marketing field. In early 2022, she rediscovered her love of reading and writing, and has barely put down a book since. *Marked by Fate* is her debut novel. She resides in Colorado with her husband and two dogs, who often make cameos in her social media posts.

@authorjaymehunt
www.authorjaymehunt.wordpress.com

www.ingramcontent.com/pod-product-compliance
Lightning Source LLC
Chambersburg PA
CBHW021210310726
48971CB00006B/1511